Caribbean
B

BACK
WATERS

A Rick Waters Novel

ERIC CHANCE STONE

ISBN: 978-1-7341626-9-1

Second Edition

10 9 8 7 6 5 4 3 2

BACK
WATERS

FIND THE OFFICIAL SYNOPSIS MUSIC AT:

ERICSTONE.GUMROAD.COM/L/BACKWATERS

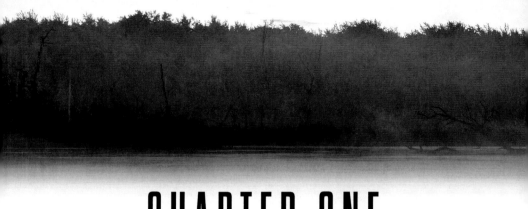

CHAPTER ONE

The *beep-beep-beep* of the heart monitor machine faded in the background as Rick tried to hear the voices outside his door in room 332 at the Hospital e Maternidade Cataratas. It was futile, as they were speaking Portuguese. He had lost track of how long he had been inside recovering. Daily visits from Rick's girlfriend Jules and his best friend Possum helped with the monotony, and occasionally, Possum would sneak Rick's cockatoo, Chief in under his shirt for a quick snuggle.

Rick's kayak had gone over one of the highest waterfalls in the world, and somehow, he'd survived. It was partly a miracle, but mostly because Jules had found him and resuscitated him. Wearing a shoulder brace, a full leg cast, and wrapped up like a mummy, he couldn't get around much and was tired of being in the hospital bed. It hurt to breathe due to his punctured lung, and his clavicle had poked through the skin when he hit the sharp rocks at the bottom of the waterfall.

The odds were against Jules finding him, yet she had, alive and in one piece. She had never given up; her love and commitment to him had given her the strength to persevere. She would've slept in the hospital room in a chair next to his bed if he'd let her, but he always insisted she get her rest at the nearby hotel, where Gary had booked two rooms for her and Possum. Gary was one of Rick's closest friends from back in high school. He won Powerball a couple years back and loved to help Rick finance his adventures and treasure hunts. He had flown back to Brazil to prove to the Yanomami that Rick and the crew had indeed recovered the Sacred Jewel of Orinoco and would be transporting it to the Smithsonian Institution to aid the tribe in their fight against the building of a dam that would destroy their homeland. The Yanomami had originally believed that the Kayapo stole the jewel, and they'd intended to commit genocide against the smaller tribe, but Rick and his crew had recovered the jewel from the late Nate Armstrong, who had acquired it in a double cross from the now also late Gina Russo.

Gina had created an escrow account in the bank of Brazil, into which she had deposited the funds from both the Smithsonian and the Museum of Natural History in New York. Both museums believed they would be the sole keepers of the stone because of Gina's scam. Gina had originally been a part of Rick's crew and a valuable asset to the Yanomami's effort, but greed had turned her and she'd had every intention of keeping all the museum money for herself and also selling the jewel to Armstrong. Armstrong was a snake, though, and Gina got bit—actually, shot through the eye on the deck of his yacht, minutes before he accidentally blew it up and killed himself and the entire crew.

Now Gary's plan was to take Davi Kopenawa, the leader of the Yanomami, to the States and convince both museums to share the jewel in dual exhibits biannually. It was the most valuable star sapphire in the world and worth well over four hundred million dollars. If Davi would agree to present the jewel in person, Gary was sure each museum would agree to the terms of two million each to continue the tribe's fight. The Museum of Natural History had already paid one million and the Smithsonian had paid two. If he could convince the famous New York museum to match it, the deal would be a win-win for everyone, especially the Yanomami.

Rick heard a familiar voice outside his door.

"Quanto tempo mais ele tem que ficar?"

It was Jules. She had been honing up on her Portuguese and helping Rick the entire time with the doctors and nurses. The door slowly opened, and Jules peeked in.

"Hola, mi amor," she said.

"Hey, baby, how are you?" replied Rick.

"I'm good. I just spoke to the doctor and he said you should be able to go home soon. Normally, you would've only been in here for five to seven days then home to recuperate. But whatever punctured your lung caused an infection. You had a pneumothorax, which is basically a fancy word for a collapsed lung, and they were able to reinflate it with a tube, but the infection caused problems and they had to go back in and clean the wound. That's what caused the setback. He thinks you can get out of here in a few days, though. Unless you are still enjoying the pampering." She smirked at him.

"Haha, no! I want out of here. You can pamper me poolside. I'm not really up to flying all the way back to Destin, but I think a few weeks back in Rio will be good for my mental and physical well-being."

"I spoke with Gary this morning, and he told me to just let him know what you need and he's got you covered. He's in Brazil meeting with Davi Kopenawa, and he thinks they both are flying to DC tomorrow. A truce has been called with the Kayapo and there is peace amongst the tribes. You did a good thing, Rick, rescuing the sacred jewel."

"*I* did? *We* did. It was a team effort."

"I guess that's true. Do you need anything? I need to go back to the hotel and make arrangements for our resort in Rio. Do you want to stay at the same one as before?"

"I'm good here, Jules. The food isn't half bad. Maybe you can sneak me in a beer or two when you come back? And how about we stay at the Copacabana Palace instead this time? The spa there is world class and every muscle in my body is sore. Even though I'm in a cast, I think they can find some spots to massage on me, haha."

"Okay, I'll head back to the hotel and book our rooms. Possum said he's coming by later and needs to discuss something with you. He wants us all here, so I'll come back with him."

Jules kissed Rick goodbye and left. Even seeing her for just a few minutes always brightened up his day. A nurse came in and took his vitals, and another man came in and set his lunch on the tray by the bed. He slowly ate, daydreaming of being outside in the sun by the pool with Jules.

After lunch, he drifted off to sleep with the TV on, causing him to dream about being on a talk show. He was awakened a few hours later by a doctor, who spoke fairly good English.

"Mr. Waters, how are you feeling?"

"I'm pretty good. I'm sore all over and it hurts to breathe deeply, but I'd say overall I'm better."

"Well, that's good. I have some good news for you. Your blood work is almost back to normal, so it looks like we've got that lung infection under control. I think you can go home in a few days."

"How long have I been here? I lost count."

"Let me see…"

The rounds doctor looked tired. He had dark circles under his bloodshot eyes. After a yawn, he opened a chart and scrolled down with his fingers.

"You have been here twenty-two days, Mr. Waters."

"Oh my God, are you serious?"

"Yes, you could've left sooner, but whatever poked your lung caused a nasty infection. I'm guessing it was a branch or something with a lot of algae on it. But we've got it taken care of now and you are on your way to a full recovery. You need about three to four more weeks in the leg cast and clavicle brace, but your X-rays look good and the bones are healing properly. Are you going to be returning to Florida?"

"Not right away. I'm gonna take some time to recover in Rio. It'll be good for me."

"I agree. A little vitamin D can do wonders."

The doctor patted Rick on his good leg and stepped out of the room.

The next few days dragged on and time seemed to stand still. Boredom was setting in for Rick. His recovery would happen, but it couldn't get here fast enough for Rick's taste.

Jules had brought him a few fishing magazines to give him something to read, but they were all in Portuguese. He still enjoyed looking at them, though, and couldn't wait to get a line wet back in Destin once he was fully recovered. Johnie had been running the charters with a hired captain the entire time, keeping his boat *Nine-Tenths* busy and in good standing at the Destin HarborWalk Marina. Johnie called every few days to update Rick on the charters and check on him. He was a great first mate, and Rick had no idea what he'd do without him.

His favorite two nurses checked on him almost hourly, and one helped him get in and out of bed a few times to avoid atrophy. Both ladies were super sweet. They also spoke a bit of broken English, so Rick had gotten to know them quite well during his stay in room 332. The youngest nurse was named Áurea, which meant "woman of gold." She had worked her way through nursing school while caring for her aging parents and two siblings who both had Down syndrome. She had gotten her BA at the University of the State of Paraná near home and done her undergraduate nursing studies in Miami, where she worked full time as a waitress and sent most of the money home to help her family. Even with a nursing degree, she didn't earn much, and most of it went to support her family members. She'd moved back in with them once she returned home.

The other nurse's name was Cássia, which meant "the fragrant one." Her story was a lot different. She told Rick that when she was young, she'd survived the house fire that killed her mother and both of her brothers, and left a bad reminder of the incident on the right side of her face and body. She was drawn to nursing because of the love and care given to her during her recovery. Her father also eventually died from the burns he had received, and she was left alone at the age of ten to fend for herself. She was abused as a child by several uncles and eventually ran away and lived on the street. She overcame many obstacles but never gave up her dream of becoming a nurse. She landed a job as a cleaning tech in the hospital and saved all her money while living on a friend's couch. Eventually, she was upgraded to an intern. She learned to use a computer from her friend and made it her full-time job to apply for a grant for nursing school. It took her three years, and during that time, she took online courses that would help toward her degree. She eventually received her grant and graduated with honors from the University of São Paulo. She had decided to come back to the very hospital that gave her a chance in the first place. She knew she could make more money at a larger facility in Rio, but she wanted to give back for all that she had received from the little hospital that first took a chance on her.

A few more days had passed, and Rick felt like the hospital room was closing in on him. The sun was starting to set, and long, angled lines ran across the wall from the window blinds. He was bored beyond belief and ready to leave. Suddenly, the door opened, and in walked Jules pushing a wheelchair with a man wrapped in gauze who looked like a burn victim or a mummy. She was wearing a nurse's uniform, and had her hair in a ponytail and an N95 mask on her face.

"What the fuck?" said Rick.

"We have to get out of here," said the gauze-faced man.

Rick knew the voice instantly. It was Possum. He stood up, unwrapped the gauze, and shoved the wheelchair behind the curtain in the shower.

"Listen up. Remember that briefcase I told you I found?"

"You mean after I fell down the falls?"

"Yes, exactly. When I opened it, I almost fainted. It was the money Armstrong had on the yacht to buy the jewel. I counted it. It's five million dollars. It survived the explosion and was floating intact near the bank where Jules and I were searching for you."

"It's real? Five big ones?"

"Totally real. The problem is that Armstrong got it from a local loan shark named Dale Clemens who relocated here from Kentucky. He used to run a bookie outfit in Louisville and was involved in a Ponzi scheme that got him in the crosshairs of the FBI. He's pretty untouchable down here, hangs out with some heavy hitters and is deep in the cocaine trade now. Somehow, he found out we were involved in the deal with Armstrong and he wants his money. Word on the street is, if he can't get paid, he'll get even."

"What's the plan?" asked Rick.

"Visiting hours are over at 9:00 p.m., in about an hour and a half. Jules grabbed some scrubs from the laundry and they are in that duffel there along with the money at the bottom of the bag. She's gonna switch back into street clothes now and meet us at the airport with Chief. Gary has arranged a charter flight with a fake flight plan and manifest bound for Miami. We will actually be getting off in Rio, though. I'll make sure that Clemens gets his hands on the flight plan. He wouldn't dare set foot back in the States. The FBI will snatch him up faster than you can say, 'Jack Robinson.' Ever since Gary returned stateside with the jewel, he's been under a lot scrutiny and his jet was searched extensively. There's no way we can bring this cash back into the States without being caught, but he says he has a plan and it involves Chief. Don't ask me how, I don't know yet. We'll rendezvous with Gary in Rio soon and he'll explain the whole thing."

"So, we are keeping the five million dollars?" asked Rick.

"Sort of. It's a long story and it's best if we go over it all in Rio. I'm afraid some old associates of Clemens's are on the inside and may strike tonight."

Jules came over beside the bed and gave Rick a huge but soft hug and whispered that everything would be okay. She slowly cracked open the door and stepped out. Possum took the duffel and stepped into the bathroom to hide. Rick knew the nurse would make one more round before visiting hours were over. There was a shift change at 10:00 p.m. They needed to get out during that time, as lots of new people would be coming and going. Every time Rick heard steps in the hallway, he tensed up.

A shadow fell across his doorway, and Rick really started to sweat. "Knock, knock," said the figure before stepping into the room. He breathed a sigh of relief, seeing a nurse with a stethoscope rather than a man with a pistol. He'd never dreamed he might be the target of an assassin for money he didn't even know he had. The irony was palpable.

At 9:53 p.m., Possum reappeared from the bathroom shower. He had scrubs on now and helped Rick sit up in bed. He slowly wrapped the gauze around Rick's face, only exposing his eyes and mouth. The hospital bill had been paid in full by Gary, so Rick didn't feel guilty about sneaking out. He only wished he could thank the doctor and nurses one more time.

"Can we leave a little something-something for the doctor and nurses?" he asked.

"Yeah, but let's hurry."

Rick grabbed some stationery and envelopes from the desk beside his bed. He put a stack of ten thousand dollars in each of three envelopes and addressed them to the doc and the two nurses who'd taken such great care of him. He knew that kind of money could be life-changing for those kind souls.

Possum helped Rick into the wheelchair with the N95 mask over his own mouth, then placed the duffel bag in Rick's lap and wheeled him toward the door. As he walked down the hall and pushed Rick, a scurry of activity was happening near the nurses' stations. The shift change was underway. Two scruffy men in scrubs walked past Rick and Possum and didn't give them a glance. As Possum turned the corner, he looked back to see one man standing outside of Rick's door as the other one entered the room.

Pew-pew-pew came from the room—the unmistakable sound of a gun being shot with a silencer. No one else seemed to hear it in all the commotion. Possum had piled up the pillows in the bed to make it look as if someone was asleep under the covers. He pushed Rick faster toward the front door and onto the curb. A black sedan was waiting, and Possum helped Rick inside. They were gone in less than thirty seconds.

"Depressa, depressa!" said Possum to the driver, who sped up toward the airport. He zigged and zagged out of traffic and pulled into the executive side, right next to an Embraer Legacy 500 mid-size jet. The door was open, and Jules stood in the entryway, waving for them to hurry. Rick hobbled as best he could with his arm around Possum for balance. They all boarded, and the flight crew shut the door. They immediately taxied for the number three runway. The pilot's voice came through the overhead speaker.

"Good afternoon, ladies and gentlemen. I'm Clay, your pilot. Jamey, our flight attendant, will be in the cabin for your service today. We will be heading directly to Caracas to refuel then on to Miami. The flight will take approximately ten hours and nineteen minutes plus the fuel stop. Please take your seat, buckle up, and enjoy your flight."

Within minutes, they were off the ground. Rick, Possum, and Jules all breathed a sigh of relief. Chief munched on a grape, indifferent to all the excitement. It would hopefully be the last time they'd have to deal with Clemens or his gang.

Gary had paid the pilot to drop them all off in Rio then continue on to Miami as per the flight plan. It was highly illegal to create a fake manifest, but it was the only way to throw off Clemens and his team, who would never set foot on US soil. The lights of Rio appeared, and the beautiful, brightly lit statue of Christ the Redeemer stood above the city with open arms, making Rick feel safe and loved. He felt a strong connection with the statue now and knew that a stronger power, along with Jules's love, had saved his life. He was at peace.

CHAPTER TWO

The plane touched down smoothly and quickly refueled, bound for Miami. Gary had arranged another car for them, and they all piled in, looking forward to checking in at the Copacabana Palace. As usual, Gary had gone all out and booked two adjacent penthouse suites on the top floor. One for Jules and Rick, and one for Possum. Each suite was over a thousand square feet and boasted an expansive veranda and a private pool on the roof. All amenities were included. They came with a catered breakfast, a full wet bar, and twenty-four-hour butler service.

The first thing Rick did after they checked in was hobble to the wet bar. He scoured through the bottles and found a fifteen-year-old rum from Colombia called Ron Viejo de Caldas, which he'd never heard of. He poured two glasses over single cubes of ice and slid one toward Jules. She took a sip and shrugged, opting for a bottle of aguardiente instead, and poured the other rum into Rick's glass as they both laughed.

She clinked her glass against Rick's. "Here's to us. Me, you, Chief, and Possum. Wait, we need to get Possum… Possum!" she yelled.

Possum opened the adjacent door and stepped in with a glass of his own.

"Great minds think alike!" he said.

They all clinked glasses and took big swigs and then had a group hug. Normally, Rick would've thought that was weird, but after all they had been though, it felt perfect. Tears welled in his eyes.

"Rick Waters, are you gonna cry?" Jules laughed as she rubbed the tears out of her own eyes.

"I love y'all so much," said Rick.

Even Possum was getting the vapors. Chief stepped off of his travel cage and walked across the bar, jealous of all the excitement. Rick handed him a lime wedge, and he held it in his claw and ripped at the pulp. They had a few more drinks and snacks and decided to call it a night. Possum moseyed back to his room, and Jules helped Rick to the bed. It felt like heaven compared to the hospital bed he had been on for nearly three weeks. He loved her soft touch but was in no shape to fool around. She held him all night as they slept. They were one.

A knock came at the door. It was only 7:30 a.m.

"Housekeeping."

"Yeah, whatever, just come in, Possum," said Rick.

Possum stepped in pushing a tray of pastries, fresh coffee, and fruit. He had preordered it from the butler before he went to sleep and ordered enough for all three of them. He poured two coffees, stirred in some Bailey's, and handed them to Rick and Jules.

"You can't drink all day if you don't start in the morning." Possum grinned.

Rick yawned and shook his head. Possum had always been a morning guy, to Rick's chagrin, but he had gotten used to it.

"I didn't just wake y'all up early because I wanted to drink," said Possum. "We have an 8:30 a.m. Zoom call with Gary, and I figured you'd wanna be wide-awake for it. It has to do with the money."

"Okay, okay, I'm up. I need to pee. I'm so sick of hobbling. Can you give me a hand, Possum?"

"I can do better than that. Hang on."

Possum jogged back into his room and returned a few seconds later.

"Ta-da!"

From behind his back, he pulled out a pair of crutches with beautiful gray fur wrapped around the hand grip and crutch pad.

"Where the hell did you get crutches, and better yet, where did you get rabbit fur?" asked

Rick.

"I got them both from the butler. I couldn't sleep last night and ordered a pizza. He came up and I got to know him. He told me he can pretty much get us anything we want. Just ask. Oh, and it's not rabbit fur. It's chinchilla. They are everywhere in Brazil."

"You sure it's not possum fur?" said Rick, holding his side from laughing.

"Haha, very funny! Feel it. It's softer than velvet."

"Damn, you aren't kidding. Possum, you never cease to amaze me. Thanks so much, man."

"Wait, there's more." He ran back into his room and opened the door wide.

Meep-meep-meep…

Possum rolled through the door sitting on an electric mobility scooter. The NASCAR Monte Carlo front end had a huge number three painted on it, and sponsorship stickers covered every piece of fiberglass. It had subwoofers and beer holders, all wrapped in flashing LED lights. "You've got to be kidding me! I don't even wanna know where you got that."

Jules was laughing so hard she started to look woozy.

"Well, since you asked, the butler got it from a gang banger who got shot and partially paralyzed. He got a new one with a Ferrari front end, so Luiz—that's our butler's name—bought it from him," said Possum, wearing a huge grin of pride.

"You don't seriously think I'm gonna ride that, do you?"

"Well, Jules and I became quite good pool buddies while you were in the hospital, so I figured you'd like to keep up. You don't wanna let her down, do you?"

"You tricky bastard! Okay, I'll ride it to the pool, but that's it!"

Jules was out of breath and fell back on the bed, covering her mouth to muffle her laughter.

"Rick, Rick, get on it. I wanna take a picture of you to send to my friends. My boyfriend is a NASCAR driver!"

Rick glared at her with devilish eyes but a wicked grin as well. He took the crutches Possum had leaned against the bed and adjusted them for his height. The chinchilla fur was luxurious and felt good in his hands and under his arms. He moved around the room and felt comfortable using them. Jules waved Rick over to have a bite before they settled out by the pool for the day. Having a butler at their beck and call was more helpful than they could have imagined. Not only was Luiz a great butler, but he was a streetwise guy who could get things done and find anything they needed or wanted. He was also very likeable. He reminded Rick of one of those guys who knelt beside the net at Wimbledon and fetched the balls as soon as one went astray. Whenever Rick called him, he was there in a flash.

"I just got a text from Gary. He said he can't make the Zoom call this morning but will call you later, Rick."

Rick looked at his phone and saw the same text. He sent Gary a thumbs-up.

After breakfast, they all made their way to the pool. It was called the Black Pool because of the black tiles lining its bottom. It was a small area and only available to guests of the presidential and penthouse suites. It had only five chaise lounges, and Rick, Jules, Possum, and Chief seemed to be the only ones checked in. Rick found out the presidential suite was vacant but would no doubt be occupied by Gary in a few days upon his return from the States.

Rick ordered some Bloody Marys for them all, and Luiz delivered them extremely fast. This kind of opulent lifestyle sure made Rick feel good. His body was still sore, but the warm water and cocktails took the edge off. He could only put one leg in, as the other one was still in a full cast, but he didn't care. It felt amazing.

Chief even liked the water and often crawled out on Rick's knee and stuck a foot in. He was a confused bird. Rick was pretty sure Chief believed one day he was a dog and the next he was a human. Either way, he was adorable and always a pleasure to be around. He was also quieter than most cockatoos Rick had encountered. He rarely squawked, and when he did it was usually for good reason—and he actually barked way more than he squawked. He also had several different barks. A *yip-yip-yip* like a chihuahua and a deeper *woof-woof* like a big dog, as well as a low growl that was always amusing.

Jules wanted a new bathing suit, so Rick arranged for a car to take her shopping. Since shopping wasn't his thing, and his mobility was quite limited at the moment, Possum offered to escort her for safety. It gave Rick and Chief some alone time at the pool. As he lounged poolside, he remembered Chief's wings hadn't been trimmed, so he contacted Luiz, who called a local pet store.

A woman soon arrived with the appropriate tools of the trade. For a change, Chief seemed to enjoy his trim. She was incredibly gentle and good at her job. She spoke softly and smoothly to Chief in Portuguese, and he cooed over all the attention. After trimming his wings, she used a Dremel-like tool and carefully took the razor edge off of his claws, which were more like eagle talons at this point; they'd left scratches on Rick's arms and knee. He was even happier that she was dulling Chief's claws than he was about her giving him the wing trimming he also needed desperately. The pool was on the rooftop, and if Chief took off, it would be a huge drop.

After the trim, she gave Rick a harness and flight suit. Rick had never seen a flight suit, and with the help of Luiz interpreting, she explained that it was almost like a bathing suit for birds that went around the wings and his lower body. It had a poop catcher and a ring on the back for attaching a leash. It was more for safety than anything else. She showed Rick the different colors of suits, and Rick chose a bright one adorned with a pineapple print. Chief didn't resist as she told Rick how to put it on him. As soon as it was snug on him, he began to strut around the pool as if he were on a cat walk. They all laughed as he made his way up and down the poolside.

Rick paid the woman as she left the pool area, his phone started vibrating and he glanced down at it and saw it was Gary.

"Wazzzzzzzzzupppp?" said Rick.

"Hey, Rick. I'm in DC with Davi Kopenawa. We finished the meetings with both museums and came to a shared agreement about the sacred gem. The Smithsonian will have a showing the first six months and then deliver it to the Museum of Natural History in New York for their round. New York agreed to match the two million paid by the Smithsonian and gave me a check for the difference. I'm flying back to Rio with Davi to transfer the funds to his tribal account. It's all gonna work out and he is grateful for everything we did. They want to have a celebration for the media and have us attend. I explained to him why that's not possible because of the heat we have on us from Clemens. I think he understands."

"Yeah, being on TV would be a bad idea at this point. I hope he's not offended."

"Nah. He wants to meet you, though, so I booked the presidential suite next to y'all's penthouse ones. He'll accompany me there tomorrow and we will all have a catered dinner in the suite. Sound good?"

"Sounds amazing. I'm stoked to meet such a highly respected tribal leader and beyond honored that he wants to meet me."

"You have to realize, Rick, that gem was God to them. It's the most sacred artifact to their entire tribal nation, and we rescued it from being sold on the black market."

"Yeah, that makes sense. When will you arrive? And what's the deal with the money in the duffel bag? I have it in the safe in my room."

"We arrive late tonight. We can catch up in the morning. It's a long story but I'll try and make it short. When I landed in Miami with Davi, my plane was searched like they thought I was bringing drugs into the country. Something or someone has put me on the radar with customs, so there's no way we can bring that money to the States without declaring it. Then we'd have to explain how we got it. Not a good idea. So, I have a plan. Have you ever heard of Bitcoin?"

"Yeah, of course. I don't know much about it, though, except that it's a decentralized, unregulated digital currency," replied Rick.

"You know more than most people; I'll give you that. Have you heard of Dogecoin?"

"Isn't that a meme coin that got popular because of a bunch of tweets from Elon Musk?"

"Yes, it's known as the people's crypto. Its blockchain technology is similar to Bitcoin and Ethereum. I found a guy who can create a new coin using the same technology. He has already started and we will finalize it soon. I will give him the money and he will launch the coin and use several hundred thousand dollars for ads to gain popularity. The plan is to release an original distribution amount of sixty billion coins. So, me, you, Davi, Possum, and Jules will all have equal shares. It will be our own cryptocurrency, and with any luck could follow in the footsteps of Dogecoin and gain popularity fast."

"I think I understand. It will be untraceable and basically a way for us to launder the money but keep it off the radar, right? What's it gonna be called?"

"That's the best part. I know you've seen that cute Shiba Inu dog on the front of the Dogecoin, right?"

"Yep, I've seen it, why?"

"Part of the reason Dogecoin got so popular is because of that dog, because it's cute. So, I am putting, wait for it... Chief on our coin. It will be Chiefcoin."

"Chiefcoin? Are you serious?"

"As a heart attack! Hang on, I'll text you a photo."

Rick's phone whistled, and he pulled it from his ear and looked at the text photo. It was a gold coin with Chief's image on it and the words *IT'S THE NEXT BIG THING, RICK,* in a circle around the outside, and *CHIEF COIN* and *WOW* on the face.

"Oh my God, that is insane!" Rick guffawed.

"It's based closely on Dogecoin and has a similar appeal that will help it gain popularity fast, hopefully. Marketing will be a big part of it. With sixty billion on launch, each coin will only be valued at a fraction of a fraction of a cent. We're talking almost less than a calculator can compute. But if it even got to six cents, our investment would be exponential. Dogecoin at one time was up to sixty-one cents.

It's back down at the moment, but just imagine if Chiefcoin ever took off like Bitcoin—each coin could be worth thousands of dollars. The numbers are almost unimaginable."

"I'm in, Gary. Do your thing. I think Chief would approve."

"Okay, buddy, it's in the works. Y'all enjoy yourselves and I'll see y'all soon. Bye for now."

"Bye, Gary."

Rick kept looking at the picture of the coin and at Chief until he remembered where the photo came from. He scrolled though his phone and found the original closeup of Chief sitting on Gary's shoulder before they hightailed it out of the Boudain Hut in Port Arthur. He had taken the picture and texted it to Gary. He shook his head, trying not to laugh at what Gary was gonna pull off. The old saying "It takes money to make money" surely applied to Gary. He was always a hard worker but came from a meager background. Once he won the lottery, he used that money as leverage to increase his wealth. It was as if a fire was set under his ass. He never stopped conceiving ideas to use that leverage. Rick was proud of him. He had come a long way from that small house he grew up in back in LaBelle, Texas.

Possum stepped onto the pool deck and greeted Rick with a big drink that had an umbrella in it. Jules followed a few minutes later in a stunning two-piece swimsuit she had picked up on her shopping spree. With the hat and sunglasses, she looked like a model or a movie star. Rick couldn't take his eyes off of her. She was simply stunning. They all clinked their glasses, and Rick caught them up on Gary's new Chiefcoin idea and showed them the photo. They all laughed and Jules applauded. Chief just bobbed up and down, showing off his own new bathing suit and raising his crown. Jules rubbed sunblock on Rick's shoulders and face and scolded him for not doing it enough. She loved taking care of him, and Rick loved it too. They all had lunch by the pool and lounged for a few more hours. In the usual fashion, as soon as Possum finished lunch, he started scheming about where they would have dinner. "Who wants cow tonight?"

Jules stuck her arm in the air like a schoolgirl.

"I want cow! I want cow!"

Rick nodded in agreement. Possum used his phone to research steak houses in the area and came to the conclusion that the best damn restaurant in Rio was right inside their hotel. It was called Restaurante Pérgula. He contacted Luiz and made a reservation for three. He read the menu aloud, and even though Rick was full from lunch, his mouth began to water.

"You can get your choice of flank steak, ribeye, or sirloin. There's also an interesting breaded filet mignon. Listen to this—*filet mignon Milanese, served with chimichurri, choice of basmati rice, broccoli rice, creamed spinach, or smoked coleslaw and smashed garlic potatoes.*"

"Damn, that sounds good," piped up Rick.

"I want a ribeye. Don't they have baked potatoes?" asked Jules.

"Darlin', at these prices and given the five-star rating this restaurant has, I'm sure they'll make anything you want," replied Possum.

Jules gave a little silent clap close to her chest in joy. They all retired to their rooms for showers and planned to meet back up around 6:50 in the lobby. Jules helped Rick clean up in the shower. She wrapped his cast in the plastic wrap she'd gotten while out shopping and gently washed him under the warm water. Rick wanted her so bad, but in his condition, it was nearly impossible. She pulled in a teak chair from the balcony and helped him sit down. After they were both squeaky clean, she carefully straddled him and they made love for the first time in a long time. It was sweet, gentle, and loving.

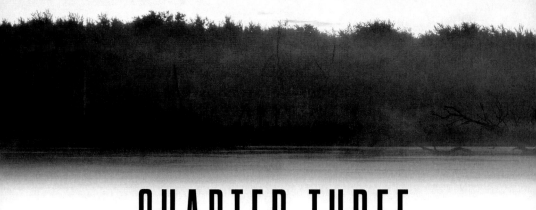

CHAPTER THREE

Jules waved at Possum, who was standing near a huge flower arrangement in the center of the expansive lobby. Rick was keeping up with her with the new crutches Possum had acquired for him. Everything about the Copacabana Palace radiated luxury, from the giant chandeliers to the enormous flower arrangements throughout the building. Possum was looking awfully debonair in his suit coat and slacks. The entire gang looked classy, but Jules outshined them all. She wore a low-cut maroon dress with a long slit up the leg. Every head in the hotel turned when she walked by. Rick couldn't have been prouder or more enamored.

"Cow?" asked Possum.

"Moo, moo," replied Rick.

The hostess sat them in a semicircular booth next to the wall that had a brightly colored mural painted on it. The restaurant had a tropical feel, the entire place adorned with colorful flowers and a mirrored ceiling. They settled around their table, and Rick took the right outside area, so he could keep his casted leg straight and comfortable.

The waiter introduced himself and presented a one-liter bottle of Caymus Cabernet, which Possum had prearranged before they sat down. Rick did the honors of approving the wine, and the waiter poured glasses for them all.

They raised their glasses, and Rick said, "Here's to Chiefcoin. May it follow in the footsteps of Dogecoin. To the moon!"

"To the moon!" they all repeated.

Both Rick and Possum went for the filet Milanese, and Jules ordered a medium-rare ribeye with a loaded baked potato. The potato alone was a meal. They all savored their food and talked as they enjoyed two bottles of the Caymus Cabernet.

Near the end of dinner, Rick's phone began to vibrate. He normally would let it go to voicemail, but it was Johnie, and since it was rather late, he felt he needed to take it. He apologized to Possum and Jules, moved away from the table, and took the call.

"Rick, how are you?"

"Good, Johnie. What's up? Everything okay with the boat?"

"Oh yeah, the boat's been steadily booked and we are getting good reviews and really starting to make a name for ourselves here as the premier charter in Destin. But that's not why I called. A woman stopped by the boat a week ago and asked if you were available to help her find something stolen from her home. She's a local. Lives in a massive mansion in Kelly Plantation. Her husband is one of the richest guys in town and responsible for a lot of the local development here. He's an investment banker. I told her you were out of town and she said she'd check back in a couple of days. She didn't seem too rushed or overly concerned, so I didn't bother you with it. I kinda put it on the back burner."

"Okay, so what changed? Does she wanna hire me now?" asked Rick.

Johnie hesitated. "This is incredibly difficult for me to say, Rick. You know I'm a good guy, but I did something I'm ashamed of and now I'm worried."

"Spit it out, Johnie. Just tell me."

"Okay, okay. Two nights ago, I ran into her again at Harry T's. We didn't have a charter the next day, so I was blowing off some steam. I was six drinks into happy hour when I spotted her. She waved me over and we started talking. She was quite buzzed too. She confided in me that her husband was abusive and cheated on her often. What she wanted you to find was a metal box with a million dollars in bearer bonds inside. They were given to her by her German grandmother. She claims that her husband stole them and hid them to punish her. He had filed for divorce and they had a prenup. If he divorced her, she would be left with nothing except those bonds."

"Okay, so let's find them," replied Rick.

"I'm not done, unfortunately. The entire story was just a ruse though. One drink led to another and another, and before I knew it, we were at her mansion. She told me her husband was out of town. I don't do things like that, but she was incredibly beautiful and persuasive. I think I slept with her, but I don't remember."

"You don't remember?"

"I think she slipped something into my drink. I woke up the next morning on the deck of the boat. I checked the cameras to see how I got there, but that section of the hard drive was blank. This morning, the sheriff's department came to the boat to question me."

"Question you about what?"

Johnie took a deep breath before he spoke.

"Her husband was found stabbed to death and burned almost beyond recognition in a field behind the old Helen Back Bar. They identified him by his jewelry. Plus, his car was found parked at Coyote Ugly with my prints all over it. The worst part is, when I came to on the boat, I realized my WÜSTHOF fillet knife was missing. You know, the one I always keep in the leather sheath on my belt. My prints were all over that knife. I'd bet anything that knife was the murder weapon. I'm being framed, Rick."

"Holy shit, Johnie! I'll get there as soon as I can. Don't go anywhere—just keep doing the day-to-day stuff. You don't wanna run. That'll make you look more guilty."

"My hands are shaking, Rick. That deputy was kinda pushy when he questioned me. They want me to come back in tomorrow for an interview."

"Don't say a thing. Lawyer up. I'm gonna text you the name of a lawyer I like from Niceville. He's been involved in some high-profile criminal cases. Remember that whatever you say can and will be used against you, so plead the Fifth and have him represent you. His name is David Swanick. He's a good guy and will take real good care of you. Don't worry. This will all work out."

"Thanks, Rick. I'm sorry to lay this all on you, but I'm freaking out."

"Don't give it a second thought. You are family and together we will sort this out. Keep the faith, buddy. See ya soon."

Rick made it back to the table and set his crutches to the side. There was no hiding the concern on his face from Jules.

"What's wrong, Rick?"

"Let's get the check and head back to the room. I'll fill y'all in when we get back."

Possum waved the waiter over to the table and signed the bill to his room number as instructed by Gary. He left him a generous tip and thanked him for his exceptional service.

Once they were all back in the suite, Rick asked Jules to pour three large rums over ice before he began to fill them in on Johnie's misfortune.

"Listen, guys, one of our own is in serious trouble. He's most likely gonna be charged with capital murder in the next couple of days. We all know Johnie and know he couldn't do anything like this. It's a total frame job. We unfortunately need to cut our recovery time here quite a bit shorter. I was hoping to be here long enough to get this cast off, but it's not in the cards."

"What?! Capital murder? Johnie?" blurted Possum.

"It's insane. I'm gonna need all your help on this one. This is what I know so far."

Rick told them exactly what Johnie had just explained to him and then pulled up the

Destin Log, Destin's local newspaper, on his phone and read aloud:

> "*Local businessman Kiefer Killian was found murdered behind the Helen Back Bar. The local sheriff's department have made no arrests but have questioned a few people as persons of interest. They have yet to name*

a suspect. Mr. Killian is survived by his wife, Pamela Killian. She has not been ruled out as a suspect. All indications point to this case not being just a robbery gone bad. According to a statement from Deputy Jason Putnam, there was no sign of a forced entry and more details will be coming soon. We will be following this story closely. If you have any information about this case, please contact the Okaloosa County Sheriff's Department or crime stoppers at 850-555-TIPS."

Rick shook his head. "I can't believe this shit! I have Johnie contacting Dave Swanick, local attorney. If Johnie gets charged, I will pay whatever the bail is. I don't want him spending any time in that rathole jail in Crestview."

He took a big swig of his rum, and Jules refreshed it, then hugged him as she put her head on his shoulder. She didn't have to speak for Rick to know that she loved Johnie too and was deeply concerned. They had all been through so much together; it was impossible for them not to have such a strong connection. The look on Possum's face was undeniable too. He had already started taking notes, and Rick knew once he was back in his room, he'd be online finding out anything and everything he could about the Killians.

It was still early, not even ten o'clock yet, so Rick piped up, trying to change the mood.

"How about we watch a movie? Something light? Have you seen the screen that comes down yet? Being all upset and worried about Johnie isn't gonna help him. He'd want us to enjoy ourselves. Let's at least fake it until we make it. Deal?"

They nodded in agreement, and Rick grabbed a remote from the wet bar and pushed a button. A huge ten-foot HD screen began to roll down from the ceiling. The projector was hanging just above Rick's head, and Jules arranged the couch so they could all sit down and have a good view. Jules rang up Luiz and ordered some popcorn and movie candy. Rick suggested they see *Captain Ron*. Both he and Possum had seen it many times, but Jules had not. It always made them laugh. Jules sat close to Rick and munched on popcorn as the movie started. They all tried to enjoy it and did laugh some, but a heaviness hung in the air that none of them could overlook.

Once the movie was over, Possum said his goodnights and headed off to his room. Jules was getting sleepy, so she went to bed. Rick kissed her on the forehead and opened his MacBook. He texted Possum and told him to focus on Pamela, and that he would get as much dirt as he could find on Kiefer. In Rick's mind, based on what Johnie had told him, neither one was a good person. The one thing Rick always knew was that if you were a bad person when you were poor, you'd be the same bad person if you were rich. Money couldn't buy class or integrity.

Once he was logged in, he signed into his VPN and then on to the NEXUS network and did a query on Pamela Killian. She was raised north of Atlanta and had graduated from the University of Georgia with a B.S. in criminal justice. She had never worked in that field and owned a small boutique store in Destin that sold high-end women's fashion and accessories. From what Rick could tell on the surface so far, she was a kept woman. He researched the annual income of the boutique, and it certainly wasn't enough to afford the kind of lifestyle and home she lived in. Her husband made all the money and gave her that boutique of hers so she would have something to do, as far as

Rick could tell. She had two cars registered in her name. Both were high-dollar vehicles less than a year old. A small BMW ragtop and a super expensive

Range Rover SUV worth well over a hundred grand.

Jules was purring quietly, and Rick checked on her a few times, trying not to disturb her. He continued to look into the background of Pamela and then came across a sealed court case against her before she was married to Kiefer. She was once married to a guy named Jacques

Hamilton. Jacques was found murdered only two years after they were married.

> We may have a Black Widow on our hands.

He texted Possum, knowing he was probably focused hard on his computer. Possum texted back and told Rick to come on over. It was too much to text.

The door to Possum's room was cracked open, so Rick stepped inside, then closed and locked the door behind him.

"Whatcha got, man?" asked Rick.

"This guy was not a good person. I found three charges against him for domestic violence. He was never convicted and all charges were dropped. He did spend some time in Okaloosa County Corrections, but each time, Pamela dropped the charges and the cases were thrown out. Do you think she killed him?"

"I'm not so sure about that. So, you're saying she made three allegations against him but dropped them all each time?" Rick frowned. "That tells me one of two things.

Either she had too much to lose financially if he went to prison, or she made false allegations. I'm leaning toward the latter."

"Why?"

"A gut feeling and the fact that her first husband was also found stabbed to death," said Rick.

Possum's eyes widened. "Really? Well, that does put a whole new spin on it. What does the charge say?"

"That's the problem—it's a sealed indictment. It's basically been expunged. I don't even know if she was ever a suspect or a person of interest. I wonder if our old buddy Carson can use his FBI contacts to get his eyes on that charge?" asked Rick.

"It's worth a try. I'll call him in the morning. Any way you look at it now, it seems to me these may have been some bad, bad people. We can't let Johnie take the rap for this."

"You got that right! Okay, let's get some sleep. We can rendezvous with Gary at his room in the morning. Sound good?"

"Sounds like a plan, Stan. See ya in the morning."

"Night, Possum."

Rick hobbled back into the room, trying to be as quiet as a church mouse, and slipped into bed. Jules just rolled over and wrapped her arms around him and never opened her eyes. It took Rick a while to fall asleep as he stared at the ceiling thinking about Johnie. He eventually dozed off.

Before he knew it, his phone was ringing and it was 8:00 a.m.

"Wake up, Rick. Possum's over here in my room and filled me in on Johnie. I ordered some breakfast. You and Jules, come on over. We'll figure this out. I haven't known Johnie long, but he ain't the kinda guy who would do something like this. Oh, and make sure to drive your racecar over!"

"Ha fucking ha! See ya in a minute."

Rick gently woke up Jules, and she bolted to the bathroom to clean her face. When she came out, Rick was sitting on his scooter.

"Want a lift, good looking?" he asked.

Jules laughed and stood on the end of the scooter as Rick drove it out the door bound for

Gary's presidential suite. At this point, he wasn't even embarrassed by it. He was just tired of Gary and Possum making fun of him, so he figured he'd drive it like he stole it. When he approached the room, Jules stepped off and knocked on the door. Gary opened it up, and Rick honked the horn and drove through the door as Gary burst out laughing. When he got inside the room, he looked to his right and saw the most powerful medicine man in all of the Yanomami tribe. He had completely forgotten that Davi would be there, and his face got red.

"This is Davi Kopenawa. Davi, this is Dale Earnhardt, the intimidator."

Davi looked confused and then Gary explained to him he was just kidding.

"Davi, this is Rick Waters. He was largely responsible for returning the Sacred Jewel of Orinoco to you."

The short, barefoot, crown feather-wearing man walked over toward Rick and stuck out his hand to shake.

"Hello, Dale Earnhardt. Hahaha."

"You speak English!"

"Yes, I spokesman for the Yanomami. I studied English in São Paulo. But I am Jeff

Gordon fan."

Rick just laughed and shook his hand. Davi was likeable from the first minute they met. It was no wonder why he was so influential in his tribe.

They all sat around the big table and drank coffee as Rick and Possum went over their notes with Gary. Davi was respectful of their meeting and stepped out to the pool to make a few calls. For a man who'd been raised without technology, he had conquered it and was probably just as at home in the rain forest as he was in an office building. Rick had to respect that.

CHAPTER FOUR

"What's the plan, Rick?" asked Gary.

"I've set him up with my lawyer, and whatever the bond is, I will pay it. As much as I hate to admit it, I've spent a few days in the Okaloosa County Corrections hell-hole. It's punishment jail, privately owned by a judge and a bail bondsman. I'm not even sure how that is legal. That's why we need jail reform, if you ask me. I personally dealt with the corruption there. I was up on an illegal possession charge because a guy I gave a lift to once from AJ's who was trashed, dropped his bag in my truck after a night of partying. I didn't even know it was there. It fell between the door and the seat and wedged itself under the seat. I have no problem with partying, but he had a bag with some weed and part of an eight ball inside."

"An eight ball, huh? You always did like pool!" chimed in Gary.

"Haha, different kind of eight ball. The judge I saw at first appearance was the co-owner of the jail, and he refused to give me bond because I was new in town and he said I was a flight risk. I did twelve days in there. Luckily, I called a friend on the outside and he vouched for me, and the second judge I saw granted me a thousand-dollar bond. I spent Christmas in there. What a nightmare. Luckily for me, the guy who dropped the bag confessed to a deputy who his supplier was after he got popped with possession with intent to sell, and also told him that the bag wasn't mine to begin with, in exchange for probation."

"Damn, dude. We need to make sure Johnie spends as little time in there as possible, or no time at all."

"That's for sure."

Rick, Gary, and Possum continued to go over what they could do to help Johnie, while Jules entertained Davi at the pool with Chief. Chief did most of the entertaining. Davi was mesmerized by him. They seemed to have an instant connection. Jules went into her suite and brought back a baggie of Chief's clipped wing feathers from his trimming. She presented them to Davi, who took them graciously and began to weave them into his headdress.

"Now Chief stays with me always," said Davi as he pointed to the white feathers.

He let Jules take a few photos of him holding Chief and pointing at his headdress. Some tribes never allowed photos, thinking it stole their soul, but Davi was used to it from being in the spotlight often while battling the building of the controversial dam.

"Davi, are you ready to go?" asked Gary.

"Yes, let's go."

Gary and Davi left for the Bank of Brazil to do the exchange for the museum money to the tribe's trust account. It was a big day for the Yanomami. Today their battle against the destruction of their sacred land would get a four-million-dollar boost. The plan was to meet up in the afternoon again in the presidential suite with a financial lawyer to draft the contracts for Chiefcoin. Rick was still trying to wrap his head around the entire thing but decided he was better off just going with the flow. He trusted Gary implicitly and knew whatever he was getting would probably lead to profit at some point. They would leave the following day bound for Destin to assist Johnie in the terrible mess he had gotten himself into.

Since this was their last day in Rio, they decided to spend as much time as possible relaxing by the pool. Rick was sick of hobbling around, and the thought of spending another three weeks in the cast was weighing on him. He wished he could heal faster, like he did before when he was stung by a centipede in the rainforest. He had spent the night in a sweat lodge with a shaman and come out as if it had never happened. Healing an infected wound was one thing, but he highly doubted any shaman could speed up the process of healing bones. It was a good thought, anyway, and he figured if anyone knew how to do such a thing, Davi would know. He decided it was worth a shot and texted Gary to ask Davi for him.

We just got to the bank, Gary texted back. *I'll ask him and let you know.*

An hour later, he texted back only three words.

Davi says yes!

Oh, thank God. Let's do this. I'm ready to get back to being myself, replied Rick, feeling a sense of relief combined with hope.

It was around two o'clock when Davi and Gary returned from the exchange accompanied by a lawyer and his assistant. They all gathered around the big table, and the lawyer passed out contracts for them all to read over.

"My name is Silva Constantine. I am here on behalf of Gary Haas and Chiefcoin. If you have any questions, don't hesitate to ask. The inner workings of a cryptocurrency are incredibly hard to explain, but I'll do my best to make it understandable in layman's terms. Basically, cryptocurrency is a digital currency in which transactions are verified and records maintained by a decentralized system using cryptography, rather than by a centralized authority. It's unregulated and cannot be affected by government interference. I hope that helps."

"I like the part about not being affected by government interference," interjected Possum.

"Me too," said Rick.

Silva was dressed like a typical techie. He wore a *Rick and Morty* t-shirt with his computer

glasses and several pens shoved into the front pocket. The only thing missing was a pocket protector and masking tape across the nosepiece of his black-rimmed glasses. He showed them where he planned to make Chiefcoin live as soon as the papers were signed. It would be listed on Coinbase, and people would be able to trade it through a website called PancakeSwap. He would start the initial coin value at 0.00005 and would release sixty billion coins divided equally at ten billion each for Rick, Jules, Possum, Gary, and Davi, leaving ten million for another person of their choosing. They immediately all said Johnie, considering how loyal he was and what he was going through. They would have to have him sign digitally, and Silva assured them that it wouldn't be a problem and that he did it all the time.

Rick texted Johnie to open up the computer on the boat and stand by for an email. Instead of trying to text it all, he stopped and called him.

"Johnie, it's Rick. How are you?"

"I'm good, Rick. I met with the lawyer and he has taken the case and will represent me in all meetings with the sheriff's department. They weren't too pleased, as you can imagine, and tried to tell me it made me look more guilty. When I told Dave what they said, he ripped them a new one and threatened to file a harassment charge against the lead detective. They backed off fast. Thanks again for hooking me up with him."

"My pleasure, Johnie. We're gonna beat this rap. Don't worry. Now for some good news. Just sign what I'm emailing you and trust me, at some point it could be worth a substantial amount of money. Are you familiar with cryptocurrency?"

"Heck yeah, I trade it all the time. A buddy turned me onto it and I bought some

Dogecoin at three cents and sold a bunch when it hit sixty-one cents. Made a nice, healthy profit. I still have about twenty thousand Dogecoins. Why?"

"The paper you are about to sign will give you possession of ten billion coins of the newest crypto on the market: Chiefcoin."

"Chiefcoin? As in Chief the cockatoo?"

"The very one sitting on Jules's lap right now chomping on a grape."

Johnie guffawed. "Oh man, that is hilarious! How did you come up with that idea?"

"It was Gary's scheme. It's a way to legally launder that five million from the briefcase."

"Say no more. I'm happy and honored to sign it. It'll give me something to look forward to when I get out of prison."

"You're not going to prison, Johnie. I won't let that happen. You have my word."

"Thanks, Rick. When are you sending the contract?"

"Right now."

Johnie's computer pinged, and he clicked open a long contract in PDF form. He saved it to his desktop, then followed directions from the lawyer to attach it and upload it to a website called PDF24, which was a place to sign and download PDFs completely free. He signed it and attached it to the return email to the lawyer while Rick was on speakerphone. "Okay, we are ready to go live," said Silva. "Who wants to do the honors?" They all pointed at Gary, since it was his idea.

"Everyone, grab a glass of champagne. I'll do a countdown," said Gary.

"Johnie, you got any champagne on board?" asked Rick.

"Nah, but I just opened a can of Destin Brewery East Pass IPA. Will that work?"

"It ain't the champagne of beers, but heck yeah, that'll work," replied Rick.

"Wait, you're right. I have a six pack of Miller High Life the captain left on board. Let me grab one. That *is* the champagne of beers."

The can made a *pssssssssssssssssssssch* sound when Johnie cracked it open.

"Okay, I'm ready, y'all," said Johnie.

Gary moved up to the MacBook sitting by the lawyer and hovered his finger over the return key.

"Three, two, one, Chiefcoin!"

"Chiefcoin!" they all exclaimed.

Even Chief yelled some gibberish from all the excitement. Rick gave him a taste of champagne and he turned his beak away.

They all toasted and looked at the computer. Silva closed the page then reopened it and did a search for Chiefcoin, and it popped right up.

"It's live now, all right," he said.

They all shook his hand, and Gary walked him out. Rick noticed Davi going through a black bag he had brought in with him and hobbled over to see what he was up to.

"Whatcha doing, Davi?" asked Rick.

"I'm getting the herbs and sacred artifacts needed to heal your broken bones. You believe, don't you?"

Rick nodded that he did, but Davi gave him a stern look like he could see right through him.

"You don't believe it will work, Rick Waters, and if you don't believe, it definitely won't work. Let me tell you a story. Many moons ago when I was a young boy, I was sitting with a wise elder. He was the shaman of the tribe. His name was Running Bear. Across the field in front of us was one of the great warriors, Gray Hawk. He was doing a tribal dance and teaching the young warriors the steps. I asked Running Bear how he got his name. He told me that when he was a young boy himself, he outran an Andean Bear and his father then gave him that name.

"'What about Gray Hawk?' I asked.

"He replied, 'Gray Hawk got his name because when he was young, a huge gray hawk used to fly over his crib. Why do you ask, Two Dogs Fucking?'"

Rick nearly fell over laughing, not seeing the joke coming. Jules and Chief were also laughing.

Davi put his hand on Rick's shoulder and said, "Now that I have eased your tension, Rick, I need you to get serious and believe what I am doing will heal your wounds and make you well again. I need you to say over and over: 'I will walk today' in your head and then aloud. You have to believe with all your heart that you will shed the cast on your leg and once again be able to walk and run. I say this with all the sincerity in the world. It is no joke. You must believe."

This time, Rick nodded and said, "I believe, Davi. I believe."

Davi got help from Jules to get Rick into a comfortable position on a sofa chair in the great room of Gary's presidential suite. He wrapped Rick's eyes with a large cloth and then lit a large roll of sage and began to wave it in a circle around Rick. In a bowl, Davi mixed several herbs and some liquid from a gourd he opened. He began to chant and dance in a circle in front of Rick. This continued for fifteen minutes. He suddenly stopped and pulled out some large animal bones from his bag, placed one on each side of Rick's cast, and wrapped them with some string. He instructed Rick to drink the potion and repeat a phrase in Yanomami. Rick did as he was told.

"*Oáke, mamáke, oáke, mamáke.*"

Rick repeated it ten times as Davi waved a feather up and down each side of the animal bones tied to Rick's cast. He began to feel a warming in his cast, as if a heat lamp had been placed in front of it. With his blindfold on, he assumed some warming device was against his leg. Slowly, the warm sensation moved up his leg toward the center of his chest, and his heart filled with warmth. Lights in his eyes under his blindfold began to spin in a counterclockwise direction, and soon he had slipped into a dream state. He felt as if he were flying, and on each side of him, eagles soared through the sky at the speed of light, then slowed to a stall and began to dive. One was pure white and the other brown. Down, down, down the three of them dove toward the rain forest into a clearing. They slowly opened their wings as Rick opened his arms, and they gently landed on the soft grass. Rick looked over at each eagle. Their eyes seemed to smile, and they suddenly took off and flew out of sight. Rick was jolted out of his dream and ripped off his eye covering.

"What happened? Where am I?" asked Rick in a confused state.

His eyes finally adjusted and he saw Davi sitting cross-legged in front of him. Davi turned his hands outward and motioned for Rick to rise. He did so, forgetting he was wearing a cast. He stood up and realized he felt no pain or discomfort in his leg. He took a few steps and still felt nothing.

"Would you like to remove the cast, Rick?" asked Davi.

"Is this real?"

"No, Rick, you are in a dream and I am ghost." Davi grinned in a mocking way, which made Rick laugh.

Rick sat back down as Gary and Jules cut away at the cast with a Dremel from Gary's tool bag. Once it was off, Jules scratched his itchy leg and calf muscle, then cleaned it with a washcloth and rubbed some cocoa butter on his legs. Rick reached down where his leg was broken and felt a slight knot but no pain. He slowly rose and carefully put all of his weight on it. "Unbelievable!" exclaimed Rick.

He took a few steps, then a few more and made a faux jump shot in the air. He had no pain whatsoever.

"Am I healed?" asked Rick.

"Do you believe?" replied Davi.

"Yes, yes, I believe!"

"Then you are ready. Now you are an eagle. Strong and swift."

"How did you...?" asked Rick

"I was the white eagle, Rick. You were the brown."

"Wait, but..."

"Rick, you have a better tan than me." Davi chuckled.

Rick just stared at Davi, too shocked to laugh but perplexed. Davi patted him on his back.

"Just a little Yanomami humor, Dale Earnhardt!" said Davi.

Rick laughed, shook Davi's hand, and thanked him.

Each step Rick took around the room gave him more confidence. His leg felt strong and the pain was completely gone. If miracles existed, this was one of them. Davi left the room accompanied by Gary, who was giving him a ride back to his own hotel.

"Jules, let's go for a walk."

"Are you sure you're ready?" she asked. "You don't want to overdo it."

"I'm ready!"

Jules held Rick's hand as they got on the elevator. He continued to take steps in place in the elevator and stretch. If someone had asked him what he thought of that shaman mumbo jumbo a few years ago, he would've laughed in their face. Now he was a true believer.

They took the rear exit and stepped onto the beach. The sky was a deep blue with a few wisps of clouds. The water lapped on the shore with tiny clapping waves. It was a glorious day, and Rick felt reborn. They walked to the water's edge, turned right, and continued to walk. People were lounging on beach towels and chairs, sipping drinks out of coconuts and soaking up the sun.

Rick pointed to the lifeguard station about fifty yards away.

"Race ya!" exclaimed Rick.

"What?"

Rick took off running before Jules even knew what was happening. She ran after him, trying to catch up, but never did. He slowed down then rolled in the sand laughing. Jules finally caught up with and pounced on him as they both laughed, rolling together with their arms wrapped around each other. Tears welled up in Rick's eyes—tears of joy. He was back!

CHAPTER FIVE

Rick and Jules stepped into the limo as the driver put their luggage in the trunk. Chief sat between them in his travel cage. His crown was up and he was speaking gibberish and bouncing up and down on his perch. He could tell they were headed somewhere and was overly excited. The driver said nothing as he pulled onto the road bound for the executive airport. Gary had left earlier with Possum and texted Rick that the plane was fueled and ready. Rick texted Johnie a few words of encouragement and let him know their itinerary. They would fly nonstop to Caracas, refuel then head directly to the Destin Executive Airport. It had been a hot minute since Rick had been home, and it would be Jules's first time to visit.

"Mr. Waters, do you need to make any stops before we get to the airport?" asked the driver.

"No, I think we're good. You need anything, Jules?" asked Rick.

Jules shook her head as the driver looked in the rearview mirror. Rick fumbled with his backpack, rearranging his electronics—a nervous habit. Even after hundreds of flights, he still hated flying and always got a knot in his stomach before taking off. Something about not being in control bothered him. He had vowed to take flying lessons one day. The cost had always been the factor, but with the big payouts on the last few cases and the creation of Chiefcoin on the crypto market, he now had plenty of comfort room to afford lessons and planned to look into it after they arrived.

The driver pulled into the Rio de Janeiro International Airport and parked on the executive side, where Gary's Embraer was. Rick tipped the driver and pulled the bags, while Jules carried Chief in his travel cage. Once on board, she let him out and set him on a perch that Rick had made out of PVC pipes and suction cups. It was secured on the desk with some newspapers beneath it. The pilot gave his briefing and they were off. As usual, Rick did a sign of the cross on his chest as Jules squeezed his hand during takeoff. He was always fine once airborne, just hated takeoffs. Gary's personal private flight attendant made them some spicy Bloody Marys. Rick drank his about halfway, then laid his head back and drifted off to sleep.

The flight landed in Caracas, and the bump from landing jolted Rick awake. For a second, he didn't know where he was. Jules was still holding his hand and leaning her head on his shoulder. She was awake but peaceful.

"Jules, you all right, baby? Hungry?" asked Rick.

Rick had been making a point lately to give Jules extra attention and make sure she was in a good state of mind. He pampered her, even. She had lost their baby very recently and he wasn't sure how it would affect her going forward, so he made sure she knew he would take care of her and loved her.

"Yeah, I could eat," she replied.

The pilot called Gary to the cockpit. He unbuckled his seatbelt and made his way there as the pilot slowly taxied toward the terminal. A few minutes later, he came back and got everyone's attention. "Hey, guys, we're gonna be delayed here. We are being escorted to another area. Customs wants to search the plane. They think I'm a smuggler or something, since I've flown in and out of here so often lately."

"Dammit, man, that's all we need," interjected Rick.

"We may end up spending the night here. Nothing to worry about. This is the exact reason why I created Chief-coin. I guarantee they would've found that briefcase and taken it. They are so corrupt here," continued Gary.

The plane came to a stop at the farthest point of the executive airport, by a rusty old hangar with a few Cessnas inside.

Jules squeezed Rick's arm and pointed out of the window. He followed her gaze and saw several black SUVs with "Customs" on the side, as well as some Policía Nacional Bolivariana vehicles. They all carried machine guns.

"It's okay, Jules. Everything will be fine. They probably want a bribe, which Gary will happily pay if they would just go away," said Rick.

The plane came to a stop. The flight attendant lowered the door and stepped back as three armed Customs agents and two national police came aboard. Gary told everyone to remain calm.

"¿Hablas español?" the first guy asked Gary.

"No, we speak English here," replied Gary.

The man waved the second guy up, and he approached Gary.

"Are you Gary Haas?" he asked.

"Yes, what is this about?"

"Please collect all the passports of your crew and passengers now."

"Why?"

"Do it now!" he said in a raised voice.

"Hey, guys, hand me your passports. This is a shakedown. Don't worry."

They all handed Gary their passports. Jules was biting her lip, a bit nervous. The man looked through them all before placing them in a plastic baggie and tucking it under his vest.

"We have reason to believe you are smuggling illegal drugs, and we are going to search the plane."

"This is bullshit! I am a businessman. Every time I come through here, y'all hassle me. Do you have a warrant?"

The man laughed. "We don't need a warrant. You are in Venezuela and we have just cause to search your plane for contraband or drug money. I suggest you cooperate and this will go much more smoothly."

Rick noticed his English was perfect and really didn't have much of a Venezuelan accent. It was more of an accent he was extremely familiar with. He had a small tattoo of a fleur-de-lis on the inside of his wrist. Rick knew right away; the guy was from New Orleans.

"May I ask a question?" asked Rick.

The man scowled at him. "No, you may not."

"How's ya mama an' them?"

The man looked at Rick, stunned at what he'd just said.

"I'm from East Texas and I have a friend in New Orleans, so I picked up a little of the lingo."

The man's scowl went away and he instantly became more relaxed.

"Okay, listen up. We are going to search the plane, and if nothing is found, you'll be on your way soon," he announced.

Everyone stepped off of the plane and onto the tarmac. Gary asked if he could make a quick phone call, and the Cajun man agreed. Gary spoke to someone out of Rick's hearing range and then said something to the agent. He waved his hand in a circle, and all the agents stepped off of the plane. He handed Gary the passports and shook his hand. He scribbled something on a business card and handed it to Gary as well. Everyone got back on the plane as the fuel truck pulled up. They all sat in silence, waiting for the fuel. Soon the door was closed and the pilot started the engines.

"What the fuck was that about, Gary?" asked Rick.

"I took your lead. As soon as you figured out he was from New Orleans, I knew what to do. I have a club suite in the Superdome. I promised him free tickets to any games he wants, any time he wants, if he could just move this along, so we could get out of here. The card he gave me is his mailing address in New Orleans. He married a Venezuelan girl and works here half of the year and works in New Orleans the other half. He owns the security company at the executive airport in New Orleans, so it's a win-win for me there too." Gary grinned.

Rick raised an eyebrow. "I didn't know you were a Saints fan."

"I'm not. I'm a Cowboys fan through and through, and also have a suite at AT&T Stadium. But I was doing a lot of trades in Louisiana, so I got the suite at the Superdome for business. I've closed lots of deals there over a Miller Lite."

"Genius!" said Rick.

Once the plane was fueled, the pilot made his quick announcement and they were off.

Next stop, Destin.

They ate lunch and discussed Johnie's predicament back in Destin while sitting around the bar at the back of the plane. About two hours into the flight, the pilot came on and told everyone to take their seats and fasten their seatbelts. The plane began to lose altitude fast and violently shake.

"What's going on?" yelled Rick as he gripped his armrests.

"I don't know. Just hang tight," replied Gary.

Rick leaned over Jules and looked out of the window. He could see a large green mountain on an island.

"We are making an emergency landing in Jamaica. Everyone, prepare for landing," said the pilot.

The flight attendant took her seat. Rick made the sign of the cross, and Jules squeezed him harder than she ever had. The plane bounced in the sky like a ping-pong ball, losing and gaining altitude in the turbulence. Rick closed his eyes and began to pray.

As the pilot approached the runway, Rick could see fire trucks with their lights on parked along the tarmac. The pilot guided the plane toward the ground, but there was a sudden change in the sound. Rick knew the port engine had stopped. The plane was coming down too fast.

"What's going on?" Jules cried.

With a loud crack, the wheels slammed into the ground, ripping one from the fuselage. The right wing scraped the asphalt, causing massive sparks. The pilot righted the plane and threw the remaining engine into full reverse. The plane skidded down the runway, past the terminal with the fire trucks in pursuit. The end of the runway was quickly approaching as the pilot desperately tried to stop, applying all he had to the brakes. Smoke was coming from the remaining wheels—Rick could see it rising up beyond the window. The plane came to an abrupt stop mere feet from the end of the runway. Just a few more feet and they would've been in the bay.

"Come on, we've gotta get out of here," said Rick, grabbing Jules's arm.

The pilot opened the door and they all exited quickly. Smoke was billowing from the brakes as the fire truck arrived. The firefighters sprayed heavy foam all over the wheels, quickly extinguishing the flames. Jules's hands were shaking, and Rick had his arm around her to calm her down. The only one who didn't seem upset was Chief, who was bouncing up and down in his travel cage from all the excitement.

"What happened?" Gary asked the pilot.

"I'm not sure. I got a warning and then suddenly lost engine number two. We're gonna be here for bit, I'm afraid, until they figure it out."

"I'm just glad to be safely on the ground. You did a great job. I'm looking for a new fulltime pilot. Would you be interested, Clay?" asked Gary.

"I do pretty well working for the association, but I have my second child on the way and something more steady would be welcome. They also provide medical insurance," he replied.

"Just give me a number, Clay, and we can work it out. Just let me know in the next couple of days. Think it over and get back to me," said Gary.

Gary waved everyone over.

"Listen, y'all. The issue with the plane will have to be investigated by the NTSB and repairs will have to be made. I can get us a charter jet but probably no sooner than tomorrow. I suggest we have an enjoyable day in Jamaica and get a fresh start in the morning. How's that sound?"

They all nodded, and Rick said, "Yeah, a cold drink on a warm beach right now is about the best idea I could think of. Where the hell are we? I know Jamaica, but where?"

Gary looked up at the pilot for an answer and he said, "We are in Kingston. This was the runway closest to where the incident occurred."

"Welcome to Kingston Town," exclaimed Gary.

"Mr. Haas, if I may interrupt," said Clay. "We shouldn't stay in Kingston. It's crime ridden and dangerous. I've flown in here several times and there are many nice resorts just an hour's car ride to Ocho Rios. It's much nicer and safer."

"First of all, call me Gary. Mr. Haas is my dad. And secondly, is there one resort in particular you'd suggest?"

He thought for a second then said, "Yes, on one of my trips last month, the owner put us all up in the Moon Palace, all inclusive. It was stunning, with a guarded private beach and even a manmade surfing pool. The food was amazing and we all thought it was the best we'd had on the island."

"Okay, Moon Palace it is. Can you arrange for a van, Clay?"

"Sure thing. As a matter of fact, I believe I still have the driver's number in my phone from the last trip. He was hilarious and drove a big luxurious custom Sprinter van with Bob Marley painted on the side. I'll see if he's available first."

An airport medical van pulled up and checked everyone's vitals, and another van escorted them to the terminal. The went through customs and waited for their luggage to be brought from the plane. As they left the customs area, an agent stopped them.

"De bird will have to stay in quarantine. We no allow animals on de island, Mon, without de proper paperwork and fees."

"How much are these fees?" asked Gary.

"De normal fee is one hundred dollars US, mista. Plus, you need a USDA APHIS

Veterinary Medical Officer Signature," said the man.

"I'm sure we can pay an expedited fee. He already has his vet papers on my phone digitally," said Rick as he peeled off three hundred-dollar bills.

The man looked around and quickly waved them through.

"Money talks. Bullshit walks," said Rick under his breath.

As they approached the curb, a man with waist-length dreads was leaning against a long black Sprinter van, which had a bright graphic on its side of Bob Marley smoking a big fatty. He was holding up a sign with HAAS on it.

"I wonder if that's our ride," said Gary sarcastically.

They made their way toward him, and he immediately recognized Clay. "Hey, Mon! Welcome back to Jamaica, Mr. Pilot Mon. How you been?"

Clay shook his hand and introduced everyone to the Rasta driver.

"This is Bunny, everyone."

"Why Bunny?" asked Rick.

"Cuz I always be hoppin' all over de island, Mon!" he said as he let out a huge laugh.

They all climbed into the luxury van. It was set up like a limo with sideways bench sofas and a bar at the back with a nice mahogany table with cupholders in the center. Bob Marley's Greatest Hits CD was playing over a powerful twenty-speaker system with huge subs. The volume was nice and they could still hear each other. Bunny turned his captain's chair around and gave his speech.

"Welcome to my Jamaica, Mon. Home of de late great Bob Marley, de magical Blue Mountain, and de best spliff dis side of de Caribbean. Please help yourself to a Bloody Bunny or rum punch and here are some brownies my wife made. Don't eat more dan one. They is de funny kind. Okay, Mon, Ocho Rios, here we go!"

Gary immediately downed a brownie and passed them around. Rick took one, and Jules broke one in half. Gary started making drinks and singing along with Bob Marley. He was in an exceptionally good mood, considering what they had just been through. Rick figured he was overcompensating to squash down his anxiety. He went with it. Gary accidentally dropped a corner of a brownie into Chief's cage, and he scarfed it up before Gary could get the door open. "Oh, shit! Chief ate a piece of brownie," exclaimed Gary.

"How big?" asked Rick.

"Just a small corner. Will he be okay?"

"Yeah, he should be fine. The guy I got him from was a stoner and he told me Chief enjoyed smoke blown on him. I never did it, so I guess we'll see. I'd actually be more worried about the chocolate, but he should be okay since it was so small. Might make him a little jumpy. Let's keep an eye on him."

Jules had a rum punch and Rick, Gary, and Possum all had some twenty-one-year-old Appleton rum over ice. The pilot waved it off, as he might have to fly the next day. Possum ate a second brownie and winked at Rick. Rick knew he could handle it. His tolerance was far greater than the rest of theirs. He'd been a stoner for quite a while. He mostly did it as a pain reliever for the botched knee replacement he'd had years back. He originally was prescribed Tramadol, but the side effects were horrible and they made him a little cray cray, so he switched to medical marijuana and never took another pill again. His knee had long since healed, but the THC mixed with some CBD had helped him sleep better than he had in years, so he continued to use it.

Rick noticed that Jules's hands had stopped shaking and figured the brownie helped. Bunny stopped a few times to point out tourist spots and tell his stories.

"Chief? Chief? Are you okay, boy?" asked Rick.

They all looked over at Chief's cage. He was hanging upside down from the top of the cage, something they'd never seen him do before. Another Bob Marley song came on, and Chief mimicked it off-key. Everyone laughed at Chief acting stoned. He just hung there singing, whistling, and raising his crown.

Bunny pulled into the resort and opened the door for everyone, and Gary paid him and gave him a substantial tip. Bunny handed Gary another bag full of his wife's brownies and gave him a big bear hug. He also handed Gary his card and told him he'd be available 24/7. Gary had arranged for adjoining rooms in the palatial resort. He handed them all their keys and tipped the bellman to bring up the luggage. "Let's go surfing! Last one in is a rotten Rasta!" exclaimed Gary.

CHAPTER SIX

With Chief in tow, Rick and Jules made their way to their room. Rick let Chief out of his travel cage and propped him on top. He was still acting goofy. Jules sat on the edge of the bed, and Rick joined her. The quiet of the room suddenly made the entire incident on the plane real, and it seemed to hit them both at once. Jules began to sob, and Rick held her tightly without saying a word.

"Rick, we could've died on that plane."

"I know, Jules, but we didn't. We are all okay and safe."

"Why is Gary acting like nothing happened?" asked Jules.

"I think it's his way of blocking it out of his mind somehow. You know, kind of fake it 'til you make it? Everyone deals with trauma differently. That's just his way of handling it. Give him some time and he'll be okay. Would you like to talk about it more?"

"I don't know what to say, Rick. It happened so fast. It may be cliché, but you know they say you see your life pass in front of your eyes? I did. I saw everything all at once, including losing the baby. I think that finally hit me as well. I'm sorry, Rick."

"No need to be sorry. It was a rough thing that happened. It just wasn't our time for a baby. We can still practice, right?"

That made Jules laugh a little and cheered her up.

"Maybe we should also fake it until we make it, Rick? I'd like to try this so-called surfing machine."

"I agree, Jules. Let's get changed. I'm gonna call Johnie first and let him know what's going on. Can you buzz Possum's room with the house phone and see if he wants to join us?" "I'm on it," she replied.

Rick stepped onto the veranda and called Johnie.

"Nine-Tenths Charters, Johnie speaking. How may I help you?"

"You've certainly got the professional phone thing down, Johnie. How are you doing?"

"Haha, I knew it was you, Rick, but I thought I'd lay it on thick anyway. I'm doing okay.

Are y'all already in Destin?"

"Not exactly."

Rick explained how they'd crash-landed in Jamaica and would possibly be stuck there for a few days. Johnie told him not to worry because he was out on bond and there wouldn't be a hearing for at least a month and a half. It was business as usual.

"Okay, Johnie. Hang in there and we'll be there ASAP and figure this whole thing out."

"All right, Rick. I'll keep the charters going and keep doing my thing until y'all get here."

After Rick hung up and came back inside, he asked, "Did you get in touch with Possum, Jules?"

"Naw, he didn't answer. Maybe he's checking out the resort. I'm sure we'll find him."

They both threw on their bathing suits, and Jules grabbed a cover-up. Rick filled Chief's bowl with some treats he found in the minibar, and he went to town on them. He definitely had the munchies. Jules grabbed the complimentary bottle of wine and put it in a beach bag with a couple of plastic wine glasses. They walked out of the veranda right to the pool.

The pool was expansive and almost the entire length of the resort. According to the map, the FlowRider Surfing Simulator was past the main pool at the beginning of the jetty. As they continued to walk, there was Possum, on a beach chair propped up under a palm tree, with an umbrella drink in one hand and a cigar in the other.

"Well, there you are, amigo," said Rick. "Jules tried to call your room, but I see you beat us to the idea of lounging. We're gonna try the surfing thing. Wanna join us?"

"I appreciate it, man, but I need to stay here and prop up this palm tree so it doesn't fall down. Y'all have fun."

Rick and Jules continued to stroll hand in hand down the path by the pools to the surfing simulator. As they got closer, they could hear someone hooting and hollering and recognized the voice; it was Gary, and he was ripping the kneeboard up and down the manmade wave slope.

"Y'all gotta try this. It's insane," yelled Gary just after he wiped out.

"That's why we're here, dufus!" replied Rick.

Jules went first as Rick watched her. She already knew how to surf and windsurf, so she was a natural and took to it right away. The same thing couldn't be said about Rick. He was athletic and had good balance, but it took him a while to get the hang of it. He was busting his butt more than standing up, and Jules laughed at him and pointed as she held her side.

After about thirty minutes, he decided enough was enough and turned the board back over to Jules. Gary had ordered a round of Flaming Bob Marley shots. They were layered from top to bottom, green, yellow, and red, just like the Jamaican flag. The green was obviously mixed with 151 proof rum, as it was on fire when the waiter delivered them. They all blew the flames out, and Rick lifted his glass in a toast.

"To Johnie, the best first mate a guy could have. May he be found not guilty!"

As they finished their shots, Clay approached them and got Gary's attention. Gary walked over as Clay spoke with him. Gary waved Rick and Jules over to hear what he had to say as well.

"I just got off the phone with one of the mechanics at the airport. They found the problem with the plane. When they drained the fuel tanks, they noticed a large amount of water in the fuel.

Now, it's normal to have a small percentage of water in fuel. Water is heavier than fuel and sinks to the bottom. I noticed that the number two engine, which we lost, was a little less efficient than the number one engine. That's probably because it was rebuilt earlier this year and not quite as broken in as the number one. That's considered normal due to condensation. Here's the catch, though. The amount of water they found in the fuel tanks was about fifty percent of the fuel tank capacity. The number two engine went through all the fuel and then began to intake the water, which is why it died. Since the number one was more efficient, there were still a few gallons of fuel floating on the water. That's the only reason we didn't lose it."

"Are you saying what I think you're saying?" asked Gary.

"If you think I'm saying that the plane was sabotaged, then yes. That amount of water had to have been purposely pumped into the tanks. There's no other explanation," said Clay.

"Why would someone do this? Who, for that matter?" said Rick.

"I have a few ideas and I wanna get to the bottom of it," replied Gary. "I'm gonna get cleaned up and head back to the airport and talk to the NTSB. If y'all wanna get some dinner, just put it on the room. I'll be back later and check in with y'all."

"You want me to go with?" asked Rick.

"Nah, I'm not even sure I can get to the right person, but it's worth a try. Y'all just hang and enjoy the resort. That includes you, Clay. If I need you for anything, I'll send a car.

They all nodded, and he turned and jogged off toward his room. They all settled in after dinner went to sleep fairly early. The next day was gonna be busy.

The next morning, Jules took another run on the surf machine, and Rick kicked back and watched her rip. When she'd had enough, they walked back to their room to get cleaned up for lunch. She opened the bottle of wine and they both had a glass. There were several choices for food at the resort, and they decided to give Pier 8 a try. It was an open-air restaurant with large ceiling fans and tables that overlooked the beach. Rick ordered the jerk pork chops and Jules got the seafood soup.

After lunch, they took a short nap on their back deck. They both dozed off fairly quickly. Feeling refreshed, they decided to do some sightseeing. Ocho Rios, meaning eight rivers, was a misnomer, since there actually weren't eight rivers. There was a famous set of waterfalls, though, called Dunn's River Falls. Jules showed Rick a brochure about the falls she had picked up, and they decided it might be worth checking out.

They threw on bathing suits with hiking shorts over the top and made their way to the lobby to find a taxi to the falls. After speaking to the concierge and learning it was only seven miles away, they decided to rent scooters and explore the city a little on the way instead of using a taxi. They were given helmets, gloves, and a quick mandatory lesson.

"Okay, Mon, stay on de main road. Don't go up into de hills. Dey will try and coax you up to buy some spleef but dey is also some undercover peeps and you never know who is who. If you wanna get some good spleef, just ask for Reggie. I am Reggie," he said with a devilish grin.

"Well, thanks, Reggie. If we are in need, you will be the first person we come find," replied Rick.

Reggie pumped his fist to his heart twice and said, "Blessed Mon!"

They took out the map that Reggie had given them. He had circled a few must-see spots. The one that stuck out the most was the Ocho Rios Market. It would require a little backtracking but was well worth it according to Reggie. They both brought empty backpacks in case they wanted to pick up some souvenirs. The little 50cc scooters were nimble and quick. They weaved in and out of traffic and got to the market in no time.

After locking up the scooters to a tree, they walked hand in hand and did the tourist thing. Rick picked up a hand-carved tree with birds on it. He thought it would look good back on the boat. Jules picked up some cold-pressed coconut oil and a nice selection of aromatherapy candles. A woman was making frozen drinks in pineapples, and they both got one. They were topped with Myer's Dark and had several spices floating on the concoction. They decided to just have one since the drinks were so strong and they had to ride the scooters.

As they approached the scooters at the edge of the market, a group of local men began to follow them. Rick noticed them right away and didn't say anything to Jules. He softly touched the small of her back so she would walk in front of him. As they got to the bikes, Rick quickly unlocked his scooter and wrapped the chain around his hand with the heavy lock hanging off of the far end of the chain.

"Jules, stand behind your scooter. Unlock it and don't move."

"What?"

Rick spun around to face the group.

"Whatcha want, bumbaclots?!" he yelled.

The group stopped, looking a little shocked at Rick cussing at them in Jamaican slang, which basically meant douchebags.

The big one in front said, "Gimme your wallet and bags."

"Now, why would I do that?" replied Rick.

Two of them pulled machetes into view and waved them side to side like the way the queen waves.

"Ah, so you think I'm gonna give you my money because a couple of you got pig stickers?

Now that's funny." Rick let out a scary evil laugh.

"We aren't playing, Mon! Do it now!" yelled one of them.

"That's too bad because I really wanted to play. Here, Jules, hold my bag. Give me your chain lock."

Jules handed it to him and placed his bag beside hers behind the scooter. She looked scared, but when Rick winked at her with a grin, her shoulders relaxed somewhat. Rick started swinging the chains like nunchucks and yelling like an insane person.

"Ahhhhhhhh, let's go, mother fuckers. Let's play!"

He started spinning the chains like a jumping rope on both sides of his body and slamming the locks against the concrete, creating sparks. The locals all got wide-eyed and turned to run when Rick moved toward them. He kept screaming and running at them, and they all ran off and disappeared into the market in all different directions. He stopped and came back to Jules, laughing so hard he could barely walk.

"That's funny, Rick? You find that funny? They could have hurt us!" said Jules.

"Nah, they were just some punk boys. I actually always wanted to try acting crazy like that to see if I could scare someone. I saw it in a movie called *I Love You, Man*."

"But what if it didn't work? Then what?"

"Well, then I would've had to split some skulls. Maybe they'll think twice about trying to rob tourists now. Those skinny machetes were no match for three-eighths-inch stainless steel chains and heavy locks," he replied.

Jules sighed. "Okay, Rick. Thanks for protecting me. Maybe next time just please give me a heads-up."

"Okay. I didn't want you to get scared and I also wanted to get the jump on them with the chains, so I kept you looking ahead. They had been following us for a while as we were leaving the market. Anyway, all is well now. Let's hit the falls."

Their route took them right past the resort again, and they swung in and asked Reggie to look after their bags while they went to the falls. He put them in a locker and told them not to worry.

The ride to the falls was beautiful with green mountains on their left and the ocean on their right. Every few hundred feet, someone tried to flag them down to buy weed. After a while, they just ignored them and didn't even slow down. Once at the falls, they locked up the scooters and began the long hike to the top. The water was cool but refreshing. The smell of skunk was everywhere. Since there weren't any actual skunks in Jamaica, they both knew it was skunk weed.

When they reached the top, Rick pulled out the little GoPro he had strapped to his waist and they took a few selfies. Jules was doing crazy poses and fooling around having a blast. They sat down in the water and let the stream run over them and down the falls. It was very relaxing and energizing at the same time. After they'd had enough, they decided to climb back down on the dry side instead of the falls trail, so they could air-dry before they got back to the scooters. About halfway down, there was a turn on the deck under some trees. A lanky local guy stepped up to them with a small knife.

"Gimme your money!"

"You've got to be kidding. Two in one day?" muttered Rick.

"Jules, step back," said Rick as he held his arm out to protect her.

She moved back a few feet against the hand rail.

"Listen, pal, we ain't got no money. See these bathing suits? There's nowhere to put money."

Rick was lying because he had a credit card and some cash tucked inside a rear hidden

pocket of his board shorts. They had put their t-shirts and walking shorts under the locking seats of the scooters.

"Okay den, give me your camera."

"This little thing?" Rick pointed at his GoPro.

"Yeah, Mon! Give me dat!"

"Okay, if you insist."

Rick unfastened the GoPro from his waist and moved toward the man. He suddenly tossed it in the air, and when the man looked up, Rick swept his legs out from under him. He fell to the deck with a hard thud. With his leg fully extended, he raised it and slammed the man square in the face with his heel bone. Blood sprayed out all over the man's white t-shirt. The knife had fallen out of his hands and landed close to the GoPro. Before the man could move, Rick rolled over, grabbing them both, and stood up. The man got to his feet as Rick moved toward him with the knife in one hand and the GoPro in the other.

"Which one do you want?" yelled Rick.

The guy started running down the stairs and bolted off into the trees. Rick broke off the blade of the knife, threw it in the woods, and tossed the handle into the river.

"Kids," said Rick as he shrugged at Jules.

Jules just shook her head.

"Let's get back to the resort. I think I've had enough attempted armed robberies for one day. How about you, Jules?"

She nodded as they continued down the path. Once they reached the scooters, they put their dry clothes back on and raced each other back to the resort, dodging coconuts and weed salesmen on the road.

They both showered when they got back to their room, and even Chief got a nice washdown in the expansive indoor/outdoor shower. As they dried off, the phone rang. Rick answered it.

"Rick, it's me, Johnie. They are coming for me. I don't know what to do," he said in a rush, sounding out of breath.

"Whoa, whoa, whoa. Slow down, Johnie. Who's coming for you? What are you talking about?"

"I just got a call from my lawyer and he said the Okaloosa County Sheriff's Department has issued a warrant for my arrest."

"But you were already arrested and released on bond. I'm confused."

"The new charge is grand larceny. Pamela Killian has a video of me stealing a jewelry case. It shows me walking into a closet and walking out with a small box. It wasn't jewelry, though. It was her box of sex toys and condoms. She asked me to go in there and get it. I had no idea there was a safe in the back of the closet with the exact same waterproof box inside it. She has me dead to rights. It's a total setup. I'm freaking out. Should I run?"

"Hell no. Just go peacefully. We're gonna be there as soon as humanly possible. I'm calling Gary as soon as we hang up and we are heading your way. Don't worry, Johnie. It's gonna be okay. I promise."

"I hope you're right, man. I'm so scared right now. I don't why this is happening to me."

"Just try and stay calm. We'll figure it out."

Rick hung up and quickly told Jules what had happened before calling Gary.

"Gary, it's Rick. Can you get us out of here? Johnie is getting rearrested. Long story, but we gotta go ASAP."

"Let me call the pilot. I think I can rent a jet from the EVO Jets in Ocho Rios. I'll stay

behind and deal with the NTSB and insurance on my jet. I'll meet up with y'all as soon as I can."

Rick and Jules packed their bags, put Chief on the luggage cart, and headed for the lobby. Rick called Possum and let him know what was going on. He was already in the lobby when they arrived. They all got in the Rasta van, and their driver peeled out, bound for Ian Fleming International Airport.

CHAPTER SEVEN

It was dark when they landed at the Destin Executive Airport. Rick called an Uber and they all hopped in for the short ride to Destin HarborWalk, where *Nine-Tenths* was docked. When Rick opened the doors to the salon, everything was clean and in its place. The only thing missing was Johnie. A note was sitting on the settee.

> *Rick, they came aboard about twenty minutes after I talked to you in Jamaica. I'm going peacefully like you said. I'm not happy, but the deputies are being pretty respectful and letting me write this note and walk to the cruiser, away from the charter, before handcuffing me. I thought that is a pretty stand-up thing to do since they know we are a business and it would look bad. My first appearance in front of the judge is at 8:00 a.m. tomorrow morning. Get me the hell out of there. Please!*
>
> *Johnie*

Rick handed the letter to Possum and Jules to read, and set his bag in his cabin. Jules put Chief back in his big cage, and he seemed happy to be home. Rustling his feathers and jumping up and down, raising his crown. Rick called the lawyer to see if he could get any more information about Johnie's arrest.

"Hi, Rick. I don't have a lot to share with you, but I was told by someone in the sheriff's department that they confiscated the surveillance video from Mrs. Killian. They said it clearly shows Johnie walking into the closet, turning toward the safe, then out of camera view, and coming back out carrying a black waterproof box with the word 'Apache' on the side. It's the kind you can get at Harbor Freight, basically a Pelican Case knockoff. She has photos of the case and its contents all listed with values that she also turned over. She claims there were over three million dollars' worth of jewels in the case. I'll be honest, it doesn't look good for Johnie. He either stole it or it's a setup. He claims the black box was just sitting on a shelf in the closet and that he never even saw a safe. What do you think? Could he do it?" asked Dave.

"No effing way! Johnie is as pure as Mother Teresa. He had no reason to steal, or commit murder, for that matter. Between the salary I pay him, his cut of Fletcher's treasure, and his share of Chiefcoin, Johnie is not hurting for money. I know for a fact he'd never do it. He is one hundred percent innocent and I'm gonna prove it."

"Okay, if you vouch for him, then I'm in too. We won't know how much or even if he'll be bonded out at all until tomorrow morning. If they do give him a bond, it will likely be quite substantial. Do you want me to set up a bail bondsman, or are you gonna do a cash bail?"

"I guess we'll have to see how much it is first."

"Okay, I'll call you in the morning after his first appearance," said Dave.

Rick hung up and filled Jules and Possum in on what had just transpired over the phone. Rick had a headache. It was a stress headache; he needed to get his mind on something else, if even just for a little while.

"Y'all wanna take the boat out? Just a little short ride to decompress?" he asked.

They all agreed, and Jules carried Chief to his cage up on the flybridge. Rick followed her up and fired up the twin Mann diesels. They purred like kittens. That was one thing Johnie took pride in. Not only was he the first mate, but he was also the chief engineer and one hell of a diesel mechanic. He had tuned the engines to perfection and used his own custom-designed computer chips for added performance.

Rick slowly motored out of the slip as Possum untied all the lines and hooked them to the dock pilings. Then he turned *Nine-Tenths* hard right toward the end of Noriega Point. There was a flurry of boat activity on the harbor. Several dinner cruises were headed out under the Destin bridge for their two-hour charters. Rick was kinda surprised so many boats were out after dark, but he didn't mind.

Instead of heading right under the bridge into Choctawhatchee Bay, Rick turned left around the end of Noriega Point toward the open Gulf. The moon was bright and the waters were fairly calm. Only a five-mile-per-hour breeze was coming off of the Gulf, and there were no whitecaps. Rick passed the center channel marker.

"You wanna steer?" he asked Jules.

It was her first time on the boat, and she seemed impressed. It took a little prodding from Rick to finally get her to take the helm. He showed her how the compass matched the numbers on the chart plotter and set her at ease when he showed her via the radar that there were no boats within five miles of them offshore.

As much as Rick tried to mentally relax, all he could think about was Johnie in that cold, dirty cell in Crestview. He could still smell it in his mind. Although he had only spent a little time there on a frivolous charge, he knew how bad the place was and couldn't stand the thought of his first mate sitting in there. His stress turned to anger and then sadness. He needed something to take his mind off of it.

As if Possum could read his mind, he handed Rick a rocks glass half filled with thirty-two-year-old Flor de Caña and one ice cube. They both clinked glasses somberly in honor of Johnie, without saying a word. Rick poured Jules a glass of Amarillo de Manzanares he had ordered special for her. It was the finest aguardiente imported from her native Colombia. He then climbed back up to the flybridge.

"Thank you, Rick," she said as she sniffed it. "Is this Amarillo de Manzanares?" she asked.

"How did you know just by smelling? You haven't even tasted it yet."

"Because it's my favorite. It comes from the coffee region of Colombia and is the only one with a hint of saffron. I smelled it instantly."

"Well, color me impressed," said Rick.

Then what seemed perfectly timed by God and the stars above, a small pod of dolphins began jumping and playing in front of the bow, as the moonlight danced on their shiny, glistening forms. Jules pointed at them in delight. For just a minute, Rick forgot about Johnie, and his stress washed away like the waves on the bow. They slowly motored for an hour then headed back in. They all were starting to feel a little tired and worn out from the flight.

Once they'd tied the boat back up in the slip, Jules offered to cook something, but since it was so late, they opted to order a pizza from Merlin's, Destin's favorite local pizza joint. Rick ordered one small thin-crust veggie for Jules and one extra-large traditional Hawaiian that he and Possum would split. He also knew Chief would want a couple of pineapple pieces, as always.

As they sat around enjoying the pizza and a few more cocktails, talk inevitably came back around to Johnie. It was around two in the morning and Jules was yawning more than talking, so Rick showed her the master cabin and tucked her in. He told her he would be in shortly. She kissed the back of his hand and squeezed it in agreement.

Rick stepped back into the salon with Possum, and one look from his friend told him they would be awake for a while.

"Rick, if it's okay, I think we should watch the surveillance videos on the boat. We can start with Johnie's re-arrest and then go back a few days before he met Pamela."

"I was thinking the same thing. I don't think Johnie ever brought her back to the boat. At least, he didn't mention it. It's not like I would be mad or anything. I mean at the moment, *Nine-Tenths* is basically his home. He has enough money to buy a place or rent a condo. And I asked him about that, but he said he prefers living on the boat so he can stay on top of things. I also think he likes the excitement of being on the HarborWalk. I know for a fact he goes up to AJ's almost every night to watch Black Eyed Blonde or whoever else is playing."

Rick backed up the surveillance video to earlier that morning, and it was just as Johnie had written in his note. Two deputies came on board and talked to him for a while, then he wrote the note and left with them. Nothing to see. Rick backed up to six days before Johnie met

Pamela, and they watched at high speed, occasionally stopping if something caught their eyes. People would stop at the stern of the boat and read about the charter up on the billboard, then either take a card and leave or add the number to their phone. Rick was trying to find a pattern or a repeat person in the videos who could be casing the boat and Johnie's daily habits.

Johnie was like the guy in the movie *Rain Man*. He seemed to do the same thing every day at the same time. When five o'clock rolled around, if there were no charters, he would open a bottle of Destin Brewery East Pass IPA, sit in the fighting chair, and watch tourists walk past the boat. He always drank one. After dark, he'd climb off of the stern and walk up to AJ's like clockwork.

"Hang on, I just noticed something," said Rick as they kept watching. He rewound a bit to play it again.

In the far left of the screen, every day for each of the six days before Johnie met Pamela, a woman showed up. She always stood in the same spot but each time had on a different outfit and hair color. Her face always seemed to be out of focus from the camera, and she kept her hair over her eyes to conceal her identity. Rick wasn't sure if it was the same woman or different women. He was basically grasping at straws. He went back several times to show Possum as he took notes.

"Bingo!" exclaimed Possum.

"What is it?" asked Rick

"Can you zoom in on her shoes with the surveillance?"

"I can try."

After several failed attempts, Rick pulled out the instructions for the cameras that he had stored in the drawer beneath the DVR. He figured it out and zoomed in.

"Okay, so what? She wears Nikes. So do thousands of other people. It doesn't mean it's the same woman," said Rick.

"Wait for it, wait for it. Pause!" replied Possum. "You see the back of her shoe when she turns to leave? There's a scuff mark just above the rubber on the left shoe. Now, go to the other days and you'll see they match. It is definitely the same woman!"

"You freaking little genius, Possum! Now, if we can just prove that the woman in the video is Pamela, we can prove that she cased the place and maybe prove to the judge that she was planning to set Johnie up. It's a long shot, but we need to find that shoe at her place. Then we'll know for sure."

"How do you plan to do that? It's not like she's gonna invite you in to look around."

"That's true, but it's also not like we ain't never worn cable company uniforms and fixed

someone's TV that suddenly went on the fritz." Rick grinned.

"Do you still have the uniforms?"

"Does a Possum still shit in the woods?"

"Well, not this one." Possum laughed.

It was 4:00 a.m. before they settled off to bed. In just a few hours, they would know if

Johnie was gonna get bail. It was also gonna be a full day playing cable repairmen.

The sun caught Rick right in his eye, and he didn't know where he was for a second until he saw the bookshelf with all the fishing guides. Jules was still sleeping peacefully. Rick quietly rolled out of bed and could already smell the coffee Possum had going. He made himself a cup as Jules stumbled into the galley.

"You're up early, boys."

"Coffee?" asked Possum.

"Please and thank you!"

As usual, Possum had made himself right at home on the boat. He already had eggs whisked to make omelets and a pan of bacon in the oven that began to fill their senses with its amazing smell.

"So, what's on the agenda today?" asked Jules.

"First, we need to find out if Johnie is gonna get bail, then Possum and I have an errand to run. If you want to, you can just chill on the boat and go explore the harbor."

"That sounds great, Rick. Will y'all be back in time for dinner? I'm happy to cook something."

"If all goes as planned, we'll be back for happy hour. No need to cook tonight. I wanna take you to the Marina Cafe. They have an amazing happy hour with half-priced sushi and other killer appetizers. And if we are still hungry, we can go to the main dining room after happy hour for entrées.

I usually get stuffed on sushi, though. Plus, they have my favorite beer there on tap—Pensacola Bay Riptide."

"Sounds amazing. Sushi would hit the spot, and I'm not picky and don't need a big dinner."

"That's one the many reasons I love you, baby!"

Jules blushed, gave Rick a big hug, and kissed his shoulder.

"I love you, too!"

"Oh my God, get a room, you two!" said Possum.

They both laughed and sat down for breakfast as Possum set the table. Chief was on his perch munching on a grape that Possum had scrounged up out of the fridge. As usual, the eggs and bacon were perfect. Rick grabbed his black duffel bag and filled it with the necessary tools and electronics he'd need for today's charade. Possum did the same.

As soon as Jules left the boat, Rick pulled the cable company uniforms out of the closet and gave one to Possum. He didn't want to worry Jules, knowing she'd either try to talk him out of it or try to go with them. He planned to drive Johnie's plain white pickup truck to the house. It looked like any other work truck. The first thing they would need to do was screw up Pamela's cable and Wi-Fi and wait for her to call the cable company.

Rick drove toward the address he'd gotten from the internet, heading for the Kelly Plantation subdivision. They told the guard at the security gate that they needed to check some of the cable junction boxes in the neighborhood, and he let them through. Rick drove around the far side of Pamela's home and dropped off Possum. Possum had one tool and one tool only in his pocket: a pair of wire cutters. He snuck around the back of the house where the cable came into the wall and with one snip, step one was complete. He walked back toward the street and hopped into the truck. Rick positioned the truck behind a bush with the passenger window facing the house. Possum put on headphones and pointed a huge directional mic toward the bedroom window of Pamela's home. He intently listened for several minutes, waiting for the sign he was looking for. Rick could vaguely hear a woman's angry voice come through the headphones. "What the hell?! The damn internet's down again? And the TVs? That damn cable company is useless!"

Possum gave Rick a thumbs-up as he continued to listen. Rick could only slightly hear her side of the conversation through Possum's headphones, but knew what was probably being said on the other end by her frustration. It was only nine, and she was told someone would be out between noon and 4:00 p.m. Now all they had to do was wait a little, then get there early and fix the problem before the actual repairmen showed up.

As they patiently waited, Rick's cell phone rang. It was Dave, Johnie's lawyer.

"Rick, I have good news and bad news."

"Go on."

"Johnie was granted bail, but the judge said due to his other charge of murder, he would set the bail at $750,000. I've already contacted a bail bondsman who has agreed to pay it. So, you will need to come up with ten percent—$75,000. Can you do that?"

"Nah, I'll just pay the whole amount."

"What? Are you nuts?"

"Nah, I just hate bail bondsmen. I know the jail is co-owned by a judge and a bail bondsman, and not only do I think that sucks, but it's also a huge conflict of interest and should be illegal. I have an errand to finish and then I'll stop by Synovus Bank and get a cashier's check for the full amount. Who do I have it made out to? Okaloosa County Corrections?"

"Yeah, that's it. I highly advise against this, though. If Johnie skips town, you're out three quarters of a million dollars."

"Johnie ain't going nowhere but to happy hour with us if we can get him out in time," replied Rick.

"Okay, I'll get the ball rolling on my end. I can meet you at the jail when you're ready.

Just text me," said Dave.

"Are you in Niceville or Destin right now?"

"I'm in Niceville, but I'll be in Destin around one. I have a 1:30 p.m. meeting."

"That's perfect. Can you meet me at the Craft Bar at one? I can give you the check and avoid setting foot in Crest-view. Can you take care of it?" "Sure, no problem, Rick. See ya at the Craft Bar."

Rick hung up, and Possum took his headphones off.

"She's been stomping through the house cussing like a sailor about the cable."

"Let's make her day. What do you say?"

"Sure, why not, maybe she'll give us a tip. Haha!"

Rick pulled up in front of her house, and with duffel bags in hand, approached the door. He rang the doorbell. She answered but only cracked open the door.

"Who is it?"

"Cable company, ma'am."

"Wow, y'all are early for once. Come on in. I checked every TV in the house and there's no signal. Internet is down too. I did a modem reset but it's just flashing."

"Okay, can you show me where the modem is?"

She walked Rick to the back of the house and pointed at the modem. Rick kneeled down and pulled out a Klein Tools Network LAN Cable Tester and pretended to screw the coaxial into it to check the signal. The tester was made for CAT5 cables, but she wouldn't know any difference. She watched for a minute and seemed to get bored.

"I'm getting a signal from corporate, but it's not strong. You check the lines outside while I check the rest of the TVs," said Rick as he pointed to Possum. "How many TVs do you have, ma'am?"

She thought for a second and counted on her fingers. "There's six—oh, wait, seven. I forgot about the one in the bathroom.

"Can you show my counterpart how to get to the yard where the cable comes into the house?"

She nodded and waved at Possum to follow her. Rick knew he had to work fast. He quickly found her bedroom and saw the closet. It was partially open. He also spotted the surveillance camera. He knew he'd be seen on the camera, so he would have to remove the DVD and replace it with a blank one in the machine. He put in the blank DVD and hit *record/pause*.

Luckily, since the internet was down, nothing was being sent to the cloud.

He opened the door and scanned the closet for the shoes. He was snapping photos like a crazy person, then he saw the Nikes. They were facing froward, so he picked them up and sure enough, there was the scrape on the shoe he'd seen on his very own surveillance cameras. He quickly snapped a photo of them and placed them back as they were. He shut the closet door and then texted Possum to repair the coax cable coming into the house.

Rick's text was Possum's cue to send Pamela back in to assist him.

"Ma'am, can you show my partner where the bathroom TV is?" said Possum. "He's not sure which of the four bathrooms to look for it in."

"Oh, no problem. It's in the master bedroom. My stupid husband wanted one in there."

She walked off, and Possum knew she had to be involved in his murder. The guy had only been dead a few days and she was calling him stupid.

No love lost there.

As soon as she was out of sight, Possum crimped on a new coaxial termination end and screwed it back into the house.

Pamela met Rick inside and showed him the bathroom. He fiddled with the TV for a bit as Possum came back in.

"I think I found it, ma'am. The coaxial coming into the house was a bit rusty. I put on a new termination end and reattached it to the house. I believe the internet will return shortly." As soon as he said that, the TV in the bedroom started blasting CNN. Rick went back to the modem and pretended to check it again.

"Okay, you're all set. We'll get out of your hair, and thanks for being a loyal cable company customer."

She just rolled her eyes and walked them to the door.

"You'll need to reset your surveillance camera DVR. When the internet goes down, they usually go into a pause mode. Just hit *play* and you should be back up and running. Have a nice day."

Rick tipped his hat, and they both began to walk off.

"Wait, wait, I really appreciate how fast and courteous you two are. Can I give you a tip?"

Possum bit the bottom of his lip and looked away, trying not to burst into laughter.

"We normally don't accept tips, ma'am," said Rick.

Pamela handed a Rick a hundred-dollar bill and thanked him again.

"Can I get your names so I can leave you a positive review for your boss?"

Rick thought fast. "Let me run to the truck. I have a comment card with our names on it. I can tuck it in the door for you, and you just need to toss it in the mail. It's already prepaid for the post office."

They both walked to the truck, and Possum climbed in on the passenger side. Rick walked around and opened the door, pretending to grab the comment card. She finally closed the door, and he hopped in and they drove off. Possum called the actual cable company and canceled the repair order for her house.

Rick pulled the Benjamin from his pocket and waved it in Possum's face.

"Looks like Pamela Killian is paying for happy hour!"

CHAPTER EIGHT

Rick pulled up beside the windowless wall of Miller's Ale House by the dumpster, and he and Possum changed back into their street shirts. Then he drove around the building to the front of Synovus Bank and left the truck running with the A/C on for Possum.

"Hi, Rick, long time no see," said an employee as Rick stepped into the lobby.

"Hi, Samantha. Yeah, I've been on sort of a walkabout. Long story. I'll have to share it with you sometime."

Samantha had started as a teller at Synovus several years back and worked herself up to Lead Loan Representative. Rick had been dealing with her since day one and they got along well. She was a sweet southern girl and a hard-working single mom. Rick respected her because of the way she was so devoted to her two kids, and because of her strong work ethic.

"Sounds good." She smiled. "What can I do for you today?"

"This is gonna sound crazy, but I need a cashier's check for $750,000 made out to

Okaloosa County Corrections."

Her eyes widened and she didn't say anything for a second.

"Wow, that's a chunk of change. Let me check your account and get on that."

She logged into her computer and typed away at the keyboard. She walked behind the teller's desk and came back with an envelope and handed it to Rick.

"Anything else I can do for you today, Mr. Waters?" she said as she gave Rick a humorous glance.

"Nope, that oughta do it."

Rick checked his watch and saw it was 12:30. The Craft Bar was just across the street in Paradise Key, across from Publix. He hopped in the truck and they drove over. Rick grabbed a high-top table by the window and waited for Dave the lawyer to show up.

"We may as well eat. They have awesome Nashville chicken here. Super spicy," said

Rick.

Possum nodded as he perused the massive beer menu. Rick texted Jules to check on her and see if she was gonna get lunch.

> Jules, we're almost done here. Need to meet with lawyer at 1:00 then we are free. Did you eat?

> *Hey Rick, I grabbed a three-cheese melt at the cutest little airstream on the HarborWalk. It's called Say Cheese.*

> *Oh yeah, they are the bomb. Love their grilled cheese. We'll probably be back at the boat around 2:00. No hurry, happy hour doesn't start until 4:00. Have fun.*

Dave walked through the doorway right on time, as usual. He pulled up a seat and ordered a pint of Idyll Hounds Brewing Company's Divide & Conch'r, a local beer with an eight percent ABV.

"Drinking during working hours, Dave?" Rick winked at him.

"Nah, this ain't drinking. It's lunch. You know, a barley sandwich."

"Dave, I'd like you to meet Possum, one of my oldest and dearest friends."

"Who you calling old, Rick?!" exclaimed Possum as he shook Dave's hand.

"Possum, huh? Interesting name."

"Yeah, it's a long story."

Rick reached into his pocket and slid the envelope over to Dave just as the Nashville chicken arrived on the table piping hot. Rick smelled it and his eyes watered. He ordered the same pint Dave had just ordered and head bobbed to Possum to ask if he wanted one. He nodded and winked.

"Well, boys, I'll leave you to it."

He started to pull out his wallet, but Rick waved it away.

"I got your beer, Dave. Just get our boy out of there. We're heading to Marina Cafe for happy hour, if you wanna join us later."

"I'm pretty slammed. Maybe. I'll head to Crestview and get this process started. I'll keep you posted if I can get him out today. If I can't get it done by five, we'll have to finish tomorrow."

"All right, Dave, do your best. Text me later," said Rick.

Rick and Possum ate their lunch, both waving their hands in front of their mouths often because of the heat. They both had a couple more beers and headed out. Once back at the boat, Rick loaded the DVD he had swiped from Pamela's surveillance machine into his old laptop that still had a CD drive in it. He assumed it would be of no use to him, since the sheriff's department had already taken the DVD after the murder. Once it started spinning, he saw that the date on it was the day after the murder. Possum wasn't really paying attention, as he was still fanning the fire out of his mouth from lunch. Rick got frustrated and hit eject. The DVD popped out and caught Possum's attention. Possum reached over and picked up the DVD and flipped it over.

"Rick, this is a double-sided DVD."

"So?"

"Some surveillance DVR machines with DVD backup will record twenty-four hours onto one side of the disk before starting the new day. It's a security issue."

"So, you're saying it's possible that Pamela gave the sheriff's department the DVD from the night of the murder and we might also have a copy?"

"Exactly. I mean, Dave's gonna get a copy of this anyway if this goes to trial as discovery, but we may as well look at it and see if anything can help us now."

Rick flipped the DVD over and stuck it back in the laptop. Both he and Possum were glued to the screen. She had several cameras but only one could be accessed with the laptop. It was the front door view. They watched as a car pulled up and two figures stumbled to the door. There was no audio, but as they approached the door, the motion light came on and Johnie came into view, looking completely shit-faced. Pamela was also wobbling. Johnie damn near fell in the door once it was opened. Then she shook her head, as if in disapproval. The lights of her car were still on. A few minutes passed by as Rick and Possum stayed glued to the screen of the lawn and the headlights. Then suddenly, she came back out of the door and walked to the car. This time, though, she wasn't wobbling. She looked perfectly sober as she turned off the headlights and came back to the house.

Rick and Possum slowly looked at each other, as if in slow motion, and said the same thing simultaneously.

"She's not drunk!"

"She definitely set up Johnie!" exclaimed Rick.

"Amigo, we need a surveillance DVR that can play all the cameras on this DVD. Do you by any chance remember the brand and model?" asked Possum.

"As a matter of fact, I do. I remember the little tiger's face on the front. It was one of the ones I was seriously considering for the boat, but I ended up getting a different one. It's actually still in my Amazon history."

Rick pulled out his MacBook and opened Amazon. He scrolled through his *Saved for Later* items. On the third page, there it was: TIGERSECU.

"I ended up ordering a different brand when I found out that they were made in China, even though they had a California headquarters address. I had a hard time finding one that wasn't made in China."

"Order it. We have to have it," said Possum sternly.

Rick placed the order. It would arrive in two days. He had no intention of keeping it but knew it could be the key to saving Johnie's ass. By now it was three in the afternoon. They both took showers and got ready for happy hour. When Rick came out, Jules had laid some items on the bed. She had picked up a few things for Rick to try on.

"Hi, baby. Did you have a fun day shopping?"

"I did, Rick. I kinda went nuts buying you stuff, though. I love shopping for you."

Rick looked at all the clothes on the bed and just shook his head and laughed.

"Can I try these on later? I wanna gorge myself on some sushi!"

"Hell yeah! Let's do it," she replied.

They all walked down the HarborWalk then up to the sidewalk beside US 98, aka Harbor Boulevard, toward Marina Cafe. They sat at a high-top table near the bar and ordered some spicy tuna rolls to start. Jules got a martini, and Rick and Possum both ordered Riptides on draft. They were about to order their second round when Dave walked up to the table.

"I've got good news and bad news," said Dave.

"Let's hear it," replied Rick.

"Well, the bad news is, you are buying happy hour. And the good news is, well, turn around."

They all turned around to see Johnie behind them sneaking up on them. They started hooting and hollering as they jumped up from their seats and hugged Johnie. Tears welled up in his eyes from all the love he was getting. He wiped them away and pulled up a seat for Dave before sitting down.

"Y'all have no idea how glad I am to see you! And to be out of that godforsaken hellhole jail they call the Crestview Hilton."

"So, what do you miss about it the most?" asked Rick.

"The food, I'd have to say. The chef there is amazing and the dining is exquisite," replied Johnie in a very sarcastic tone.

"Whatcha want? A beer? Sushi?" asked Rick.

"D—all of the above."

Rick waved his finger in a circle to the waitress, and she brought everyone another round and took their orders for more sushi.

"Now, don't you be running off, Johnie. That'll cost me more money than you can imagine."

"Yeah, Dave told me. I can't even begin to thank you. I ain't going nowhere."

They all devoured the sushi and drank until their eyes were floating. Rick paid the bill, shook Dave's hand, and the crew headed back to the boat. On the way there, Rick got Johnie up to speed on what they had discovered on the surveillance DVR. He was excited to hear and better yet, see it. When they got back to the boat, Rick showed it to Jules and Johnie.

Johnie let out a sigh of relief. "Hopefully this'll be enough to clear my name."

"Now, you realize that we are only seeing one camera view. I've ordered the DVR brand that these cameras use, and we will be able to see all the different views," said Rick.

"When will that get here?" asked Johnie.

"The day after tomorrow. Until then, I think we should focus on what Mrs. Killian is up to and see if I can dig up any dirt on her. When is the funeral?"

"It's on Sunday at Beal Memorial."

"Okay, we need to be there. Everyone but Johnie. I want us all to scout any unusual people at the funeral who might be acting strange. Possum and I will have to go in disguise since she's already seen us. Jules, you can just wear black. I'll set up my GoPro hidden in a hat for you," said Rick.

"What can I do to help?" asked Johnie.

"I have the perfect job for you. Do you think you can access the roof of the old Families First building? The one beside the Mitsubishi dealership?"

Rick opened up Google Earth and zoomed in on the building. It was right beside the Beal Memorial Cemetery.

"It looks like there are some undeveloped woods behind the rear parking lot," said Johnie. "I can drive there tomorrow and scout it out. I'm not sure how old this photo is. They may have developed it since these were taken. I'll find out."

"Possum, you up for a little recon? I need to be able to access her computer and phone. Do you have a way we can do that without her knowing?"

"The computer will be easy," said Possum. "All I gotta do is tap into her cable modem. When I repaired the cable coming into her house, I put a sleeve with a t-connector on it. All I have to do is hook up a GSM listening device to the connector. Her backyard is overgrown where the cable comes in. She'll never know it's there. I can hide a hard drive with a receiver in range, and everything she types, sends, or receives will get stored on the hard drive. We can swap out hard drives every few days. They are 4TB drives, so they should get everything. The cell phone is a bit harder. We need a bug and it will have to be planted inside the phone. That's FBI/CIA stuff. Can you call in a favor from our FBI profiler buddy?"

"I'll give Carson a call in the morning, replied Rick. How long will it take for you to get your GSM stuff?"

"I have it in Houston, but it'll be faster just to order one and have it FedExed here. I'll do it now," replied Possum.

Possum pulled out his own computer and went to his favorite spy shop online. He ordered a few things he thought would help. A few GSM listening devices, two hard drives with receivers, and a couple of motion-activated video cameras he would plant in the tree on her property.

"I just thought of something," said Johnie.

"What is it?" asked Rick.

"I remember when I met Pamela that night at Harry T's and asked if she was a regular there, she told me that she loved their happy hour, but the one place she never missed was ladies' night at McGuire's. Every Thursday from ten to two is ladies' night there, and tonight is Thursday."

Rick looked over at Jules with a little devilish grin.

"Jules, you wanna make a friend tonight?"

"Yay, I get to help." Jules clapped her hands. "Yes, please. I'm so excited."

"Okay, I need you to get close to her and see if you can win her over and get to know her. Think you can pull it off?"

"Did it work on you the first night, Mr. Waters?" She waggled her eyebrows at him.

"Touché!"

Jules went to the master cabin to get all spruced up for ladies' night. Rick gave her a tiny lapel mic she could hide under her shirt that he hooked up to a credit card-size recording device. All she had to do was hit *record* and speak normally.

They arrived at McGuire's around 10:15. The place was packed. Jules went ahead of Rick, who had put on a reverse baseball cap and a huge Fu Manchu mustache. It took everything Jules had not to burst out laughing every time she looked over at him. She grabbed a chair at the bar and ordered a Cosmo. Rick was in her peripheral and would cue her whenever Pamela entered the bar.

At 10:30 p.m., she walked in and took a seat at the bar a few seats down from Jules. Rick rubbed his eyebrow, and Jules knew it was her. Two girls got up and moved to a table, so Jules hit *record* on the recording device tucked inside her bra, moved over, and got the bartender's attention. She was about to order another Cosmo when he delivered a lemon drop martini to Pamela.

"What's that?" asked Jules as she pointed to the drink.

Pamela looked up at Jules with an ugly look.

"It's a lemon drop martini."

Jules gave her the biggest smile, blowing off her stank eyes.

"That looks delicious. I'll have what she's having," Jules told the bartender.

He whipped one up for her and set it down in front of her.

She picked it up and said, "Cheers!" and moved her glass toward Pamela's. She reluctantly clinked her glass against Jules's.

"Hi, I'm Valentina," said Jules, making up the name on the spot because of the hot sauce on the bar with the same name.

"Okay," responded Pamela, as if Jules was bothering her.

"And your name?" asked Jules.

"Pamela."

She took a sip of her drink, and Jules noticed the pendant she had on her necklace. It was a deep blue dolphin surrounded in yellow gold.

"Oh my God, I love your pendant. I love dolphins, and that color perfectly matches your eyes. I wish I had beautiful blue eyes like you. And your blonde hair is so lovely as well."

Pamela seemed to let down her guard a bit and smiled for the first time. She looked over at Jules.

"I love dolphins too. Valentina, is it?" She stuck out her hand to shake Jules's.

"Yes, Valentina. Very nice to meet you. Do you live here or are you on vacation?" asked Jules.

"I live here. Hopefully not for too much longer, though. I'm planning to move."

"Oh, okay. I moved here a few months ago. I'm probably gonna head back to Colombia this fall, though. I clean houses for a living and while there's plenty of work here, it's very expensive to live in Destin."

"You clean houses?"

"Yes, I also do commercial cleaning. I just finished a job at Destin Commons." "We should get together again sometime," said Pamela.

Pamela pulled out her phone, and Jules took notice that it was an iPhone 11 with a dolphin case on it.

"What's your number, Valentina?"

"I'll call you so that way we'll both have it. What's yours?"

Pamela gave Jules her number and saved it. Jules excused herself and asked her to watch her drink while she went to powder her face. When she got into the bathroom, she pulled out her phone and quickly changed her voicemail message.

Hi, this is Valentina. You have reached A1 House Cleaners. Leave your name and number and someone will get right back to you.

She felt pretty proud of herself for thinking on her feet. If Pamela called her, it would solidify her story. She was starting to feel like a real spy. She returned to the bar as two more martinis arrived.

"I hope you didn't mind. I ordered two more for us," said Pamela.

It was obvious she was warming up to Jules. They made small talk for a while, and after splitting an appetizer and paying the bill, they hugged goodbye and promised to meet again for the next ladies' night, if not sooner. Jules walked out right past Rick and winked at him. He followed her a few seconds later and they met back at his truck.

"Mission accomplished. My name is Bond, Valentina Bond."

CHAPTER NINE

Back at *Nine-Tenths*, Rick transferred the audio Jules had recorded to his MacBook. He would listen to it later. He could tell Jules was chomping at the bit to tell him what had happened. She was jumping around like a rabbit. He couldn't help but laugh at her excitement.

"Okay, 007, spill the beans."

"You'll never guess what my new job is."

"Spy?" asked Rick.

"Nope, well yeah, but also a house cleaner. She wants me to clean her house. I just made it up on the spot. This way I can get even closer to her."

"That is perfect, Jules!"

"Call me Valentina. I need to stay in character."

Rick laughed. "Okay, Valentina. What else transpired?"

"She did mention that she would be moving soon. She didn't say where and I didn't wanna sound too suspicious, so I didn't ask her. I'll find out, though. I even changed my voicemail, so when she calls, she'll think it's a business."

"Wow, Jules—ahem, Valentina. I am impressed."

She was strutting around like she'd just won the lotto or figured out the cure for cancer. Rick thought it was so cute. What she had done was in fact going to be a huge help to them. The one thing that couldn't happen was for Pamela to see Jules on the boat or near Johnie. Rick decided to rent a month-to-month condo over at The Palms of Destin. He and Jules could stay there, away from the boat, and more importantly away from Johnie. It wasn't too far from HarborWalk and it was even closer to where Pamela lived. Things would go back to normal. Johnie would continue to run the charters with a hired captain, while Rick, Jules, and Possum would turn The Palms of Destin into home base.

Rick made up some cleaner business cards with Jules's number on it, and emailed the design to Office Depot. They would stop at Dollar Tree in the morning and get her some supplies to round out the farce. It was 2:00 a.m. before they settled off to bed and both fell asleep.

Everyone was moving slow the next morning.

"Morning, hombre. Still trying to wake up?" asked Possum.

"Yeah, man, long night. We got in about one in the morning and crashed somewhere around two, I guess."

"What's the plan this morning?"

"We are moving. I'm gonna rent a place over at The Palms and we are all, except for Johnie, gonna head over there for a while. Jules can't be seen on the boat or near Johnie. She got some killer intel last night from Pamela and she's gonna start cleaning her house. It's a great cover."

"Smart!" replied Possum.

Rick got on the phone and called his favorite real estate agent, Jessica, and told her he was having some work done on the boat and wanted to get a place for a month or so. She called back within fifteen minutes and told him there were three units available, including a furnished two-bedroom on the top floor. He chose that one and planned to meet her later to sign the papers. Johnie and Chief would stay on the boat and keep business running as usual.

After breakfast, Jules and Rick drove over to Dollar Tree to get her some cleaning supplies. He called Office Depot and learned the cards would be ready around two in the afternoon. They decided to kill some time and go to Grayton Beach and Seaside. Jules had never been and Rick still wanted to show her how beautiful the beaches were in the area. He had no intention of working her to death as a double agent spy, although she really enjoyed it.

They stopped at Grayton Beach, and Rick took her into the Red Bar. It had burned down a few years ago and been rebuilt. He hadn't even seen it since then. It looked similar to before, only cleaner. It didn't have quite the same charm but was still inviting. Knowing how good their fish dip was, he thought he'd give it a shot.

They sat down at the bar, and Rick ordered the fish dip and a Grayton Beer 30A Beach Blonde for Jules and Fish Whistle IPA for himself. The fish dip was just as good as he remembered. After their quick snack, he drove down past Watercolor to Seaside. He showed Jules a quick clip from the movie *The Truman Show*, which was filmed there, then drove around the town square, showing her all the cool landmarks. He parked on the street in front of Bud and Alley's, and they strolled over the boardwalk to the beach.

"It's so beautiful, Rick! Just like you described it. The sand looks like sugar. Look how rough the water is, though!"

"I know, right? It's pretty rough today. The beaches from here to Orange Beach are all really nice. Wait until we have a day off and I can take you fishing on the bay. Johnie has a flats boat and I think I've used it more than him. I can show you how to fly fish. There's a ton of reds and specks out in the bay."

"Reds and specks?"

"Sorry, redfish and speckled trout. Good-eating fish and so fun to catch, especially if you hook up to a big ol' bull red. The fight of your life."

"I can't wait, Rick. Let's go today."

Rick just laughed and gave her a hug. "We will, hun, I promise, as soon as we get a jump-start on Johnie's deal."

She nodded in agreement.

"You see those double red flags? That means there's a risk of a riptide and people are supposed to stay out of the water."

"Riptide. Like the beer."

"Very good, Jules. What a memory."

She laughed. They decided to walk down the beach toward the west for a while, out of view of most tourists.

"Why are the waves so big, Rick? It's so different from the other night out on the boat."

"There's a storm kicking up in the Gulf causing the waves to build."

Seagulls fought the wind as killdeer and sandpipers ran up and down the beach, eating snails and whatever they could get as the water rose and fell on the sand.

"Did you hear that, Rick?"

"Listen."

They both stopped and listened. Suddenly, they heard it. It was faint but it was certain.

"Help!"

Rick scanned the water, looking for someone. All he could see were white foam and waves at first, then about twenty-five yards farther west, he saw something dark bob up for a second, then disappear. He put his palm up to his forehead to block the sun and kept looking.

"Help!"

He saw it again. An arm was waving out in the water.

"Jules, someone's in trouble. Go to the lifeguard station back by Bud and Alley's and tell them to hurry. I'll keep an eye on the person."

Jules started running, and Rick hurried down to the water's edge to try and spot the person again. Whoever it was had been pulled out past the second sandbar, and they were struggling to stay above the water. Jules was beyond his sight and the lifeguard was too far away; he was afraid they wouldn't make it in time.

He kicked off his shoes and took off his shirt. He knew he was taking a huge risk and could end up in the same boat as whoever was out there. He looked both ways down the beach and there was no one close. He had to go in. He let the riptide do most of the work and got to the first sandbar fairly quickly. The tide was pulling hard parallel to the shore. Swimming against it was impossible. Rick swam as hard as he could toward the person flailing in the water. When he got close enough, he realized it was a teenager. He yelled to get the boy's attention. His arms were thrashing around on the water, and Rick knew better than to swim up on him, as the kid might pull him down with him.

"Stop thrashing. Calm down!"

The boy was in pure panic mode. He was struggling and obviously tired. He kept going below the surface and reappearing. He was spitting out seawater and coughing.

"I'm here to help you! Do you understand?"

The boy finally nodded and waved Rick over. Rick swam closer and did everything to calm him down. He got his arms around the boy's chest from behind and lifted him out of the water a little, which seemed to calm his nerves some.

"Now, listen. There's no way we can swim straight in. We have to swim with the current at an angle. Do you understand?"

The boy looked completely done. He finally let out an exhausted, "Yes."

"We'll swim back to shore, okay?"

The boy nodded, still trying to catch his breath.

"What's your name?" asked Rick as he kicked backward with his arm still tight around the boy's chest.

After a few breaths, he murmured, "Devon."

"Okay, Devon, we're gonna be fine. Just try and relax."

Motionless, the boy just hung there under Rick's control. Rick kicked and kicked, occasionally looking toward the shore and making progress. He passed the second sandbar and noticed the lights of the lifeguard pickup truck coming. He was halfway to the first sandbar when he heard someone yell. It was the lifeguard on a huge longboard. He tossed a line to Rick, who wrapped it around the boy and held on to the float. The lifeguard turned the board around and started paddling as hard as he could toward the shore at an angle. A wave offered some assistance, pulling them close enough to touch the bottom. Rick dug his toes into the sand and pulled the boy toward shore, where the lifeguard slung his board onto the beach and ran over to help Rick. As they got to the beach, Rick realized the boy was unconscious. He had ingested gallons of saltwater.

Rick flipped him over onto his back and checked for a pulse. The lifeguard asked Rick if he knew CPR. He nodded and began to start CPR as the lifeguard ran to get his phone. Jules was on her knees right beside them, shaking with tears in her eyes. Rick got a few rounds in before the lifeguard took over. Within minutes, he heard a chopper. It landed on the beach a few yards away from them. The boy still wasn't breathing.

The lifeguard continued CPR as the guys on the chopper ran over with a stretcher. Just as they got within a few feet, the boy coughed and water came out of his mouth. The EMTs on the chopper took his vitals and then put him on the stretcher, loaded him up, and flew off.

Rick collapsed in the sand from exhaustion. The adrenaline had worn off and he'd hit a brick wall. He just lay there breathing hard.

Jules grabbed his arm. "Are you okay, Rick? You're scaring me." She was crying now.

"I'm okay, Jules, just out of breath," he struggled to say.

She put her head on his chest and squeezed his arm until he was breathing normally again. He sat up, staring at the water.

"Mister, you saved that kid's life," said the lifeguard.

"I just did what anyone would do. Where'd they take him?"

"Sacred Heart. He's gonna be fine. It's a precaution when someone inhales saltwater. There's a thing known as dry drowning where the lungs fill with fluid because of all the salt. You got to him just in time."

"Can I visit him?"

"I'm sure he'd want that. His full name is Devon Hill, of the Watercolor Hills. The family who developed the entire area. You can probably see him later today."

The lifeguard took down Rick's info and a statement about the near drowning. He gave Rick a card and told him to feel free to call him anytime in regards to the boy or anything else for that matter. He patted Rick on the back and hopped back into his pickup. Jules gathered Rick's shoes and shirt from down the beach and helped Rick to his feet.

"I didn't plan on swimming today. Otherwise, I would've worn my Speedo."

His joke cleared the air, and Jules wiped away her tears and smiled.

"You're something else, Rick Waters! But never scare me like that again. You should've waited for the lifeguard."

"I wanted to, but I also knew if I waited any longer, we'd be pulling a body out of the Gulf instead of a kid with his whole life in front of him."

Jules hugged him so tight she almost squeezed the air out of him. They walked back down toward Bud and Alley's. Rick carried his shoes and shirt, trying to air-dry his body. When they got near the lifeguard shack, applause broke out from the crowd gathered on the boardwalk. The lifeguard gave Rick a big thumbs-up and a smile. They made their way back to the truck as people patted Rick on the back as he passed. He was definitely the hero of the day in South Walton County.

CHAPTER TEN

Rick's hair was still wet when he pulled into the parking lot of Office Depot. Jules ran inside and picked up her cards. What had started as a regular little tourist sightseeing day to kill some time had ended up being an adrenaline-filled lifesaving adventure. They drove back to the new condo to sign the papers. Jessica gave Rick the keys and also some printouts of vacant land on the bay. She always did that. She knew Rick wanted to live on the water and kept pitching properties to him. He didn't mind because she was so nice and not the least bit pushy, and she was probably right. At some point, he wanted to build his dream house on the bay. It wasn't the right time.

Once inside the condo, Rick went straight to the shower as Jules started unpacking and putting things away. After she was done, she called Possum and gave him the address so he could take an Uber over. The bedrooms were identical, so Jules picked the one Rick had already showered in for them.

"Feel better, baby? All clean and shiny?"

"So much better. I think I need to start surfing again. I forgot how great a workout paddling against waves is. Surfing in Destin is usually pretty crappy 'cause there are no waves or it's all blown out. Anyway, I'm just rambling now."

"Ramble away, Rick. You know I'd like to join you on a surfing safari. We'll have to plan one. Maybe a nice place in the South Pacific?"

"I like the way you think, Jules!"

Rick dried off and got dressed about the time that Possum knocked on the door. Jules let him in and got him up to speed on Rick's big adventure of the day. Rick stepped out of the bedroom as Jules and Possum sat at the bar in kitchen.

"Where's your cape, amigo?"

"My cape?"

"Well, according to Jules, you are Superman. Or maybe I should say Aquaman."

"Haha, very funny! How do you like the place?"

"I like it a lot. Did you see the pool down there? It looked like a damn waterpark. We gotta hang there with a few brewskis sometime."

"I'll give that a big Texas-sized ten-four. They also have a restaurant and bar on the property. It's called The Palms Bistro. It's sort of a beach bar/sports bar. We should check it out later," replied Rick.

"Cool, I'm game."

"How's Johnie?" asked Rick.

"He's great. You'd never know that he has capital murder and grand larceny hanging over his head. He has an afternoon charter today. He told me to let you know he's got it all under control. He's already stocked the boat for the trip, and the captain has worked the boat several times. The family going specifically asked if Chief could go on the trip, so I expect a nice tip for the boat."

"If y'all don't mind, I think I'd like to rest my eyes a little."

"I think you earned it, Rick," said Possum.

"Mind if I join you?" asked Jules.

He smiled. "As if you have to ask."

"I'm gonna walk down to the pool and play tourist," said Possum.

Rick nodded and stepped into the bedroom, and Jules followed right behind him. He closed his eyes and fell asleep almost immediately, with Jules's head on his chest.

Rick slept for an hour and groggily woke up with Jules still holding him tight. He kissed her on top of the head, and she kissed his chest. One kiss led to another and before he knew it, they were making love. It was passionate and slow and lasted a long time. They were entangled in each other and deeply in love. Rick had never had a love like this and had no intentions of letting her go. They both got cleaned up and decided to go down and find Possum. Possum wasn't alone when they arrived.

"Hey, amigo. This is Liz. She's staying on the eighth floor for a month. Liz, let me introduce you to Super...ahem, I mean Aquaman and Jules. It's actually Rick and Jules. I already told her about your huge lifesaving event today."

"Very nice to meet you, Liz," said Rick.

They all shook hands, and Rick pulled over two more lounge chairs. He looked at his watch and it was 4:15. Johnie's charter had just gotten underway.

"Who's hungry?" asked Rick.

They all nodded in agreement.

"Shall we check out the bistro?"

"Way ahead of you," said Possum as he reached under his lounge chair and passed Rick a menu.

"Hmmm. Pizza and wings. Works for me."

"Yeah, we can go in or order and have it brought right here," replied Possum.

"You wanna stay here, Jules?"

"It's nice out. Let's chill here."

Rick gathered up what everyone wanted and stepped into the bistro to place the order. He got Jules and himself the drink of the day, which was the cucumber chill. The waitress said she'd bring the rest out when it was ready.

Possum and Liz seemed to be hitting it off nicely. They all got a few drinks and did the "ha-ha, clink-clink" for a few hours. Time got away from them and it was eight o'clock before they decided to call it. Possum got Liz's number and they all planned to meet again. Rick, Jules, and Possum made their way to the condo on the top floor. Rick turned on the sixty-five-inch TV and kicked his heels up and chilled on the couch with Jules to watch some mindless show and relax.

His phone rang. It was Johnie.

"What's up, Johnie? Good charter?"

Johnie's reply came tumbling out. "Hurry to the boat. Something's happened."

Rick fumbled for the TV remote to turn down the volume. "Slow down. What's up, Johnie?"

"Someone took a shot at me while I was spraying off the deck. The bullet shattered the sliding glass door. I hit the deck. Whoever it was ran off. I went inside, and Chief was lying on the bottom of the cage and there's blood all over the sole of the boat."

"What?!! Oh my God. Is he breathing? Was he hit?"

"There's glass in the cage and a bullet hole in the galley wall. I don't think he was hit by the bullet; I think some glass hit him. His right wing is straight out and bloody. I grabbed some baking soda and packed it on there to stop the bleeding. He bit the crap out of me, but I don't care. He's scared."

"I'll be right there."

He hung up and threw his shoes on.

"What's happening, Rick? I'm scared," said Jules.

"I don't have time to explain. Possum, let's go. Jules, stay here. I'll call you as soon as I can. I promise."

Rick's hands were shaking as he and Possum ran out of the door. He peeled out of the parking garage and sped down the back road toward HarborWalk. He threw the truck into park at

AJ's and bolted to the boat.

Chief was still lying on the bottom of the cage, breathing so fast he was hyperventilating. Rick grabbed a towel and carefully picked him up.

"Johnie, call the police. I'm taking Chief to Airport Vet Clinic. They have a twenty-four-hour hotline. Possum, can you call while we walk to the truck?"

"I'm on it."

Rick carefully placed Chief on the seat in between Possum and himself. The bleeding had stopped thanks to Johnie's quick thinking. They got to the veterinary hospital and no one was there. Within a few minutes, a car pulled up. The vet unlocked the front door and turned on the lights as Rick carried Chief inside. He placed Chief on the stainless-steel table and pulled over a huge light. He looked closely at Chief, who was still hyperventilating.

"I can't help him. He has a broken wing and a large cut in the tendon from something. He needs surgery or this wing won't survive."

"You do surgeries here, right?"

"Yes, but only minor surgery and mostly on dogs and cats. You need an avian specialist. There's one in Tallahassee. I can call him."

"Okay, call him."

He stepped into his office and came back a few minutes later.

"Dr. James in Tallahassee thinks he can help. He's gonna wait for you, but you need to leave now," said the vet.

Rick called Jules and let her know what had happened. She told him she'd run down to the lobby and meet him on Commons Drive. Rick put Chief back in the truck and Possum climbed in. He sped back to The Palms and through the roundabout. Possum jumped out and Jules climbed in. Rick floored it, smoking the truck tires. Chief had grown attached to Jules; her voice seemed to calm him down and he began to breathe slower.

Rick made the three-hour trip to Capital Circle Veterinary Hospital in two and a half hours, setting a new ground speed record for the 1962 Ford. They had already prepped for surgery when Rick and Jules burst through the front door. Chief's breathing was shallow now and he couldn't hold up his head anymore. He started making a moaning sound that sounded like a hurt puppy. A man all dressed in white stuck out his hand to shake Rick's.

"I'm Paul James, the veterinary surgeon. How much blood did he lose?" he asked.

"I don't know. There was quite a bit in the cage and a small three-inch puddle under it."

"That's a lot for a bird this size. We've got it from here. Just go to the waiting room and pray. I'll do everything I can."

The surgeon spun around and disappeared into the operating room. Rick was inconsolable. Jules hugged him and tried to calm him down, but he couldn't stop pacing. Every few steps, he would look at his watch and then at the clock on the wall. Time seemed to stand still.

"That little guy didn't deserve this!" exclaimed Rick.

"I know, Rick. Whoever did this should pay. Who would take a shot at Johnie, anyway?"

"I don't know, Jules, but I'm damn sure gonna find out. Poor little Chief was just in his cage minding his own business and probably enjoying a grape. It just makes no sense."

Rick continued to pace. Jules walked over to make him a cup of tea from a Keurig machine in the lobby. He tried to sit down but didn't last more than a few minutes before he went back to pacing. Forty-five minutes had gone by and they were still in the operating room. He continued to pace, holding his palm to his head and trying to pray.

An hour and twenty minutes had gone by when the doors opened up at the rear of the vet clinic. The surgeon walked out of the operating room toward Rick, pulling off his mask as he approached.

"Mr. Waters, I'm afraid it's not looking good. I'm so sorry. It could go either way. He lost a lot of blood."

Rick collapsed to the floor. Jules began to cry, and she kneeled down to assist Rick. He looked up at Jules with bloodshot eyes full of tears and disbelief.

"No, no, no!" he said.

Jules threw her arms around Rick and didn't say anything. He began to sob and couldn't speak. She rubbed his back and kissed him on the forehead as the tears continued to flow.

"He has to survive! He has to survive!" repeated Rick.

Rick sat on the floor in complete disbelief, sobbing. With Jules's help, he finally got to his feet.

"Mr. Waters, there's nothing you can do here now. You can come back tomorrow, or I can call you tonight if there are any changes. I know this is difficult. He is in a sort of birdie coma. Would you like to see him?"

Rick wiped his eyes and nodded. He and Jules followed the vet into the back room. As they approached the stainless-steel table where Chief lay, Jules broke down completely. Rick helped her over to the table. They both just stared down at his tiny body. His eyes were closed, and the little powder-blue outline around his eyes made Rick smile a bit. He loved him so much.

With tears in his eyes, he rubbed Chief's head and said, "I love you, boy. You are one of a kind. Please don't leave us."

CHAPTER ELEVEN

The alarm in the room next to Rick and Jules went off and buzzed and buzzed, waking them up. Rick hadn't really slept much anyway. He was still in shock that Chief might not make it. He'd been way too emotional to drive back to Destin the night before, so they'd gotten a room at the TownePlace Suites. He hugged Jules and she pulled him close, kissing his chest and trying to console him. It was 8:05 a.m., according to the clock radio. They hadn't eaten since happy hour the day before.

"I'm gonna go down and get some coffee. Can I get you something, Jules?"

"Sure, Rick. A bagel and coffee, or whatever. You want me to go with you?"

"No, just relax. I'll be back in a few minutes."

Down in the lobby, Rick grabbed a couple of toasted bagels with cream cheese and four coffees in a cardboard cup carrier. He also grabbed a couple of free toothbrushes and toothpaste from the front desk. A sign on the wall read

Pets Allowed—$100 Refundable Deposit. It made him think of Chief and the many times he had snuck him into hotels under his jacket. They had been on so many adventures together. It was still unbelievable that he might actually die. Like a bad dream he couldn't wake up from.

Rick rang the hospital to check on the kid who'd nearly drowned. He was told the boy was stable and recovering and would most likely be released that day. That made Rick feel thankful, and his mind drifted back to Chief. The veterinary clinic opened at 9:00 a.m. Rick needed to settle the bill and check on him. He realized no one back in Destin even knew yet. That was going to be a hard call to make. Chief had become one of the crew and was beloved by everyone. If he died, it would be like a family member dying.

Rick munched on the bagel back in the room with Jules and told her his plans. She offered to call the boys back in Destin to give them the touch-and-go news. Rick agreed and stepped into the living room of the suite to call the vet. He gave the vet his credit card number and let him know they'd be by shortly to check on Chief.

The doctor told him there were no changes and his BP was dangerously low. "If I were you, I would plan for the worst," he said in a heavy voice.

Rick walked back into the bedroom just as Jules hung up. Tears were welling up in her eyes, and Rick gave her a huge hug.

"Let's get going, baby."

Jules sniffled and grabbed her purse off of the nightstand. She brushed her teeth and splashed her face with water. Rick did the same after she was done, and they headed out.

"Mr. Waters, we are closely monitoring his condition," said the vet when they arrived. "It appears the setting to his wing went well. We just need to pray that he wakes up. Just like humans, when animals are mortally wounded, the body will shut down in order to heal itself. We just never know if they'll come out of it."

"Thanks, Doc. That means a lot. I really appreciate the update. Can we take a look at him again?"

The vet had Jules and Rick follow him into the back room. Rick was in a deep funk and felt more like a zombie than a human. After gazing at poor little Chief on his soft birdie hospital bed for a few minutes, he headed out. Jules sat close to Rick, consoling him, not with words but feelings. Her squeezes on his arm said a thousand words.

"Rick, Rick," she said, trying to get his attention. He was lost in deep thought.

"Yeah, Jules. What is it? I'm sorry, I was racking my brain trying to figure out who would do this."

"I know Rick, me too. It's all just so unnecessary. I'd like to do something for you and Chief, if you'll allow me."

Rick was silent for a second. He was struggling to focus on understanding what she'd said.

"Sure, what would you like to do?"

"I'd like to organize a prayer vigil for Chief on the boat or wherever you'd like."

"I'd like that, Jules. But let's do it down on Princess Beach. It's the first place I took Chief when I became his dad. I drank a couple of beers down there, and Chief caught his first buzz on beer that day. It's a special memory for us."

"Okay, the beach it is. I'll take care of the whole thing. You wanna do it today, maybe at sunset?"

"That's a great idea. Make sure you get some twenty-four-ounce aluminum beer cans.

Chief would approve. That's what I had that day with him."

"Don't worry, I'll get a whole cooler full of them."

A tiny smile crept over Rick's face as his put his hand on Jules's thigh.

After a long conversation with Dr. James and him reassuring Rick that the best thing for Chief was to let him rest and recover, they made the decision to head back to Destin. They arrived at midday. Rick drove straight to the condo and was met at the door by Possum. He hugged Rick like he had never hugged him before. Silence stretched between them; nothing needed to be said. Rick knew what Possum meant without speaking. Jules walked in behind Rick. She told Possum what she had planned for later that day at the beach, and he said it was a wonderful idea.

"I'm so sorry, Rick. I look forward to the prayer vigil today. Listen, I got a call from Johnie. The police recovered a .40 caliber bullet from the galley wall. On a hunch, I went to the boat, and the detective came back to ask Johnie a few more questions. I stood in front of the stern and held my hand up to try and see if I could detect the angle of the shot. I got permission from AJ's to go on the roof to the right of the outdoor big-screen TV with the detective. He recovered a .40 caliber shell casing. It was the perfect angle toward the stern of the boat, and with the music pumping that night, no one ever heard the shot. The detective thinks it came from a tactical rifle, possibly with a silencer, though that's unclear at the moment. They are gonna review the

surveillance cameras and see if they can come up with anything. They are treating it like an attempted homicide."

"Thanks, Possum. How's Johnie doing?"

"He's okay, a little shook up and worried, as we all are,
but holding up pretty well, I believe. I got some grocer-
ies and I'm grilling some ribs on the veranda if y'all are
hungry."

"I'm not really hungry. I might just have a little. Jules?"

"I could eat," said Jules. "That bagel didn't quite do it
for me. I need energy to plan the event today."

They all sat down at the table and ate ribs and baked
beans and reminisced on all the funny things Chief had done
over the years. It was a wonderful meal, so full of happy
stories and tears of joy and sadness at the same time. Rick
didn't know what he would do if Chief passed.

"Jules, I rented an SUV for the month when y'all left, so
I wouldn't have to depend on Rick's old Ford. He never lets
me drive it anyway, haha. You're welcome to use it to go
get supplies for the vigil."

"Thank you, Possum. I appreciate that. What time do
you wanna head down to the beach,

Rick?"

He thought for a second and said, "Let's all go down
there around four-twenty. That would make Chief laugh.
Well, I'd laugh and he'd mimic me."

Possum tossed Jules the keys, and she bolted out of the
door to get everything needed for the afternoon prayer.

After Jules left, Rick and Possum drove down to the
boat to debrief Johnie and put their heads together about
who could have done this. The sheriff's department had
removed the crime tape from the scene, and Johnie had

already ordered a new rear glass door for the boat. He had
to cancel a couple of charters, but Rick didn't care under
the circumstances.

"Rick, you got a package this morning from FedEx,"
said Johnie.

"Oh great, it must be the surveillance DVR."

Johnie had already cleaned up all the glass and removed
the sliding door. They all sat down around the settee, and
Rick unboxed the DVR and plugged it in. He popped in
the DVD they had gotten from Pamela's house. Rick was
excited to see what was on the DVD's other camera angles.
He hooked up an external hard drive to the laptop so he
could record a copy of each camera in separate file folders.
Glancing back, he spotted Chief's cage in the corner of the
galley, and anxiety gripped him again.

Once Rick had copied all the files to the external hard
drive, he began to go over them in slow motion as Possum
leaned in close to assist. The first camera was a view of
the kitchen and didn't reveal a lot. It was empty most of
the time, so Rick fast forwarded until he saw motion, then
slowed it down. Possum took notes and scanned the entire
room, looking for anything that would resemble a clue. They
went through all eight views and saw nothing new. They did
see Johnie enter the house on a few different cameras and
how badly he was stumbling, obviously hammered. Frustrated, Rick turned it off.

"Well, that was a waste of time. I may as well return the
DVR back to Amazon," said Rick.

"Do you mind if I take it back to the condo with the original DVD? I wanna go over it a few more times and see if
I can come up with anything," said Possum.

"Knock yourself out."

Rick unhooked the external hard drive from the laptop, put that and the DVD back in the box, and slid it toward Possum. Rick sat there silently staring into space. Possum kept quiet and let him sit there.

After a few minutes, he said, "Amigo, how about let's crack open a beer and toast Chief."

"Better yet, crack open one of those bottles of thirty-two-year-old Flor de Caña. Johnie ordered two bottles last week."

Possum poured two heavy pours in rocks glasses over a cube of round ice, and slid one to Rick.

Rick picked it up and clinked Possum's glass.

"Here's to Chief, the best bird a man could ever have. May the grace of God return him to us from his coma."

"Here, here. To Chief."

They both took a big swig, and Possum patted Rick on the shoulder. They sat there silently sipping on the rum.

"Okay, that's enough of that. Let's get busy saving Johnie's ass. Chief will be okay. I feel it in my bones."

"I agree, hombre."

They both hopped into Rick's old Ford and were driving back to the condo when Rick's phone rang.

"Hello."

"Rick, it's Carson. I got your message about getting a phone bug. I've been retired for a while but I still have friends in high places. Now, you have to realize whatever you get on recordings is not admissible in court. Plus, I'm going out on a huge limb getting you this equipment. We can't let anyone know. You're gonna owe me one."

"You name it, Carson!"

"I'd like to go out on a charter on that boat you're always talking about."

"Anytime, Carson. Just come to Destin."

"That's just the thing. I just landed at the Destin Executive Airport. I didn't feel comfortable shipping the bugs, and I need to show you how they work and how to install them in person. Can you come pick me up?"

"Hell yeah. I'm on my way."

Rick dropped Possum off at the condo, then turned around to pick up Carson. Carson was overdressed as usual in a black suit. Rick pulled up to the terminal and waved at him to get his attention. He hopped in.

"Thanks for coming. What a surprise. Did you book a hotel yet?"

"No, not yet. I was hoping you could suggest one."

"Well, you can take the couch in our condo…wait."

Rick picked up his phone and called his real estate agent.

"Jessica, can you tell me if there is a unit on our floor I can rent for…hold on…how long, Carson?"

"Let's say a week."

He removed his palm from the phone. "Can you find a unit on our floor for one week? I can wait on the line."

After a long pause, she came back on.

"Yes, actually, the unit right beside yours is available. It's a one-bedroom. Will that work?"

"Book it, Danno. Can you bring the keys and the contract by my unit soon?"

"Yes, I'm at the property now. Thirty minutes, okay?"

"Perfect, see ya then, bye." Rick ended the call. "You're all set, Carson. The unit beside me is open. I got you covered."

"You don't have to pay for it, Rick."

"I know I don't, but I want to. No arguments."

Carson nodded in agreement. Rick pulled into the parking garage and led Carson to their unit. Possum was in his room sitting at his desk going over the DVR again.

"Oh, Carson, I forgot to tell you. Do you remember me talking about my cockatoo, Chief?" asked Rick.

"Yes."

"There was a terrible accident. Not actually an accident. Someone took a shot at Johnie on the boat, and a piece of glass broke Chief's wing and punctured his chest."

Carson's eyes widened. "I'm so sorry, Rick. Will he be okay?"

"We don't know yet. He's at the vet now."

Jules returned a few minutes after they arrived.

"Oh, hello," she said to Carson.

"Jules, this is Carson. He's a friend of mine from the FBI," said Rick. "He's going to assist us in tapping Pamela's phone."

Carson shook Jules's hand, and they all gathered around the kitchen table. Carson pulled a padded manila envelope out of his jacket and pulled a clear plastic baggie out of that. Inside were a couple of tiny SIM cards. He also laid down what looked like a walkie talkie, only smaller.

"Okay, who's gonna be planting the bug?"

"Probably me," piped up Jules.

"You see this little SIM card?"

She leaned in to get a closer look.

"This is preprogrammed to trace any outgoing or incoming calls, texts, or instant messages. It delivers the data to another number that is stored on a hard drive. Whatever phone it's installed in will not change the way the phone works, and they'll never know it's in there. Rick told me you said it was an iPhone 11, right?"

"That's right."

"So, you need to get her phone somehow to make the switch, then hold this device over it for three minutes to activate it. Can you get her phone without her knowing?"

A big devilish grin creeped over Jules's face, and she reached into her purse and pulled out an iPhone case. She removed it from the plastic to reveal a dolphin on the case.

"I was over at Destin Commons today getting supplies for Chief's prayer vigil, and I saw this case at T-Mobile. It's the exact one she has on her phone. I also have the same color iPhone 11 that she does. She called and asked me to meet her today for a drink over at Bric à Brac. I noticed when she was at McGuire's she always kept her phone face down on the bar beside her. She checked it often for texts but always put it back face down. If I put mine in airplane mode and swap them out while she's not looking, I should be able to run to the restroom and make the SIM card switch and activation. I can switch them back without her noticing, hopefully."

"Jules, you truly are becoming a secret agent," said Rick.

She smiled ear to ear, patting herself on the back and laughing. It was 3:45 now and time to head to the beach.

"Carson, would you like to join us? I know you really didn't know Chief, but the beach is quite beautiful."

"I'd be honored, Rick. You have spoken so highly of him. I don't really have anything to wear other than this suit, though. I planned on buying some fishing-appropriate clothes tomorrow."

"I got you covered, hombre. I just picked up some fishing shorts and tees at Bealls. We look to be about the same size. They haven't even been worn yet," said Possum.

"Thank you kindly, Possum."

Possum took Carson into the bedroom and showed him the clothes, then stepped out to let him change. Jessica rang the doorbell while he was in Possum's room, and Rick signed the contract and took the keys from her. She left him a few more printouts of vacant land, as usual. When Carson reentered the living room, Rick handed him the keys and showed him the unit.

After a few minutes, they all took the elevator down to where Possum's Navigator was parked, and headed to Princess Beach on Okaloosa Island. Possum backed into a spot and helped Jules get the large cooler and supplies out of the back of the SUV. She had thought of everything, including an aluminum fishing cart she'd picked up at Bass Pro Shop. She put tiki torches on the rod holders, and Possum placed the cooler on the cart. Rick and Possum pulled the cart down to the beach. There was a large easy-up set up on the beach, and several chairs sat under it with a table. A guy was sitting in one of the chairs looking out at the Gulf, smoking a cigar. As they got closer, he turned around. It was Gary.

"What the hell are you doing here?" asked Rick.

"When Jules called me and told me what happened, I chartered a flight and came straight here. I'm so sorry, Rick. I had to be here to say my prayers as well."

Rick hugged Gary and thanked him for coming.

"I wouldn't miss it for the world," said Gary.

Rick pulled the cart around in front of the easy-up and opened the cooler. He passed out tall boys to everyone and cracked one open himself. The sun was starting to go down but still hung above the horizon.

"This is the first place I took Chief after he came into my life. I gave him a few sips of my beer and we bonded. He got a little buzzed and never drank beer again after that. Smart bird."

Rick asked everyone to think of the good times with Chief and try to stay positive. They all gathered around and took turns saying something nice about Chief. Jules was a trouper and held back her tears, mainly for Rick. He kneeled down in the sand and began to pray.

"Dear Lord, I know I'm not the greatest Christian. I honestly can't remember the last time I went to church. I'm not here to make a deal with you per se, but if you can see it in you to save Chief's life and bring him home healed, I'll try and do better. I've always lived my life by the words of Christ. I do unto others as I would have them do unto me. Please save Chief. He's loved by so many people."

It was more than Jules could take, and she turned around to hide her tears. Rick stood up as the sun began to touch the water.

"To Chief.

"He likes to sit up on his perch and stare out at the dock.

He likes to raise his crown and squawk at kids that he would mock.

He likes to sneak out of his cage and laugh when he escapes.

But only thing he really loves is me and those damn grapes. To Chief!" they all

exclaimed, raising their tallboys and clinking them together.

The sun slowly sank beneath the waves, and they all drank their beers and each said their own prayer.

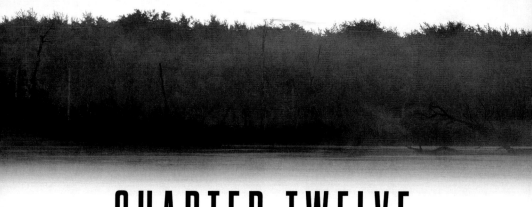

CHAPTER TWELVE

Jules walked into Bric à Brac dressed to the nines. After a few minutes, Rick walked in and took a seat on the farthest side opposite her at the bar. Pamela hadn't arrived yet, so Jules took off her shawl and placed it over the bar seat next to her to hold the seat. She ordered a Cosmo and waited patiently, occasionally looking over at Rick in the mirror behind the bar. She cracked a grin and tried not to laugh at the fake Fu Manchu mustache on his face. Rick was just there in case things went sideways and had no intention of being spotted by Pamela. She was so self-absorbed, they figured she probably wouldn't remember him anyway from when he had posed as a cable company repairman at her house.

Pamela came in, spotted Jules, and waved. She made her way to the bar, and Jules removed the shawl and pulled out her bar seat.

"Why thank you, Valentina."

"My pleasure, Pamela. Whatcha drinking?"

She thought for a minute, looked at a few other drinks people were having, and decided to order a rum runner. She sipped on the tall frozen drink and made small talk with Jules, checking out every guy who walked into the bar. She kept looking over Jules's shoulder toward Rick.

"Who's that cute guy with the funky mustache? He looks familiar."

Jules looked over and rolled her eyes sideways for Rick to leave. He didn't see her hint.

"I'm gonna go introduce myself to him," said Pamela.

Shit!

"Uh, uh, okay. I'm gonna run to the ladies' room. I'll be right back."

When Pamela took another look at Rick, Jules snatched Pamela's phone and slid hers in its place. Pamela picked up the phone, zipped it into her purse, and walked around the bar toward Rick. Now Jules's phone was in Pamela's purse, and she knew somehow, she'd have to get it back before Pamela realized.

Rick noticed Pamela making a beeline for him. He was blocked in and couldn't sneak away. He saw Jules scamper toward the bathroom and had to think on his feet quickly.

"Hi, I'm Pamela. What's your name? Have we met? You look so familiar."

In a dry, husky voice, he said, "I'm Reggie. I just got into town today. I don't believe we've met."

"New in town, huh? How'd you find this place?"

"Uh, I'm staying at the Sandpiper and I just drove by and popped in for a beer. Never been here before. Pretty cool, though."

"If you're looking for some great food while you're here, try the Local Market just up the street."

"Oh yeah, I passed that on my way here. I'll have to give it a shot."

Rick was starting to sweat thinking she would recognize him. There was no law against pretending to be a cable company worker and then seeing her again at a bar, but he'd have a hard time explaining the fake mustache. She was blatantly flirting, and Rick kept looking over her shoulder for Jules to reappear.

"I can give you my number if you wanna meet up for happy hour or want me to show you around. Let me grab my phone."

Oh shit!

Jules was still in the bathroom when Pamela unzipped her purse and pulled out the phone. It didn't unlock, of course. She punched in the passcode and that didn't work either.

She frowned. "That's weird. I can't seem to unlock my phone. My face recognition isn't working and my passcode isn't working. I wonder if I'm using the right one…"

"Maybe you don't have a signal," suggested Rick.

He pulled out his phone, pretending to check for a signal.

"No, I have four bars. This is so weird."

"Let me text you instead," said Rick.

Jules was coming back from the bathroom, and Rick waved his head at her to join them. When Jules got closer, she saw Pamela trying to get into her phone and her eyes grew wide. She rushed up to them.

"Hi, who's your friend, Pamela?"

"Valentina, this is Reggie. Reggie, Valentina."

"Pleasure to meet you, Valentina."

"I can't get my phone to unlock."

"Let me see it. I was having the same problem in the bathroom with mine."

Pamela handed Jules her phone, and Rick put his hand on Pamela's shoulder and pulled her over and pointed at the draft taps.

"What beer is that one with the 30A on the handle?" asked Rick.

When she leaned closer to look, Jules swapped the phones back and put hers in her back pocket.

"That's 30A Beach Blonde. It's more of a girly light beer. You look like an IPA man. You should try the Destin East Pass. I hate it, but guys seem to love it."

"Here, Pamela, try your phone now."

She picked it up and it immediately opened.

"That's so crazy. Okay, Reggie, what's your number?" Rick quickly made up a number, and she plugged it in.

"I'll text you now so you have mine," she said.

"Got it," said Rick, pretending to see her text on his phone. "Ladies, I hate to say this, but I need to go. I'm meeting a friend. Nice to meet you both. Pamela, I'll be in touch. Y'all have a great night."

Rick scurried out of the front door to his truck parked behind the building to wait for Jules. He let out a sigh as soon as he got out the front door.

That was close.

Jules sat back down at her bar stool, and Pamela stepped into the restroom. She came back a few minutes later and was visibly upset.

"What's wrong?"

"That guy I just met totally blew me off."

"What do you mean?"

"When I got to the bathroom, I texted him to ask him if he would like to meet me for lunch tomorrow. Look at his response."

She held the phone up for Jules to read.

It was nice to meet you, Reggie. Wanna meet me for lunch at Dewey Destin's on the bay?

Who is this?

It's Pamela, we just me a few minutes ago in Bric à Brac.

You have the wrong number. This is not Reggie and I haven't ever been to Bric à Brac.

I'm sorry. My bad.

"That son of a bitch gave me a bogus number."

"Maybe not. Maybe you just inverted the numbers?"

"No, because when I texted him before he left, he said he got it." "Well, that's his loss, Pamela. His mustache was weird anyway."

"That's true. Fuck him! Let's get another round," she said.

"How about mojitos instead?" asked Jules.

"Deal! Bartender, two mojitos please."

Jules sipped her drink, then texted Rick to go ahead and go back to the condo, and that she would get an Uber.

You sure? he texted back.

> Yes, I'm sure. I've got it under control.

As Jules tucked away her phone, Pamela said, "Let's get out of here. How'd you like to come see my house and give me an estimate on cleaning it? I must admit, I do feel kinda weird having you clean it since we are pretty much friends now."

"Don't feel bad. It's what I do. Plus, I have a great crew. It won't be me actually cleaning it every time. I'm more of a supervisor. Don't get me wrong, I'm not afraid to get my hands dirty and I do help out, but things go way smoother when I delegate."

"Smart lady. I like you, Valentina. Did you drive here?"

"No, I took an Uber."

"Okay, you are riding with me. You can Uber back home from my place. I have some amazing wine I had shipped in from New Zealand. I'd love for you to try it. I also have some great cheese I got from Chan's Wine World too."

"Sounds like a plan, Pamela. Let me hit the ladies' room real quick and we can go." Jules popped into the ladies' room and texted Rick.

> Change of plans, she invited me to her place. I'm gonna do some recon. 007, over and out!

> Be careful, Valentina Bond. LOL

Pamela hit the button on her fob, and her BMW beeped. Jules climbed in on the passenger's side and sat on the plush leather seat. Pamela backed out and peeled out toward Harbor Boulevard. She turned left at The Palms, and Jules looked up and spotted the unit she was staying in with Rick. They pulled into Kelly Plantation Estates, which was only two miles from The Palms, and into Pamela's driveway.

"Home sweet home," she said.

"Wow, what a beautiful place."

Pamela shrugged. "It'll do for now. Like I said before, I'm gonna be moving."

"Where to?"

"I can't really say right now. Let's just say it's warmer."

"Okay, gotcha. I won't be nosey."

"Oh, it's not that. I'm just waiting for some insurance money. If it all goes as I planned, I'm out of here. Wine?"

"Wine not. Haha."

Inside the house, Pamela opened her huge Sub-Zero refrigerator and pulled out a bottle of Destiny Bay Magna

Praemia. She poured two glasses and set out some cheese that she had cut earlier in the day.

"New Zealand is known for its Sauvignon Blanc, but this red is so amazing. It's spendy. Three-fifty a bottle."

Jules nearly spit out the sip she'd just taken.

"Three hundred and fifty?!"

"Don't worry about it, sweetie. My former husband paid for it."

"Oh, you're divorced?"

"You don't know?"

"Know what?"

"My husband was murdered recently."

Jules gasped aloud, trying to sell her surprise. "Murdered?"

"Yeah, they already caught the guy who did it. I was fucking him. I really fucked him, if you know what I mean."

"No, what do you mean?"

"Never mind. Listen, my husband was a piece of shit. I heard he had filed for divorce. I didn't really care. It's not like we were in love anymore. He had his flings and I had mine. I signed a prenup and I was guaranteed to get pretty much nothing. But after we were first married, he added me to his will. He wanted me to get a hundred thousand dollars in case something ever happened to him. A measly hundred K? What would I do with that?! Then I found out he had changed the will, so it reverted back to the prenup, which meant I wouldn't even get the hundred K. But luckily, the guy who killed him also stole the jewels I had in my safe. I had them insured for $3.5 million. He's gonna rot in jail and as soon as I get my insurance money, I'm gone, gone."

"Wow, that's insane. I had no idea," replied Jules.

"So, the jewels were never recovered? What if they are found?"

"The insurance company has issued a one-million-dollar reward for the return of the jewels. I guess they figured one million is better than 3.5. Once I get my payout, I don't give a shit if they find them or not."

"So, who's the guy that killed your husband?"

Anxiety swept over Jules as they were discussing Pamela's husband's death. Her heart was racing but she tried to remain calm.

"Some boat guy I met at Harry T's. He was so drunk I don't even think he knows he did it or didn't do it."

"What do you mean, did or didn't?"

"All I know is the evidence points to him. I was asleep. I'm just guessing that my husband showed up and his ego and testosterone took over. He was found stabbed several times, and the prints on the knife belong to the guy I met. It was probably self-defense. Who knows? Not my problem. He actually did me a favor when you think about it."

They indulged on the wine and cheese and before they knew it, it was almost midnight.

"I need to get going, Pamela," said Jules. "It's late."

"Are you sure? You can take the spare bedroom, if you wanna stay."

"No, I really need to get going."

"Okay, let me call you an Uber. I'm gonna get changed. I'll be right back. What's your address?"

"Oh, I can do it on my phone. I'm gonna use Lyft. I have a free ride coupon."

"I don't have Lyft. Let me get changed first, so I can say goodbye."

She disappeared into her bedroom before Jules could argue. She texted Rick that she would be leaving soon. A few minutes later, Pamela came back in wearing a quite revealing outfit. Jules thought it was odd since they were alone.

"Well, thank you, Valentina, for a wonderful night. I had a lot of fun."

She walked up behind Jules and stroked her hair.

"You have such beautiful black hair. It's silky."

"Thank you. I try to take care of it."

Pamela bent down and smelled her hair. She was acting differently than before. Jules got a creepy vibe.

"Valentina, do you think I'm pretty?"

"Umm, yes, I told you that before."

"Well, I really think you're pretty. Your body is so amazing."

"Are you coming on to me?"

"I thought we had a connection. It seemed obvious."

"I'm not lesbian, Pamela."

"I'm not either, but I just love how soft women are. Aren't you curious?"

"I'm no saint and I did experiment in college a little, but even if I was curious, I don't really know you that well yet," said Jules, playing along.

"I respect that."

She kissed Jules on her neck, and she jumped.

"I'm not ready for this. I need to leave."

"I'm sorry, Valentina. I didn't mean to come on too strong. I just find you so attractive. I don't wanna ruin our friendship. But please think about it, okay?"

"Oh, okay. I'll talk to you soon—my ride is almost here. I gotta run, bye."

Jules ran out the door and jumped into her Lyft, which arrived just in time.

When she got back to the condo, she was still in shock and couldn't wait to tell Rick. He opened the door as she came in and wrapped her arms around him.

"She came on to me!"

"Like, came on to you sexually?"

"Yes, apparently she's bi. She wants to see me again. I don't know what to do."

"I guess you're gonna have to take one for the team, Jules—I mean, Valentina," said Rick, bent over laughing.

"Not funny, Rick Waters! I don't swing that way."

"I know, honey. I'm just messing with you. But maybe you can get to know her a little better and just let her know your boundaries."

Jules bit her lip. "That's true. I mean, we didn't even know she liked women. Maybe that info can help the case?"

"It's possible. I'm gonna try and find out if she went out with any women. It didn't even cross my mind before," said Rick.

"She also told me that the jewelry Johnie was charged with stealing was insured for $3.5 million, and that she had a prenup where she'd get nothing. Apparently, the insurance company is offering one million dollars for the return of the jewelry. Have you ever heard of such a thing? Do insurance companies offer rewards?"

Possum chimed in. "I've been going through all the files in her computer, through the hard drives I switched out last night. She indeed had the jewelry insured through Lloyd's of London for three and a half million dollars. They are a unique insurance company and will do things most insurance companies won't do. They insured Betty Grable's legs, Tom Jones's chest hair, and Springsteen's voice. They have in the past offered rewards, including a reward for the return of jewels stolen from an exhibition in the French resort city of Cannes."

"So, if someone finds the jewelry, they will receive the reward, no questions asked?" asked Jules.

"That's correct. Even if they are returned by the thief himself. Now, I'm sure Okaloosa's finest will have questions, but Lloyd's of London will pay the reward. Period," said Possum.

With that comment, Rick glanced over at them both with a wicked grin on his face.

"Treasure hunt?"

"I'm already on it, Rick. I'm going through every email and message she's sent. It's tedious, but she's a drinker, and at some point, I'm sure the alcohol will override her better judgment, and she's gonna slip or already slipped and left a clue. It could mean a million-dollar jackpot reward and more importantly, clearing Johnie of any wrongdoing," replied Possum.

"I wanna play!" piped up Jules.

"You've been playing since day one, Valentina," said Rick.

Jules punched him playfully in the arm.

CHAPTER THIRTEEN

Rick drove down US Highway 98 towards Sandestin. Chief was on his mind, and the gravity of the entire event replayed over and over. He wished he had brought Chief to the condo instead of leaving him with Johnie on *Nine-Tenths*. There was no going back and he had to accept it. He tried to put on a strong front, but thinking of Chief brought tears to his eyes, and it took all he had to keep it together.

He stopped at the Donut Hole to hopefully help him stop worrying about Chief. He ordered a chocolate angel and thumbed through a *30A* magazine. The magazine featured celebrities and the upper crust of the redneck riviera from Panama City to Destin. He flipped pages just to kill time, not paying much attention to what he was looking at. He didn't hang out with those people in the pages but knew who some of them were. He spotted the mayor of Destin and some of the area's biggest movers and shakers.

As he continued to flip pages, something caught his eye. A photo of a woman receiving an award at a gala held at the Emerald Coast Theatre Company. As he looked closer, he recognized Pamela. It was no surprise to see her in the magazine, but what was shocking was the woman standing behind her. It was hard to make out and they were a little out of focus, but it was obvious the woman behind her had her palm in the small of Pamela's back. The woman was wearing a long, dark blue flowing gown and had bright red hair.

He kept scanning the photos of the gala, and toward the bottom of the last page of the story, he spotted her again, holding up a champagne glass by the bar with several other people. The man in the forefront of the photo was named and the others were just in the background. But she was in focus this time. Rick held his iPhone close to the photo and snapped a picture. He pulled up the photo, cropped her face in the center, and saved it. After opening Google image search, he uploaded the cropped photo and instantly got a hit. Her name was Michelle Tangier. He did a search of her name and found out she was a popular local realtor. He did a deeper search of her on Facebook and Instagram and saw she was always with women. He went to her About section on her Facebook profile page and then to her Basic Info, and it said she was interested in women.

Bingo! She might be a love interest of Pamela.

"Here ya go, honey. Can I get you anything else?" asked the woman behind the counter.

"Nope, this oughta do it."

After a quick stop at Chevron for a tall boy, he drove over the Destin bridge and glanced down at Crab Island. Over fifty boats were already anchored there. It was a beautiful day with not a cloud in the sky. The tide was in and the water was a mix of light and dark blues. The Gulf had settled down and looked like glass. Rick backed up to the fence that had access to Princess Beach. He kicked off his shoes and grabbed the beer from the seat. As he walked toward the water, he once again reflected on the first time he had come down here with Chief. He plopped down on the sand a few feet from the water and cracked open the beer.

"God, I know you are listening. I know we already had a prayer vigil, but I need to talk to you alone, man to man. I know you're looking down at me right now. I just want you to know that if I could take Chief's place, I would. I'm gonna find out who did this. They will pay for it. I'll never be the same if Chief dies. Please, God, please save him."

Rick took a huge swig of his beer, got to his feet, and started to wade out into the water. When he reached the first sandbar, he stopped and look up at the heavens. He took another big swig of the beer and said a personal prayer for Chief. He stood there on the water for several minutes, gazing at the horizon and praying, then walked back to where he had parked. There was nothing more he could do and it was in God's hands now.

He fired up his old red Ford and headed toward *Nine-Tenths*. When he arrived, two men were installing the new sliding glass door on the boat. Johnie was standing on the dock trying to stay out of the way.

"I got a charter this afternoon, Rick. You wanna come along?"

"Um, maybe, I'll let you know. I think we'll skip the funeral recon. We don't need it now. I gotta meet the gang back at the condo. Carson is here and he's helping us."

"That's great. Any word on Chief? I got it all under control here. If you decide to go, just text me. We're pulling off of the dock at six. It's a two-hour sunset trip today."

"Nothing yet. I hope the vet calls with good news soon. This worrying is for the birds, haha. That one's for Chief."

Rick headed back to the condo. When he opened the door, it looked like a scene from *True Detective*. Papers were spread all over the table, and Possum, Jules, and Carson were all buried in their laptops. Photos were taped to the wall, and the couch had been moved out of the way in order to set up a command center.

"Hey, Rick," said Carson.

Possum nodded, and Jules jumped up and ran over to hug Rick.

"Any news?" she asked.

"Not yet." Rick lifted his good luck necklace and kissed the sailboat pendant hanging from it.

He walked over to Possum and airdropped the photo he had cropped earlier.

"I need you to find anything and everything you can on this woman. Her name is Michelle Tangier. All I know about her is she is a real estate agent and connected to Pamela in a sexual way, I think. Carson, can you search her in the FBI database?"

"I certainly can," he replied. "I also have been working on a profile for the killer of Pamela's husband. Since there are usually multiple victims I can use to develop a profile, it makes this single murder a bit harder, but I'll come up with something."

Rick took a shower to get the saltwater off of him and joined the gang back in the war room. His hair was still wet and he jumped up and down, trying to get the water out of his ears.

"You look like Chief when he bounces on his perch," said Jules. She quickly cupped a hand over her mouth. "I'm sorry, Rick. I don't know what I was thinking."

Rick just laughed.

"It's okay, Jules. I haven't stopped thinking about him since we left the vet anyway."

He walked over, hugged her, and kissed her on top of the head. She looked up and gave him a big smile.

"Rick, I may have found a lead," said Possum.

Rick stepped over to Possum's laptop and looked over his shoulder. Possum pulled up a file.

"You see this? It's from the app HumminbirdPC. It's a copy of a route that was taken on her boat. She keeps her boat over at Legendary Dry Dock by Lulu's. The day before the murder, the boat left Legendary on a route near Hogtown Bayou."

"So what? Lots of people fish at Hogtown. That's not weird."

"Look at the time," replied Possum.

Rick leaned over and squinted to see it. The boat had left Legendary at 2:07 a.m., routed to Hogtown Bayou, arriving at 2:27 a.m., and left again at 2:29 a.m. It was back at the Legendary dock by 2:57 a.m.

He frowned. "That is weird."

"Guess what the weirdest part is?"

"What?"

"Legendary is only open for launching from 8:00 a.m. to 4:00 p.m. How did the boat leave at 2:07 a.m.?"

"So, in order to launch the boat that early, someone who worked there would have to have done it. Can you get a list of all the employees there and see if there's any connection?"

"That's exactly the next step, Rick."

"Great job, Possum! Not sure where it's gonna lead, but it certainly is odd and interesting. Maybe I should drive over and check things out. Wanna go look at some boats, Jules?"

"Yes, please!"

Rick handed Possum the company credit card and told him to order some food for everyone.

"Has anyone spoken to Gary?"

"Oh yeah, sorry, Rick, I forgot. He said he called you and got your voicemail. He had to leave to sort out some stuff back in Jamaica."

Rick pulled his phone out and saw the missed call. Gary had called when he was at the beach and his phone was in the glovebox. He would have preferred for Gary to stick around, but knew he had to deal with the authorities in Jamaica about the crash, and would likely return as soon as humanly possible.

"Let's roll, Jules," said Rick.

They pulled up to Legendary Marina around 3:15 p.m. The place was hopping. A line of boats bobbed, waiting to be pulled out by the massive forklifts. It was an impressive sight. They ran six forklifts. Rick and Jules walked around, looking at the various boats on display. It wasn't more than fifteen minutes before a salesman approached them.

"Howdy, Billy McKissick. Y'all looking for a boat?"

"Hi, I'm Rick and this is Jules. We're thinking about it. I have a charter sport fisher in Destin harbor, but I'm thinking about getting a flats boat or something to fish the back waters."

"You've come to the right place. Do you want a trailer or you wanna use dry storage?"

"Umm, probably dry storage. Are the rates good here?"

"If you buy the boat here, you'll get a monthly discount on storage. Plus, we have a boat club with an infinity pool over there next to Lulu's."

"Nice. Can you give me some paperwork about the storage rates and other amenities at the marina?"

"Sure, follow me into my office. I can also print out a list of boats that fit your needs."

Rick and Jules trailed after Billy into his office.

"LSU alum, huh?" said Rick, pointing at the big LSU Tiger hanging in his office.

"Geaux Tigers. There's only one Death Valley!"

Rick laughed. He was a Texas Longhorn fan through and through, but he played along.

"What are the haul in and out times?" he asked.

"Basically, out by 8:00 a.m. and in by 3:30 optimally. We close at 4:00 p.m."

"What happens if you're running late? There ain't no way I'm watching a clock if I get into a mess of reds."

"I heard that. If you get in after four, you can tie up to the dock. We have an app that you can use to schedule your launches and pickups. Let me show you."

Billy stepped out of the office and returned with a clipboard.

"They are logged in here via the app. The forklift guys run a line though them when they are done. See, this is from last week."

He slid the clipboard over to Rick.

"Can you launch a boat before four and tie it up to the dock if you wanna get an early start the next morning before y'all open?" asked Rick as he and Jules looked down at the clipboard.

Then Jules blurted out, "I know Pamela Killian. We are good friends."

Billy nodded at Jules and continued. "Oh yeah, people do it all the time. As you can plainly see, Pamela Killian launched her boat at 3:00 p.m. and had it put back in storage the next day at 1:00 p.m. She probably went for an early fly-fishing trip the morning after she launched. A shame what happened to her husband."

Rick looked closer. "Whoa, her boat was put back in storage the same day as the murder."

Billy looked down at the clipboard. "You're absolutely right. What a horrendous tragedy. I hope they fry that son of a bitch who did it. I heard he's out on bond. Pamela and her husband have kept their flats boat here since they bought it. I haven't seen him a lot in the past few years, but she's an avid fly-fisherman and goes out all the time by herself."

"Life is short. You just never know, right?" replied Rick.

"Do you have a boat in mind? Here, let me give you a copy of our listings. I also have boats over in Panama City and Orange Beach. Honestly, if you want it, I can get it," said Billy.

"I appreciate your time, Billy. We're gonna grab a bite over at Lulu's. I'll go over the list and give you a call."

"Sounds good, Rick. Nice to meet you, Jules."

They both shook his hand and walked over to Lulu's. Rick looked at the marina docks on the way there and saw cameras on the dock. He needed to see what those cameras had caught of Pamela's late-night excursion. If he had to buy a boat to do it, he would. Whatever it would take to get inside the building after hours. They sat down at the bar, and Rick ordered an East Pass IPA for himself and a 30A Beach Blonde for Jules.

"I wanna look at the gift shop," said Jules.

She jogged over to the gift shop like a little girl. Rick loved that about her. She was a badass woman but had the heart of a child at times.

Sipping his draft, Rick flipped though the listings. He had actually considered buying a flats boat because he felt bad about using Johnie's all the time. The only thing he hated about flats boats was how wet they were. It only took a slight crosswind to get spray above the freeboard. Plus, a flats boat had no head, and he knew Jules would wanna go with him as much as possible. He started thinking maybe a cuddy cabin with a shallow draft might work better. He searched on his iPhone, but most of the cuddy cabins in the twenty-two to twenty-four-foot length drew a foot-and-a-half draft up and a three-and-a-half-foot draft down.

Halfway through Rick's beer, Billy walked in and waved at him. Rick waved him over.

"Hey, Rick, you mentioned Lulu's and I got thirsty."

"Let's get you one, Billy. Whatcha drinking?"

"Thanks, umm, I'll take a Tito's and soda."

Rick got the bartender's attention and ordered his drink.

"Anything in there catch your eye, Rick?"

"I like a few of them, but to be honest, I'm kind of leaning more now toward a cuddy cabin. I just want something with a shallow draft. The little lady over there at the gift shop would also appreciate a marine head."

"I have the perfect boat for you! I ordered it for a guy and he never came back. He put $5K down as a deposit. I've called him a dozen times. I'll gladly give you his deposit and drop another $5K off of it. My boss is pissed that I ordered it without twenty percent down. It's been in the yard for two months. If I don't sell it soon, I'm gonna have to buy it. I'm not trying to pressure you, just being honest. You said a shallow draft? How does a ten-inch draft grab you?! It's a killer boat. It's a Judge Yachts Chesapeake 24. It has a Suzuki 225 with a twenty-horse kicker, and it's loaded with electronics and a walk-around cuddy. It's known as the utility boat. Pretty rare around here. I've never actually seen one in the area. They are built up in Maryland. If you want, I can show it to you in the morning."

"All right, I'll give you a call in the morning and come over," said Rick.

Jules returned to the bar with a bag of goodies she'd bought from Lulu's gift shop. She set Lulu's *Gumbo Love* cookbook on the table.

"Oh, hello again," Jules said to Billy.

"Hello, Jules."

"Rick, now that we are in the condo with a full kitchen, I'm gonna cook you some Cajun food! How do Lucy's Signature Summer Seafood Gumbo and Crab and Corn Fritters sound to start?"

"Sounds like I'm getting hungry! Let's order something," replied Rick.

Rick got a menu from the bartender, and Jules leaned in to get a better look.

"You ever have fried crab claws, Jules?"

"Nope."

"Okay, we'll take a large order of fried crab claws and crazy sista's crab dip," said Rick as he passed the menu back to the bartender.

Billy excused himself and came back a few minutes later with a brochure he'd had printed of the Chesapeake 24.

Damn, he sure is persistent.

Rick said goodbye to Billy, and he and Jules flipped through the pages. Her eyes lit up. It was obvious to Rick that she liked it.

They finished their meal and headed back to the condo to brief Carson and Possum on what they'd learned. It looked like they hadn't left their computers. Empty boxes of Thai food from Thai Delights sat in the middle of the kitchen table.

"Hey, Rick, did you buy a boat?" said Possum with a chuckle.

"You laugh now, but I actually may buy one tomorrow. Let me tell you why."

"I'm all ears."

"We found out how she got her boat back to Legendary in the middle of the night. They have some finger docks behind the boat club. She launched the boat the day before and tied it to the docks. That night after they closed, in the wee hours, she returned and took it to Hogtown Bayou then returned it. They have lots of cameras on the docks. I need to get to the hard drives for a copy of the files. I have an idea of how to get inside after they close. If I buy and store a boat there, I can have it launched, and Jules and I can take it out, pick you up after a while. We can wear similar colors and those long-billed hats and shades. Then we can return it and I'll hide in the cuddy cabin and after they close, I'll put on a mask, copy the hard drives, delete the footage of me inside, and sneak out. It's foolproof. What could go wrong?"

"I guess you'll find out. It does sound like a solid plan. You picked out a boat?"

"No, a salesman named Billy picked one out for me," said Rick as he passed the brochure to Possum.

"Noice! Now that's a dry boat."

"That's what I was thinking."

"When do you wanna do this boat rendezvous?"

"Probably tomorrow. I'll buy the boat and have it dropped and tied to the dock. I'll make up some story that I wanna take it out for a test run midday because I have errands to run. We can return it just before closing with you behind the helm and me hiding in the cuddy. They will be super busy and not paying attention. It's our best bet to do the switcheroo."

Rick went to his bedroom and returned with matching bright yellow fishing shirts and long bill caps. He passed one set to Possum.

"Just wear those blue Columbia beer can shorts you got at Bealls, and your white slipons. We'll be twins. I'll pick you up at the Cessna Landing boat launch in Hogtown Bayou."

"Will do, Rick."

"Guys, we're gonna go to the bedroom and watch a little TV and call it a night."

They waved goodnight, and Carson called it as well. It had been a long day and his eyes were bloodshot.

"I'm gonna stay up and keep working," said Possum.

Jules was in the shower when Rick closed the bedroom door. He snuck in the bathroom.

"Room for two?"

She peered out from behind the shower curtain.

"Get your butt in here."

Rick didn't hesitate; he kicked off his shoes and threw his clothes in the hamper and climbed in with her. He washed her hair gently as he kissed her neck, occasionally running his hands down the small of her back. She scrubbed his chest and dug her nails in just enough to let him know she was ready for him.

When they were all rinsed off, they made love in the shower first, then on the bed for a long time, slowly. They spent more time snuggling and kissing than anything else. Rick had already turned the TV on for cover noise. Possum was so enthralled with his laptop; he wouldn't have noticed the lovemaking sounds anyway.

Rick set an alarm for 7:00 a.m. Possum was already awake when Rick stumbled like a zombie into the kitchen for coffee. He munched on an everything bagel, trying to wake up. He wanted to head to Legendary as soon as they opened. Jules got dressed and packed a cooler with sandwiches, a few beers, and some bottled waters. Rick threw on his yellow fishing shirt, and they were off.

He arrived fifteen minutes after they opened. He found Billy and followed him to the yard to look at the boat. Jules climbed in, all giddy to check it out. Rick paced around it, trying to not look too interested. He knew he was gonna buy it, but he also wanted a good deal.

"I'll be honest, Rick, there's a guy coming at two o'clock to look at it," said Billy. "He's from Maryland and very familiar with Judge yachts."

Rick didn't know if it was true or just a sales ploy. Either way, he didn't care.

"Let's get down to brass tacks. How much are you really wanting for it?"

"Come to my office and we can go over all the details."

Rick helped Jules down from the boat, and they followed Billy into the office. Rick scanned the area and didn't see surveillance hard drives. They had to be in the dry dock building, which was exactly what he'd hoped.

"The list price on the boat is $119,229. I took a five-thousand-dollar deposit. I can knock another five off of it. Do you want the trailer?"

"No, I'm gonna dry store it here."

"Okay, that will knock another $3,900 off, bringing it to $105,329 plus tax and dealer's fee."

"I tell you what. I'll give you $95K out the door for it. That's my first, last, and final offer."

Billy looked shocked, and Rick did his best poker face. Bill scratched his head and crunched numbers on the large calculator. He was looking frustrated but determined.

"I'll be right back. I'm gonna speak to the sales manager."

Rick knew what that meant. He'd come in and try to throw something into the deal, like an extended warranty or some other bullshit to get the price they wanted. After a few minutes, Billy and the sales manager returned.

"Mr. Waters, I'm Tracy Brewer. Billy got me up to speed on the boat you're interested in. The best we can do is $105K out the door. That will require around twenty thousand down for financing."

"I'm paying cash."

"Cash?!"

"That's right."

"In that case, we'll take $100K for it."

Rick stood up and started to walk out the door. "Thanks for your time. I'll look somewhere else."

"Wait, wait. How long will it take for you to get the cash?"

"I can call the bank and go pick it up in ten minutes. I have things to do. Do we have a deal?"

"Okay, $95K it is. Billy will do the paperwork while you go to the bank. A cashier's check is fine. Same as cash to us."

They shook hands, and Rick called the bank to get the check started. Synovus Bank was just down the street, and by the time they arrived, Samantha had the check ready. Rick signed a couple of documents and headed back to Legendary. Step one was complete.

He signed all the paperwork and explained to Billy that he wanted it in the water and would take it out around two and return it just before closing. Billy showed him the dry storage and gave Rick a few choices of spots on the rack. He chose one closest to the floor. He didn't know how hard it would be to climb down from the boat after hours. He spotted a room that he guessed must hold the hard drives for the surveillance cameras. It was a metal door, but he recognized the lock brand on it and knew it could be picked in seconds.

They left and returned to the condo. Rick put together a go-bag with a few things he'd need. A long-sleeve black tee and a ski mask, his lock-picking kit, and a prybar just in case. They drove down to *Nine-Tenths*, and Rick grabbed his fly-fishing rig, while Jules waited in the truck. Johnie was off buying bait and other supplies for a charter they had set for the afternoon. It was 1:30 when they headed back to Legendary. Everything was set. They would meet Possum at the Cessna Landing around three.

The boat floated on the water and was smoother than Rick expected. He was pleased. Possum was on the dock at Cessna Landing when they got there. He came aboard, and Rick handed him the keys to his Ford. They motored back toward Legendary, and when they reached within a half mile of the marina, Rick climbed into the cuddy, changed clothes, and hid under a blanket. Once the boat was docked at the end, Rick felt the boat bob a little, and he knew Possum and Jules had stepped onto the dock.

After twenty minutes, one of the employees came aboard, fired up the outboard, and steered it toward the forklift area. Rick felt the boat rock as it was lifted out of the water. They sprayed it off and put it in the rack. He didn't move and just listened.

Another hour passed, and a few more boats were loaded inside. At last, he heard the big doors to the dry storage building close. He waited a few more minutes, listening for any straggling employees. It was 4:45 p.m. when he peered out from under the blanket. The lights were off but there was enough to see because of the huge skylights on the aluminum building. Rick had seen the top of the roof many times when flying into Destin. The entire roof was painted with an American flag, and the second attached smaller building read, *God Bless America*. It was painted in homage to the flyboys over at Eglin Air Force Base. The side of the building was covered in whales, courtesy of Wyland, the famous artist. It had actually been the largest Whaling Wall in the world up until 2015, when he painted the one at the

Long Beach Convention Center, which knocked Destin's into second place. The flag mural still held the record for the largest flag mural ever painted.

Rick donned his ski mask and snuck quietly out of the boat, being as quiet as a church mouse. He quickly found the metal door he'd seen earlier, picked the lock, went inside, and closed it behind him. There were four cameras in the dry storage. He found the hard drive and backed it up a few minutes.

There he was, plain as day, right on camera three, climbing out of the boat. Luckily, it was an older unit that recorded directly to a DVD. He popped the DVD out, replaced it with a blank one, and hit *record*. Inside a file cabinet were rows and rows of DVDs. He found the one for the day Pamela had launched and returned her boat. He took the DVD and swapped it with a blank one. He used the Sharpie in the drawer and copied the handwriting as best he could, onto the blank one with the same date, and put it back in the cabinet.

This is too easy.

He had let his guard down a bit and didn't take time to see if the coast was clear. When he exited the room, at the end of the giant aluminum building, he spotted a security guard, and the guard spotted him. He came running full speed toward Rick. He was fast.

When the guard got to him, Rick tossed his duffel bag into the air. The man tried to catch it, instinctively. Rick swept his feet out from under him, and he and the bag hit the ground with a thud. The man was trying to pull his night stick out, but Rick kicked him in the side, knocking the air out of his lungs. He snatched the duffel bag and began to run. There was only one problem. There was no way to get out. The only door he could see was locked up tight from the outside.

The guard got to his feet and came at Rick again. Rick set down his bag and pulled out the prybar. The guard swung at him with his night stick, and Rick blocked it with the prybar. There was nothing for it—he had to take this guy out. He jabbed him twice in the nose, making his eyes water, and slammed the prybar into his chest. When he bent over, Rick swung with all his might with an upper cut and connected to the man's face, lifting him off the floor. He toppled back down, out cold.

It turned out the door was not only locked but also had a coded alarm on it. He had no choice but to climb to the top of the rack and bust out of one of the skylights. He hated heights and it was the last thing he wanted to do.

Once on the roof, he carefully made his way to the shorter building, swung the duffel bag onto his shoulder, and climbed down the gutter downspout, cutting his hand a little on the fascia bracket. When he reached the smaller building, he found a ladder used to check the HVAC and climbed down it. He ran to the front side of the large building and waited until no cars were coming off of the Mid-Bay Bridge, then bolted across the Spence Parkway to the One Water Place Condominiums.

He found a small wooded area and changed back into his fishing shirt and baseball cap, stuffing the black shirt and mask back into the duffel bag. He called Possum and arranged to be picked up beside Bonefish Grill. Possum pulled up a few minutes later in the Navigator rental, and Rick wrapped his hand with a napkin in Possum's glovebox.

Luckily, it was more of a scrape than a cut and wouldn't require any stitches.

"Phew!" said Rick.

"You got what you needed?"

"We'll see. Let's hit the condo and check it out. Where's Jules?" "She's where shopping is a pleasure. Said something about gumbo."

"Ah, Publix. Cool. Let's roll.

CHAPTER FOURTEEN

Rick loaded the DVD from the Legendary surveillance cameras into the machine. Possum had attached it to the 4K sixty-five-inch TV so they could get more detail. Rick fast-forwarded the DVD until about 1:30 a.m., then ran it at normal speed. Just a few minutes before two, headlights could be seen entering the parking lot. The car was out of view of the camera and parked closer to Lulu's.

A few minutes later, a silhouette of a person could be seen walking toward the docks, carrying something. It was too dark to make it out. The night-vision cameras made it impossible to tell what color the person's clothes or hair was, but it seemed to be a woman. Rick paused the DVD image and zoomed in. Her hair was much longer than Pamela's, though. He pushed *play* again, then switched to the camera facing toward the buildings at the end of the dock. He switched around to different cameras and found one that was pointing toward Pamela's boat. As the woman got closer, he paused again. She was wearing a bucket hat and it was pulled down. He zoomed in closer and saw some embroidery on the hat. It read *30A*, which had to be refer-ring to the popular area just past Destin where Seaside, Water Color, and Grayton Beach were located. A favorite of tourists and locals alike.

Could she be Michelle Tangier? thought Rick.

Rick pulled up Michelle's Instagram account and scrolled through the photos. She loved taking selfies. As he contin-ued to scroll, he suddenly stopped. There it was. The same hat with *30A* on it.

"Busted!" said Rick aloud as he spun his MacBook around. They all looked at Rick's laptop and then back up at the dark image on the TV. Same build, hair, and hat. It was most likely her. They hadn't seen her face in the cameras well enough to make a positive ID. They could just make out the silhouette of her features but nothing concrete.

"Rick, please forward both of those images to me," said Carson.

"Are you going to enhance them?" asked Rick.

"No, I'm gonna send them to Langley and have facial recognition done on them. We know the woman on Insta-gram is Michelle Tangier. They take a measurement of her eyes, nose, etc. and use biometrics to map facial features. If it's her on the dock, we will know for certain."

Rick forwarded the images to Carson, who called someone he still had connections to at the FBI and texted the images to him. After a few minutes, he hung up and joined Possum at the kitchen table as he continued to search the original surveillance footage and listen to audio obtained from Pamela's house.

Jules returned with several Publix bags, excited to make dinner for the crew. Once Rick showed her his hand, she doted over him and cleaned the injury. It wasn't bad and he didn't really need any medical attention, but he knew it made Jules happy to take care of him. Rick got a text from Johnie and with his right hand, he read the text while Jules wrapped his other hand with gauze, as if it had nearly been cut off by some whacko with a machete.

Rick, we have a full boat, heading out at 6:00 for a shark trip. Monitoring channel 23 and my cell if you need me. Johnie

Okay, text when you're back at the dock if you need a hand. Swing by condo later, Jules making Cajun.

Woohoo! Save me some.

Jules propped up the Lulu's cookbook in the kitchen, and before long, the house smelled like New Orleans. She had diced up the holy trinity—onions, bell peppers, and celery—and stirred them with a wooden spoon, into the big pot of roux she had made. The roux came out perfect. She used an equal mix of oil and flour and browned it to a dark brown thickness. Altogether, she had the base for some amazing gumbo, complete with large shrimp, blue crab claws, and loads of blue crab lump meat. She'd even picked up some fresh French bread for dipping. In addition to the gumbo, she planned to make Key West Tuna Burgers with fresh ginger, cilantro, and red pickled onions, on wasabi mayo-laden toasted brioche buns.

"Jules, since you are on a roll cooking, maybe you can do up some shark if Johnie scores any small ones tonight on his charter," said Rick.

"Don't laugh, Rick, but I have an amazing recipe for Shark 'N Bake I got while visiting Trinidad."

"Shake 'N Bake?"

"No, Shark 'N Bake. It's actually called Bake and Shark, but I thought it was funnier to say Shark 'N Bake, like Shake 'N Bake. It's usually blacktip shark fillets inside a fried bread pocket, with mango chutney. It's amazing!"

"I'm game!" exclaimed Rick.

"Shark 'N Bake," said Possum in the character voice of Ricky Bobby from the movie *Talladega Nights*.

Jules shot him a strange look, as she had no idea what he was going on about. Possum just laughed as he stepped into his bedroom. Rick had set his phone face down on the counter, and it started to vibrate. He picked it up and saw the name on the screen: Capital Circle

Veterinary Hospital. Rick took a deep breath and picked up the phone.

"Hello, this is Rick."

"Rick, it's Dr. Paul James from Capital Circle. Are you driving or in a safe place? Sitting down would be better."

Rick's heart sank and all the warmth drained from his face. He looked over at Jules, and her eyes showed that she instantly knew it was about Chief.

"I'm home, Doc. Just tell me."

"I was about to lock up tonight and I had checked on Chief a few minutes before and he was still in a coma with no changes. I was waiting for the night staff to show up. When I have a critical patient, we always have someone here to monitor vitals. I heard a noise from the recovery room, and I stepped in to see what it was. I looked over at the recovery cage, and to my absolute amazement, Chief was standing up trying to get out of the cage. The noise I heard was the stainless-steel water bowl hitting the floor of the cage. I was stunned. I called back the lead assistant and we took his stats. Except for the soft cast, which needs to stay on for a few weeks, he seems to be in good shape. I wanted you to know right away. He is one lucky bird."

"Oh my God, Doc, you just made my day—hell, my week. No, my century! When can I pick him up?"

Tears were flowing down Rick's face, and everyone in the room was watching him with hopeful excitement in their eyes.

"I wanna keep him for a couple more days, maybe three, but he should be able to go home after that."

Rick thanked the vet several times and set down the phone. You could hear a pin drop as everyone waited for Rick to speak.

"Chief survived! I can't believe it!"

They all cheered, and Jules ran up to Rick and jumped on him, wrapping her legs around his waist. She was crying, but this time they were tears of joy. Even Possum, who had returned from his bedroom, was welling up with happiness. A beautiful fervor filled the room. Rick, Jules, and Possum had a group hug, and Carson patted Rick on the back, happy to hear the news, even though he hadn't met Chief yet.

"Woohoo!!!!" repeated Rick.

He ran to the liquor cabinet and grabbed a bottle of thirty-two-year-old Flor de Caña.

"Carson, you indulge?"

"Not too often, Rick. But I'd be honored tonight."

Rick pulled out four of the crystal-clear round ice cubes he kept in the freezer and poured everyone two fingers of the golden-brown nectar. They all stood in a circle, and Rick raised his glass.

"To Chief, the bird with nine lives!"

They all clinked glasses and hooted and hollered about the great news. Rick texted Johnie and Gary to let them know Chief was gonna make it. Rick was still in shock. Up until the phone call, he had been trying to prepare himself for the fact that Chief might die. Part of him was still in disbelief. He was happy but filled with anxiety at the same time.

Jules returned to the kitchen to finish dinner, dancing around and humming, filled with joy. The boys all sat around the kitchen table celebrating Chief's good luck and the grace of God that had been bestowed upon them. Rick helped Possum clean all the electronics and papers off of the kitchen table, which had been transformed into the war room to help solve Johnie's case.

"Dinner, boys!" exclaimed Jules.

Possum had already set the table, and Rick opened a couple of bottles of wine. Just before Jules prepared the dishes, he excused himself and went to the bedroom. He washed his hands and looked into the mirror. A sense of calm overcame him. Before he reentered the dining room, he got down on one knee and prayed.

God, thank you. I asked for your help for Chief and I got it. I am forever a believer and I will from now on be the best person I can be and spread love every chance I get.

In God's name, I pray. Amen.

He wiped away a little mist from his eyes and joined the gang for dinner. Just as he sat down, Johnie texted him a congrats about Chief and let him know they had hooked into a huge shark that had been on the line for over thirty minutes. They had also caught a few small spinner sharks and planned on filleting them.

"Cajun food tonight and Trini food tomorrow, thanks to Jules!" said Rick.

"Johnie got some sharks, Rick?" asked Jules.

"Yep, some small spinner sharks. Very mild white meat. It should work great for your Shark 'N Bake."

"Shark 'N Bake!" interrupted Possum in his Ricky Bobby voice again.

"What are you doing, Possum?" asked Jules.

"It's a character from a movie, Jules," said Rick.

"We should watch it tonight, Rick," said Possum. "We could all use a good laugh, and since Chief is out of danger now, that's a damn good reason to laugh and celebrate."

"Hell yeah, let's do it!" said Rick.

They all sat down around the table as Jules filled their bowls with the gumbo she had made. Before anyone took a bite, Rick said, "I feel like we should say grace, after the news we just got."

"I got this, Rick," interrupted Possum.

Jules sat down, clasped her hands together, and closed her eyes.

Possum began, "'Dear Lord Baby Jesus, or as our brothers to the south call you, 'Heysuz.'" He continued with thanks for the fast food, family, and friends, quoting the movie *Talladega Nights: The Legend of Ricky Bobby* perfectly. Before Possum got halfway through it, Jules opened her eyes and stared at him in bewilderment. Rick was biting his bottom lip, trying not to laugh, but as soon as he saw the look Jules was giving Possum, he burst out laughing and almost fell out of his chair. Everyone in the room but Jules has seen the movie *Talladega Nights: The Legend of Ricky Bobby* and knew what he was up to. They all laughed, and Jules just shook her head. Rick gave her a quick hug and explained to her she would understand better after they watched the movie.

"Jules, you nailed it!" said Possum.

They all agreed. Considering it was her first time making Cajun food, she'd absolutely hit it out of the park.

"Thanks, guys! And coming from a great cook like you, Possum, that's a huge compliment."

They took their time eating, enjoying every morsel, sipping wine and talking about both Chief's amazing recovery and Johnie's case. After they finished, Rick helped Jules clean up and she made Johnie a plate. Carson tried to excuse himself, but Possum talked him into staying to watch the movie. Just as they all sat down to start it, someone knocked on the door.

"Come in!" yelled Rick.

It was Johnie. He opened the door with a double-bagged Ziploc full of shark fillets. Jules heated up his meal, and Rick started the movie. Johnie sat at the edge of the coffee table and ate. It was a great night, and even Jules started saying, "Shark 'N Bake," like Ricky Bobby by the end of it. It was near midnight when it ended, and everyone was yawning. Carson and Johnie said their goodbyes and everyone went to their bedrooms.

The smell of coffee and biscuits woke Rick from a dream. He had been dreaming that he was playing poker at a casino and was about to win the hand when Bruce Willis turned over four kings and a ten and swiped the chips toward himself. Rick was glad it was a dream as he had just gone *all in*. He rubbed Jules's hair, kissed her head, and softly snuck out of the bed to join Possum for some quick coffee and a meeting to go over the day's plans.

Jules joined them shortly after, yawning and gripping her coffee cup like a precious treasure find. The sun had just peeked over the dunes as Possum called them over to the table for some biscuits and gravy. Carson joined them, but Johnie had decided to stay on the boat and do some routine maintenance. He planned to change the oil and all the fuel filters. He texted Rick that the afternoon charter had been canceled due to some sick family members.

"Carson, you wanna take that fishing trip I promised you? We have an opening this afternoon," said Rick.

"Hell yeah! What time?"

"I'll call Johnie, but we can leave a little earlier than normal afternoon trips if you'd like more time. We can try to spot some near-shore cobia first, then head out to the drop."

"Count me in. I just need to get some fishing attire. All I got is the suits I brought. Where should I go?"

"I'll take you. I have some discounts at Bealls and we can swing by Bass Pro after. They have a cool indoor saltwater tank you gotta see," piped up Possum.

"Jules, you wanna go fishing?" asked Rick.

"Does a deer shit in the woods?" replied Jules.

"It's a bear."

"What's a bear?"

"Never mind, haha. I'll take that as a yes."

Rick called Johnie and told him he'd swing by after breakfast to help him out with the boat and get supplies for the afternoon trip with Carson. For a change, Rick would captain *Nine-Tenths*.

Nine-Tenths backed out of the slip just before three. An electric energy filled the boat as Rick steered it around the end of Noriega Point. The sky was a light blue with very few clouds. A new moon could be seen, and baitfish danced on the water. The day seemed like some kind of postcard turned into real life. Rick was hoping to get into some big fish for Carson. Being behind the helm of the mighty sport fisher made Rick feel alive. Johnie and Possum were busy setting lines and prepping the ballyhoo rigs.

Rick gave Jules the image-stabilizing binoculars and explained to her what to look for when trying to spot a cobia. Sight casting could either be one of the most exciting days or the most boring event a person could experience. Johnie had already rigged up two spinning rods and reels with two-ounce yellow bucktail jigs.

"Look, Rick!" yelled Jules as she pointed.

Rick took the binoculars and looked and spotted what Jules was hollering about. A huge manta ray was making its way down the coast. Rick looked behind the ray and spotted what he was hoping for—three cobia in tow. He yelled down to Johnie to get Carson ready. Rick motored toward the cobia then turned the boat to be parallel with them. Johnie instructed Carson how to cast in front of them and cross their path. He cast and began to reel. Within a few seconds, his rod bent over and his reel whizzed.

"Fish on!" yelled Johnie.

Rick threw *Nine-Tenths* into neutral, set the SeaStar Optimus 360 auto-helm system, and climbed down to the deck to join in on the fun. Jules was filming with her iPhone from the flybridge. Possum launched the Mavic Mini drone and flew over the fish as it jumped. Carson grinned from ear to ear as the mighty fish thrashed on the surface repeatedly, trying to throw the hook. Within a few minutes, Carson dragged the fish to the boat, and Johnie cast over his shoulder at the sight of another even bigger one. Rick gaffed the cobia and pulled it in as Johnie set the hook and handed the second rod to Carson. The second cobia was nearly twice as large as the first, and Carson struggled to maintain control. He'd gain a little ground then the big fish would make a huge run, nearly pulling all the line off of the reel. Possum was getting some amazing footage of the catch from the drone.

"Woohoo!" yelled Carson.

Sweat was rolling off of his forehead and his face was red. After twenty minutes, the fish was almost to the side of the boat. It gave one more futile attempt to escape, and Johnie gaffed it as it passed beside the hull. He pulled it in, and Carson nearly fell down when it hit the deck. His arms felt like spaghetti and he collapsed in the fighting chair, trying to catch his breath.

"Oh my God, that was fun! I had no idea it could be this amazing," exclaimed Carson, still out of breath.

"That's a lot of fun, but if we get into a big tuna or marlin on the drop, you will truly know what a fight is about," said Rick.

"Can I catch my breath first?" asked Carson.

"Nope, time to take pics," replied Johnie.

He helped Johnie get the fish into position after Possum landed the drone. Possum pulled out his Canon 80D and took several photos to memorialize Carson's first big catch. Rick climbed back up to the flybridge and pointed *Nine-Tenths* south, then brought it up to plane, bound for the big drop. The boat seemed to glide like a bird on the small swells, and the engines roared as they continued to the deeper, darker water offshore. The first stop was Whitehill Reef, about six miles due south of the east pass in about eighty feet of water. With any luck, they could get into some amberjack, grouper, or snapper and maybe tag a mahi mahi on the way out. Regardless of what they caught, Rick was gonna make sure Carson got the fishing trip of his life.

Rick spotted some birds and bait moving to the port of *Nine-Tenths*, got Johnie's attention, and steered the boat in that direction. Once the boat got closer to the schooling fish, Rick slowed them down to a perfect trolling speed of six knots. He tracked the boat directly through the school of baitfish with four rods on the stern. Within seconds, two reels sizzled. Two bull mahi mahi leapt into the air simultaneously. Johnie handed Carson the port rod, and he took the one on the starboard side. Rick set the autopilot then he and Jules reeled in the two other rigs to get them out of the way.

The beautiful bull dolphins, as they were known by locals, jumped high in the air, spinning and shaking their heads to dislodge the hooks from their mouths. Their silver and blue scales glistened in the afternoon sun. Johnie got his in first, and Rick gaffed it and threw it onto the deck. Its silver and blue colors faded to a soft grey as the fish also faded away. Rick tossed it into the cooler as Carson continued to fight the larger one. It took him around fifteen minutes to get the fish to the side of the boat. Johnie gaffed it and pulled it in, and hung it on the scale.

"Seventy-one pounds, eight ounces. Damn, homie, nice one!" yelped Johnie.

Possum took some photos with Carson holding his catch. He couldn't stop smiling, and it made Rick smile as well. They did a few more passes then began to head out to the famed hundred-fathom curve. Johnie set the bigger rods with bright green and yellow skirts and ballyhoo rigs. The rigs worked well with both marlin and tuna. Rick set the GPS parallel with the reef and trolled at a little under seven knots. Johnie passed out bottles of water to everyone to stay hydrated. Carson was still recovering from his last catch and his arms were sore.

"You ready to catch a big one, Carson?" asked Johnie.

"A big one? That last one wasn't big enough?"

"You ain't seen nothing, son. There's some big fish out here. A few years back, Tommy Browning caught the Florida state record blue marlin not too far from here."

"How big?"

"I believe it was 1,046 pounds. Still the record."

"Dayum!" exclaimed Carson.

Rick continued to troll back and forth, scanning the water for any signs of fish. A tick came on the starboard side reel. Everyone spun around to look at it. It was just one tick.

Sometimes the rigs would hit a patch of sargassum seaweed, which would cause the reels to tick. Nothing happened for a minute or so, then another tick. Johnie led Carson to the fighting chair and strapped him in.

"I've got a gut feeling," said Johnie.

The reel ticked again, then again, and then it began to sizzle. Johnie passed the rod to Carson and set the drag.

"Wait for it," said Johnie.

He held one finger up in the air, watching the line run from the reel.

"Now!"

Carson pulled hard on the rod, and it bent over as more line flew off of the reel. Rick put the boat in neutral and spun around to watch. They all looked out over the water, waiting for the big jump. The great fish was running just below the surface away from the boat, then turned and leapt into the air, spinning its massive body. A collective gasp filled the air.

"Oh my God," said Rick.

"Exactly," repeated Johnie.

It was a massive blue marlin. The sun was still above the horizon and sunset was still over an hour away. Every time Carson gained ground on the big fish, it would take out all the line reeled in and sometimes more.

Two hours into the fight, the fish still wasn't any closer to the boat. Carson's arms were spent, but he refused to give up. Rick turned on the spotlights on the flybridge. Another hour went by and Carson had made some progress. The fish seemed to be tiring. Johnie rubbed Tiger Balm on Carson's arms and poured a bucket of water over his head. It refreshed him and he fought harder. Possum took the handheld spotlight and kept it on the fish as best he could.

Three hours and twenty minutes into the fight, the fish was close to the boat. Possum filmed as much as he could with his Canon 80D, and tried to stay out of the way. The massive marlin spun and drove straight toward the port and turned. Johnie leaned over the rail and jammed the gaff into the fish's side. Rick held him and kept him from going overboard. Possum wrapped a stainless cable around the marlin's bill, and the three men pulled with all their might. The giant fish thrashed on the boat, and Johnie got slashed on the shoulder by its bill. They grabbed on and pulled, and the fish flopped on the deck. It was so big it didn't fully fit inside. Its tail hung way over the stern, and the fish was lying on the deck, no longer moving. Carson collapsed in the fighting chair. His arms lay by his sides. He was completely spent but still grinning from ear to ear.

Jules cleaned up Johnie's shoulder gash and put some steri-strips on it to stop the bleeding. He probably needed stitches but would assess that back at the slip.

"We're gonna weigh this puppy back at HarborWalk. You may have a record here, Carson," said Rick.

"I can't believe we got it." Carson grinned. "I had no idea fishing could be like this. Thank you so much, Rick."

"I should be thanking you; this fish is gonna really increase my business!"

Jules pulled out a big bottle of Moët and Chandon Impérial Brut Champagne, and poured it over Carson's head. She handed him the bottle and he shook it up, spraying it everywhere, and took a huge chug. She opened two more bottles, and they all began to drink and spray each other. Rick got on the radio.

"HarborWalk Dockmaster, this is *Nine-Tenths*. Are you receiving?"

"Go ahead, *Nine-Tenths*. This is Bruce, dockmaster."

"Can you proceed to channel twenty-three, Bruce?"

"Channel twenty-three, go ahead."

"Bruce, this is Rick Waters on *Nine-Tenths*. We have landed a possible record-size blue marlin. Can you let the press know and set up the big scale behind my slip? This will be a great boost for our tourism."

"What's your ETA?"

"We are at the hundred-fathom curve; we can be in the channel in about forty minutes."

"Ten-four, we'll have it all ready. Back to sixteen."

"Back to sixteen," replied Rick. To the others, he yelled, "Let's go, y'all. Time to hit the scales!"

Rick pushed the throttle forward, and the big yacht lifted up then planed out, bound for

Destin HarborWalk.

CHAPTER FIFTEEN

A large crowd had gathered beside AJ's as Rick backed *Nine-Tenths* down into the slip. Cameras were flashing, and *oohs* and *ahhs* could be heard as people got glimpses of the mighty fish lying across the deck of the boat. Johnie was prepared for the onslaught and had a pocket full of business cards.

"How's your shoulder holding up?" asked Rick.

"It's hurting a little, but Jules did such a good job of cleaning and bandaging it, I'm gonna skip the walk-in clinic. I'll have her put on new bandages after I've met with the potential customers."

He popped a few Advils to take off the edge.

Once the boat was tied off, several men helped the crew pull the fish to the dock. They tied it up to the huge scale that had been placed behind Rick's slip. A reporter from the *Northwest Florida Daily News* and his cameraman were waiting to interview Carson about his catch. The Florida state record was 1,046 pounds. Two men began to pull the fish up on the scale. It bounced above 1,046 to 1,100 then came back down, settling at 1,031 pounds, just shy of the state record, but the second-largest catch ever brought into Destin HarborWalk. If this had been the Emerald Coast Blue Marlin Classic Tournament held in October, Carson would have won hands down. The largest fish ever taken in that tournament was 889.6 pounds. The catch put Carson and *Nine-Tenths* into some impressive company, as they joined the group for the top one hundred fish ever caught in off-shore history.

"Congrats, Carson," said Rick as he put his arm around Carson to take some photos for local magazines and news-papers.

This catch would put the boat and crew into Destin's Who's Who. *Emerald Coast Magazine* had the entire crew gather around the fish behind the stern and pose for a cover photo.

The celebration continued for well over an hour, and then Johnie and Possum began the process of filleting the smaller fish, while Rick made arrangements to get the marlin over to Sexton's Seafood Market and get it on ice. Big blues like this were rarely eaten, although sometimes the meat was smoked. Rick planned to donate the fish to the Florida State University. They would study the striations in the meat. Big pelagic fish like this were often studied by the Biological Oceanography program to help identify the migration of the species. The weight along with measurements would be given to the International Game Fish Association and recorded in the database. Carson and the crew would receive an award as the top one hundred all-time big game-fish. Rick requested five pounds of the cleanest meat so he could smoke it. He hated killing anything and not eating it.

He was so good at seasoning and smoking that he could've made shoe leather taste good. It would be his homage to the great fish.

"Are you gonna get a mount of the fish, Carson?" asked Rick.

"I don't know. How much does that cost?"

"Ask Johnie. He knows all about that stuff."

Once the boat was all cleaned, the entire crew, except for Johnie, headed back to the condo. Everyone was tired and planned an early night to sleep. After everyone had showered and changed, Rick ordered some pizzas from Merlin's, and they all enjoyed it and a few beers over at his unit. Carson thanked Rick again and headed off to bed.

"He's gonna be sore tomorrow," said Rick.

"Yeah, his arms were shaking toward the end. He did a hell of a job, though," replied Possum.

The sun was just above the water and Possum was on the balcony with a cup of coffee, admiring the orange and red colors in the sky. Rick poured a cup just as Jules walked out imitating a mummy, her arms extended in front of her.

"Cawwwwwwffyyyyy!" she moaned.

Rick gave her a cup and texted Carson and Johnie to see if they wanted to join them for breakfast. Johnie had work to do on the boat, but Carson said he'd tag along.

After the amazing pancake breakfast, Carson asked where he could get a massage. His arms were sore and he wanted to nip it in the bud. Rick gave him a number from his phone of a place he went to in Sandestin sometimes. Carson made an appointment for 1:00 p.m. and they all returned to the condo.

"Jules, you ready to play 007 again?"

"I sure am, Rick."

"Can you get ahold of Pamela and see if she wants to get together at her place? Tell her you have a bid for her house cleaning, and we can make up something on the computer."

"Okay, Rick, I'll call her."

She disappeared into the bedroom then came back.

"She wants me to stop by around six. She's having a few friends over for dinner as a remembrance of her late husband and was planning on asking me to join anyway. She has a date, which I thought was in poor taste, but she said I could bring a friend if I wanted to. I don't wanna go alone."

"Maybe Carson can be your date. He's old enough to be your father, though. Wait, let me see what time Gary is landing. He would do it."

Rick texted Gary and he said he'd be in around 4:45 p.m. Rick explained the plans for later and he was all in.

"I was thinking a lot about what you said about her wanting to move to a warmer place," Rick said to Jules. "We haven't seen any air reservations or received any texts or messages on the bugs regarding an imminent trip. Can you get into her office and see if you can find anything that'll give us a heads-up to what she has planned?"

"I'll do the best I can, Rick. That I promise."

Gary arrived at Rick's condo and opened the door without knocking.

"Hey, y'all, I'm here. Do I have a story for you!" said Gary.

"Hi, Gary. You must be popular. Five minutes ago, someone dropped off this envelope for you."

Rick handed Gary the large manila envelope, and he ripped it open and dumped the contents onto the table.

"This is part of the story," said Gary.

"I'm all ears," said Rick.

"Me too," added Jules.

There was a knock on the door, and Johnie peeked in and Carson was behind him.

"Okay, good, the gang's all here, so I don't have to tell this twice. Hi, Carson. Good to see you again. You too, Johnie. Why don't we all sit down, and let me tell you one hell of a story."

They all gathered around the kitchen table, and Rick grabbed a couple extra chairs off of the veranda.

"Okay, here goes. When I got to Jamaica, I met with the NTSB. They determined beyond a shadow of a doubt that the jet was sabotaged. It happened in Caracas. I had the plane insured for more than its value, and they cut me a check immediately. Because there was a breach in security in Caracas and my plane was compromised, the Caracas airport is being held responsible. I put my best lawyers on their ass right away and threatened to sue them for one hundred million dollars.

"This next part is on the down-low, so it can't go beyond this room. I know I ain't gotta worry about it from y'all. Anyway, they didn't want the word to get out that someone breached their security. The business they could lose from the private jet industry would be devastating. Long story short, they settled for seventy-five million. Chump change to them. So, with the insurance money I got for the jet and the settlement I got from Caracas, I needed to invest some of it for taxes. That's the last part of the story, which brings me to the manila envelope. I just bought this." He gestured around the room.

"This rental unit?" asked Rick.

"No, this building. Actually, both towers and the restaurant downstairs."

Rick fell back in his seat with his mouth wide open.

"You bought the building—ahem, buildings?"

"Yep, I originally was gonna just buy the top floor, but when your real estate agent told me the entire facility was available, I jumped on it. It's eighty percent rented now. I don't own every single unit, but the ones that were for sale, I took. Plus, the entire infrastructure and parking lot and restaurant. Needless to say, Rick, you now own this unit if you want it. It's on me. I'm taking the end unit and the one beside it for my own personal use. I'm gonna tear down the wall and make it all one giant bachelor pad."

They all just sat there in silence as Gary sipped on his Busch Light, and they gazed at him in awe and disbelief. He was quite a guy.

"Oh yeah, Rick. Jessica told me to tell you to thank you, thank you, thank you. She made enough off of this deal to retire. She wants to throw a party downstairs to celebrate. We are all going, of course. It'll be a couple of days from now. I'm gonna keep the same staff and chef, but I wanna rename the place. I was thinking Chief's Cockatoo Cafe. You like it?" asked Gary.

"That's a great name, Gary. Chief would approve! Speaking of him, I need to call and see if I can go pick him up tomorrow. Why don't you show everyone your new unit on the end? I'll call the vet and meet y'all over there shortly"

Rick stepped onto the balcony and dialed the vet's number.

"Hi, Doc, it's Rick. I'm just calling to check on Chief. How soon can I come get him?"

"He's doing amazing, Rick. I don't see any reason why you can't come get him tomorrow or the next day. Whatever is convenient for you. He'll need to wear the wing brace for about five more weeks, but after that you can take it off. It's held on by Velcro. I can show you how to remove it when you come to Tallahassee to pick him up. I know he's ready to get out of here. He's saying your name all the time."

"That sounds great, Doc. I'll head over there in the morning. If something comes up and I can't make it, I'll let you know, but I should be able to. We want him back as much as he wants to come back. Trust me."

Rick joined the gang over at Gary's units. Gary gave them a tour and shared his plan to turn them into one fifty-one-hundred-square foot bachelor pad. Possum helped Gary get all of his suitcases upstairs, while Jules returned to the unit with Rick to get ready for the event at Pamela's. She put on a dark dress and high heels that made her calves pop. Rick helped her put on a strand of pearls. She looked stunning. Gary said he'd dress to impress yet be conservative. She planned to meet him around five-thirty in the lobby. They would Uber over. The best bet was for Jules to distract Pamela and send Gary into her office.

The Uber dropped them off at 6:10 at Pamela's. Several high-end cars were parked in the driveway. A Ferrari and several BMWs, as well as a Mercedes-AMG S 65 with the custom license plate, *RDHEAD 1*. Jules snapped a quick pic of it and texted it to Rick before she went up and rang the bell.

A man in a tux opened the door, and Jules and Gary made their way to the great room where everyone was gathered. Pamela ran up to Jules and hugged her.

"Welcome, Valentina. I'm so glad you could make it. Who is your friend?"

"This is Gary. Gary, Pamela."

"Sit down, sit down. This is Michelle."

They all shook hands and sat down, as several servers came walking around carrying silver trays with appetizers and champagne. It was an odd vibe for a Celebration of Life gathering. Pamela's husband had only been dead for a little over a week and a half. Pamela sat down next to the lovely redheaded woman and it was clear that they were a thing. Gary glanced over at Jules and gave her a wink. Michelle was stunning. Even Jules could see why

Pamela was attracted to her. Everyone in the room was. After appetizers and a few drinks, Pamela clinked a knife against her champagne glass to get everyone's attention.

"Thank you all for coming. For those of you who attended the funeral, I know Kiefer and I also appreciate you coming here tonight. This is much more Kiefer's style. As most of you know, my husband Kiefer and I were mostly married on just paper for the past few years. It was no secret. He had his life and I had mine. He still did not deserve what happened to him. Even though we weren't really a loving couple anymore, we were still friends. The man who killed my husband will be convicted, but life must go on. I don't want anyone to be sad tonight; Kiefer would want everyone to party. So, let's do it. I have lobster and steak in the main dining room. Please take your seats for dinner."

She held up her glass to make a toast.

"To Kiefer. May God rest his soul, and may we continue to live life to the fullest!"

They all slowly made their way to the huge dining table as the wait staff began to serve the filet mignon and lobster tails. No expense was spared. Several bottles of Cristal were in the center of the table as well as caviar and pâté. Pamela sat at the end of the table with Jules to her left and Michelle to her right. Gary sat beside Jules diagonally from Michelle. The entrées were exquisite, and crème brûlée was served for dessert. After dessert, they poured glasses of incredibly expensive port wine.

Michelle kept making eyes at Gary and Jules. Jules paid her no attention, and she moved her desires more toward Gary. She slipped off her heels and began to rub her feet up Gary's leg. Gary didn't stop her. She continued up his leg and began to rub his crotch and lick her lips. She glanced at Pamela and then at Gary and it was obvious what she wanted. Jules excused herself to the bathroom and texted Gary to do whatever he had to do to get them alone and away from everyone. Several couples left after dessert, and soon only four other guests remained and were all out on the screened-in patio smoking cigars.

"Shall we?" said Michelle, waving her head toward the bedroom at Gary. She took his hand and eyed Pamela.

Pamela quickly said goodnight to all the guests. "I'm feeling a little overwhelmed tonight. Thank you all for coming. Please stay as long as you wish and let yourselves out. There's plenty of liquor, wine, and champagne. Help yourselves. I'm sorry, but I feel I must call it a night for myself."

One couple saw themselves out, but one stayed to finish a cigar and left shortly after. The staff started cleaning up and leaving too. Jules told Pamela she was not feeling well and needed to head out.

"Pamela, Gary and I are just friends, so you guys have fun. I need to leave."

"Are you sure, Jules? I really wish you would join us. In my home three's *not* a crowd and four is even better."

"Ummm, not really my thing, Pamela. Like I said, y'all have fun. No judgment from me. Let Gary know I'm taking an Uber."

Pamela gave her a hug and stumbled after Michelle toward the bedroom. Gary went along. Jules was pretty sure he wasn't doing it because he was undercover; the heavy desire in his eyes told her he wanted to be the filling to this sensual lover's sandwich.

Jules opened the front door, turned around, and gave Pamela a little playful goodbye wave as she closed the door behind her. She waited a minute until she heard the bedroom door close, and quietly stepped back inside. She stepped out of view of the closest surveillance camera and unplugged her Wi-Fi. That would leave a blank space on the footage, but at least she wouldn't be seen while searching. She made a beeline for Pamela's office. She went inside and pulled the double doors closed behind her.

She began to search for anything she could find that might give a hint as to where she planned to disappear to. Time wasn't on their side, as she knew Pamela's insurance settlement could come any day. She looked in all of her filing cabinets and in the leather case she carried her laptop in. Nothing. She opened the desk drawer and inside was a calendar with three days from today circled in red. She lifted up the calendar, and under it was a book titled: *How to Dis-*

*appear: Erase Your Digital Footprint, Leave False Trails,
and Vanish Without a Trace.* Inside the book, she found a
page listing countries without extradition. Two were highlighted— the Maldives and Cape Verde.

Jules took pictures of everything and quietly slipped out
of the office and out the front door. She grabbed an Uber
and was back at the condo within fifteen minutes.

"What happened?" asked Rick.

Jules showed Rick the photos, and told him Gary was
still there.

"That dog!" said Rick.

"Yeah, he's taking one for the team—actually, two for
the team," replied Jules.

Jules got undressed and showered. She came out in a soft
blue teddy. Possum had long since fallen asleep. Rick took
the hint and closed the door to the bedroom.

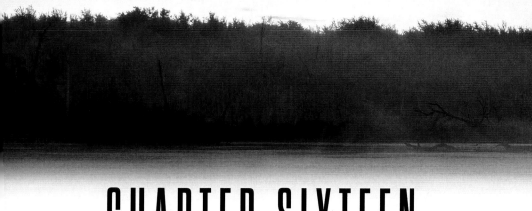

CHAPTER SIXTEEN

Rick's cell phone was vibrating and it woke him up. It was 3:22 a.m. Rick picked it up and saw it was Gary.

"Rick, I need a ride. I can't get an Uber to show up. Can you come get me?" he said, terribly slurring.

"Okay, can you find the main gate of Kelly Plantation and make it to Commons Drive? It's one street over from Pamela's. Just walk out of the driveway, take a right, and follow it until you get to the guard shack. Take the sidewalk to the main street—that's Commons Drive."

"Okay, I think I can find it. I'm walking with one eye closed. I'm so drunk, you'll see three of me."

"You always say that when you're drunk. Haha. Hang tight. I'll be right there." "What's going on, Rick?" asked Jules as she rubbed her half-opened eyes.

"Go back to sleep, baby. I'll be right back. It's Gary. He's sloshed and can't get an Uber."

"Please be careful, Rick. It's really late."

"I will. Don't worry, I'll be back shortly."

Rick threw on some jeans and a t-shirt and took off to rescue Gary from his sexual escapades. He rounded the corner near Kelly Plantation and saw him sitting on the curb with his head in his hands.

"Get in, man. No puking! If you're gonna puke, ride in the bed."

"I'm fine. I'm hammered but I'm not sick."

"So, spill it. What happened?"

"Basically, I was manhandled by two women. The redhead was in charge and she didn't play. I'm not gonna go into detail because a gentleman never tells. But I will say, I think it might be broken!"

"You're something else, man. Thanks for playing along."

"Are you kidding? Hell, I'd pay you to do that again! I think I'm in love. Twice."

"You're forgetting one thing."

"What?"

"It's highly likely that one or both of those women are murderers. And that's not all."

There was a long silence. Gary's head was bobbing from the liquor he'd consumed as he squinted at Rick, waiting for him to share the rest.

"You also just had Johnie's sloppy seconds."

"Pull over, pull over, I'm gonna puke!"

Rick slammed on the brakes and almost ran up on the curb. Gary started laughing his head off.

"I'm just fucking with you, man. I was with the redhead and the redhead was with the blonde. Get it?"

"That's enough imagery for one night," said Rick.

Gary leaned back in the seat and seemed to pass out. It was a short ride to the condo. Rick helped him to the elevator and into his unit. He collapsed face down on his bed.

He's a big boy. He's on his own.

Eight o'clock came early. It had taken Rick a while to get back to sleep after retrieving Gary. Possum had coffee going, and he and Carson were already at the command center—aka the kitchen table—going over the latest surveillance videos they'd picked up from Pamela's devices. Rick caught them up on Gary's late-night sex antics. It wasn't like he was telling a secret or spreading rumors. There was no doubt in Rick's mind that as soon as Gary dragged his hungover ass to Rick's unit, he would be bragging about his threesome, like a D student who'd just passed

Algebra.

Jules was dressed and ready to go with Rick to pick up Chief. They were both super excited.

"Okay, y'all, we'll be back by dinner. We're gonna go pick up Chief in Tallahassee."

"Did you want me to fix some BBQ, Rick?" asked Possum. "I need to break in that Traeger on Gary's balcony."

Rick just shook his head, knowing Gary had probably ordered that from Amazon on his private charter from Jamaica. There was no telling what else was piled up in his new condo. He loved to buy new toys.

"That sounds great, Possum. Can you also smoke some of that blue marlin?"

"I'm way ahead of you; it's already marinating. I'm gonna make some jerky and fish dip with it, if that works for you."

"Do what you do, hombre."

Out in the hallway, Rick put his ear to the door of Gary's unit and could hear him snoring through the door. He just laughed, put his arm around Jules, and pushed the button on the elevator.

The ride toward Tallahassee was foggy at first but cleared up around Mariana. Jules had made a thermos of coffee and put some KIND bars in her purse. It was just enough to take the edge off. They were both excited, yet anxious to see Chief. It seemed like a miracle that he'd recovered and come out of his coma. According to the vet, he'd lost nearly a third of his blood.

They pulled into the parking lot just before eleven. Jules climbed out of the same side as Rick, damn near climbing over him. She had taken a real liking to Chief and was just as happy as Rick that he had pulled through. Once inside the vet clinic, Rick hollered, "Chief! Chief!"

He heard Rick and started squawking loudly and laughing. The nurse walked in the back and carried him out. Rick set his travel cage on the desk, and Chief nearly jumped off of her arm to get to Rick. His poor little wing was wrapped up tight with a ballistic nylon brace with Velcro straps. Half of his chest was bare and the stitches were covered with a small bandage. The vet had placed a soft neck collar on him, so he couldn't pull off the bandage. He was quite a sight.

Jules kissed the top of his head, and he snuggled with Rick, making kissing sounds. Rick carefully placed him in the travel cage and pulled out a small baggie of red grapes he'd brought with him. He handed one to Chief and placed a few more in his dish. He joyfully munched on the grapes. Rick and Jules both thanked the vet and staff for saving his life and hopped back in the red Ford with Chief sitting between them.

"You hungry, Jules?"

"I am now. It is lunchtime, after all."

"Let's go to this cool place on the beach on 30A. They allow pets and it's right on the water," replied Rick.

Rick drove west on I-10 and took Greensboro Highway just past Quincy to 331 then down to Seaside. He pulled into Stinky's Fish Camp in Santa Rosa Beach just after one-thirty. They got a high-top table by the edge of the deck and put Chief on one of the backs of the chairs. Several people stopped by to take pictures of him and ask what happened. He always seemed to draw a crowd anywhere he went.

Rick ordered a fried shrimp po' boy, and Jules had the seafood and corn chowder. Both meals were prepared perfectly, and they both had a mimosa. Jules shared a few bites of corn from the chowder with Chief, and he was a happy bird.

After lunch, they took a short stroll down the beach with Chief on Rick's shoulder. It was a perfect day. Chief tried to flap his wings when he saw some young kids and nearly fell off of Rick's shoulder. Rick took him down and carried him like a baby until they got back to the truck. He didn't squirm or try to move at all. He looked like he was about as happy as he'd ever been. They all were. They made it back to Rick's truck and his phone began to vibrate.

"Hello?"

"Rick, it's Gary. I got a Destin phone. Save the number. Listen, Rick, someone attacked Johnie. He's been taken to

Sacred Heart Hospital. Someone snuck up behind him and hit him with a bat or something. They beat him pretty bad. The first cowardly hit from behind apparently knocked him down; he hit face first on the car ramp down to AJ's, and it knocked several teeth out. He was also beaten on his chest and arms. He has a couple broken ribs."

"What the fuck? First someone took a shot at him and now someone attacked him?" asked Rick.

"I don't know. But we need to find out who the hell did this before it happens again. I'm heading to the hospital. Where are y'all?"

"We're just leaving Seaside. We aren't that far from Sacred Heart. We'll see you there."

"What happened?" asked Jules, her eyes wide. "Who was attacked?"

"Johnie."

Rick fired up his Ford and smoked the tires to get them on their way.

Chief was comfortable and content so Rick cracked the windows and parked in the shade. Gary and Possum were already in the waiting room when they arrived at the hospital.

"How is he?" asked Rick.

"A nurse just came by and said he's stable. He has a concussion and they have him medicated pretty heavily," replied Gary.

"When can we see him?"

"She said she'll let us know. They are waiting for the results of his MRI. He's awake and responsive, but they don't wanna upset him until they know the extent of the damage. All we can do is wait."

"Where's Carson?" asked Rick.

"He's at the condo. I told him to stay back behind and hold down the fort. He's meeting with the Okaloosa Sheriff's Department later today to see if he can review the surveillance video and offer any assistance. His FBI history carries some heavy weight," replied Gary.

About thirty minutes later, a doctor stepped into the waiting room.

"Hi, I'm Dr. Cannon. Who here is family for Johnie McDonald?"

"Hi, Doctor. I'm Rick Waters, his employer. We are pretty much all his family as he has no one he's related to in Destin."

The doctor flipped over some of the papers in his folder.

"Oh yes, Mr. Waters. You are listed as his emergency contact. He sustained some serious injuries to his rear cranium and upper abdomen. He has two broken ribs and a small fracture on his right arm. The main thing we are watching for is swelling in the parietal ridge."

"Layman's terms, Doc," said Rick.

"It's the area just above his right temple. He took the biggest blow there. He's very lucky. If he had been hit in the temple, he most likely wouldn't have survived."

"Can we see him? Is he conscious?" asked Possum.

"He's quite conscious. He was going on and on about somebody named Chief and how he didn't wanna ruin the reunion."

"That's just like Johnie. Always putting other people first. Chief is my pet cockatoo. He is returning today from the vet with his own injuries. It's a long story," replied Rick.

"I'll send the nurse out as soon as it's okay to visit. Probably pretty soon, I think."

The doctor shook everyone's hands and disappeared behind two doors. About twenty minutes later, a nurse appeared.

"I can let three of you in at a time to visit. Who'd like to go first?"

Gary nudged Possum forward.

"Y'all go. You've known him longer."

Rick, Jules, and Possum followed the nurse to Johnie's room.

"Hey there, bud. How you feeling?" asked Rick.

"I have a splitting headache and I can barely breathe because of the pain in my ribs, but other than that I'm awesome," said Johnie with a half grin.

"What happened? Did you get a look at who hit you?"

"I was walking down to the boat and took the car ramp that goes down to AJ's. I usually go that way. All of a sudden, *WHAM!* I felt something hit me in the back right side of the head. It knocked me to the ground and I slammed my face into the concrete. I spit out two teeth. I flipped over, trying to protect myself. The person swinging was wearing a hood and sunglasses. The bat hit my arm when I tried to block it. That cracked my left arm bone, I mean ulna, as the doctor called it. I reached up after taking several more hits across my ribs and tried to grab the guy. At first, I didn't know if it was a guy or a girl, but when I grabbed his shirt, I ripped it and I saw chest hair."

"Did you get a look at his face?"

"Not very well. All I could tell was that he had a beard. But when I ripped his shirt, I did spot something important. There was a tattoo on his chest of the skull of a goat on top of an upside-down cross. I've seen that symbol in movies about Satan. It freaked me out. He was about to swing at me again when someone yelled. He ran off and I passed out. The next thing I knew, I was in the ambulance."

"Man, that is freaking weird. Was he a biker?"

"I don't think so. Maybe? When I ripped his shirt, his hood pulled down too and I could see he had short hair. That doesn't mean anything. I only saw the side of his face, but for some reason he appeared to be clean cut. His beard was tight, not scraggly, and no earrings. That's what was so odd about the tattoo. It didn't seem to go with his look. Maybe like a secret thing he's into? I'm not sure," said Johnnie.

"Okay, take care of yourself. We'll be back to visit. We need to get you out of here and up to the condo soon. I'll send Gary in. Maybe he can get you some lunch."

They all walked back to the waiting room, and Gary took their place. Rick and Jules headed back to the condo, while Possum waited in the lobby for Gary to return.

Once back at the condo, Rick introduced Chief to Carson and then gave him the lowdown on Johnie's condition. Chief seemed content as he munched on a grape on top of his travel cage. Rick needed to get him a bigger cage for the condo and planned to do so later that afternoon.

"Carson, this is weird. The guy who attacked Johnie had a satanic tattoo on his chest. It was a goat over an upside-down cross. Does that mean anything to you?" asked Rick.

"Hmmm, funny you should say that. I was doing some research on Pamela on Facebook and I found out she's a member of a Facebook group called Mephistopheles Cocoa, and so is her love interest, Michelle. It's a satanic group that practices on the private island of Cocoa in the Maldives. There is serious money on that island. Half of the island is private and the other half has a super high-end resort on it called COMO Cocoa.

"Jules, didn't you say Pamela had highlighted two destinations on the brochure on her desk?" asked Rick.

"Yep. One was the Maldives and the other was Cape Verde," replied Jules.

"Carson, is there any sort of connection between Cape Verde and the Maldives?" asked Rick.

"They are nowhere near each other, I can tell you that. Let me see if I can find out anything about them both."

Rick got on Facebook Marketplace to see if he could find a big cage for Chief. He checked with PetSmart, but all they had was one that would accommodate a smaller bird. He found one in Fort Walton and messaged the guy. It was a large macaw cage that he had found in a storage auction. Rick talking him into taking a hundred and fifty dollars in cash. It was a great deal, as a new cage that size would normally fetch eight hundred or more.

"What do you want for that rolling tree stand and box full of bird toys?" asked Rick when they reached the seller.

The man thought for a minute then said, "How about an even two hundred for all of it, and I'll throw in these metal feeding bowls."

Rick agreed, knowing full well the stainless-steel bowls came with the cage anyway, but the tree stand and toys were well worth three hundred dollars on their own. They stopped at the Rub-a-Dub Car Wash off of Kelly Avenue and thoroughly pressure-washed the cage, stand, and toys. They would be air-dried by the time they got back to the condo.

Possum, Gary, and Carson pulled into the Okaloosa County Sheriff's Office a little after three. Carson went first and made sure it was okay for Possum and Gary to be in the meeting with the deputy. He told him they were his tech assistants and he didn't seem to care, as Carson was such a high-profile former FBI agent—an actual FBI celebrity. Several people from forensics introduced themselves to Carson and gushed over him a little.

"Mr. Trimboli, this is Gary and Possum, the tech assistants I mentioned."

"Call me Jim. Nice to meet you, Gary and Possum—is that right, Possum?"

"Yeah, it's a long story."

A special investigator from the Florida Department of Law Enforcement joined the group. Since Johnie the victim was also Johnie the suspect in a murder case, they wanted to see if the assault on Johnie was related in any way to the two cases against him. Special Agent Halsey let Jim Trimboli do most of the talking.

"We scanned the surveillance video from both AJ's and the Galati Yachts next door. The man who assaulted Mr. McDonald was smart. We saw him on all cameras, and under his hoodie, you can clearly see him carrying what looks like an aluminum baseball bat. He keeps his head down and glasses on the entire time. You can see he's wearing gloves. The attack happens just between camera angles, as if he knew it was a blank spot. If you watch to the very end, you can see someone running up to aid Mr. McDonald. We followed the Galati cameras and saw the attacker tossed the bat into the bushes in between AJ's and Galati. I sent a deputy to find it but someone must've picked it up. It's not every day you find a free bat sitting near a parking lot. A fish head probably snatched it. I'm gonna go over the footage and see if I can find who took it and retrieve it."

"If you find it, will it even help? I mean, he was wearing gloves," said Possum.

"You never know. Maybe we can find out where it was purchased, or before he donned gloves, maybe there were trace prints on it. We really want it. If the victim had died, that would be the murder weapon, if that gives you better context," replied Trimboli.

"Are you looking for his transportation as well?" asked Carson.

"As you can see here, the perp rode off on a bicycle. He wasn't stupid, knowing if he drove there, we might see his vehicle and plates. He may have ridden the bike all the way from his residence if he lives nearby, or parked in one of the lots across Highway 98 and then transferred to the bike. Most but not all of those lots have security cameras. I'll be going over them this week."

"Excellent," said Carson. "In any of the camera views, can you see his chest? Johnie said he saw a satanic tattoo of a goat and an upside-down cross. I already ran it through the FBI database, and the only hit I got was for a guy currently doing time in Ohio for grand theft. He was inside during the time of the attack and doesn't fit the body description anyway."

Sergeant Trimboli took notes about the tattoo, and they brainstormed ideas for a while until they called it about four-thirty. He traded cards with Carson, and Halsey gave him his cell number too.

Once back at the condo, they all settled down for some BBQ Possum had put together. Rick set up Chief's new cage and tree stand and let him play with all the toys. He had destroyed two before dinner was even over.

It was Thursday, and Jules knew Pamela would be going to ladies' night at McGuire's. She texted her but got no response. She called her and her phone rang and rang. She frowned.

That's odd.

"Rick, can you give me a ride over to Pamela's? She's not answering her texts or calls. Maybe I should take an Uber?"

"Naw, I'll take you and drop you a couple houses down and swing around the backside. She doesn't know my truck anyway."

They left and took Chief with them. He wanted to go everywhere they went. Rick dropped off Jules and turned the corner onto the street behind Pamela's house.

As Jules walked up to the front door, she noticed there were no cars in the driveway. She knocked on the door and rang the doorbell. No lights were on in the house. She used her iPhone flashlight to look inside and was shocked when she saw the entire place was vacant. Not a single piece of furniture anywhere.

Jules texted Rick: *Coast is clear. Come over—quick.*

He parked the truck and jogged around to the front of the house. When he saw no sign of life, he went back to the truck and got his lock-picking kit and two small flashlights and some gloves. Within seconds, they were in. The place was completely empty. They checked every room and then a folder on the bar. It was from WeBuyHouses.com. Rick opened it and asked Jules to snap some photos. The house had been sold for cash for $975,000, made payable to Pamela Killian, power of attorney for Kiefer Killian.

"What the fuck?" said Rick. "I thought he was divorcing her."

"He was," said Jules, her brow furrowed. "I wonder if she created a power of attorney after he died? She has a lot of powerful lawyer friends. I'm sure for the right amount of money, anything can be forged."

Rick pulled up the house on Zillow, and the value of the house was at least seven hundred thousand dollars higher than what she'd sold it for. This had been a fast transaction, as if she wanted to get away ASAP. Rick texted Possum to see what he could find out and said they'd be back over shortly.

They pulled into McGuire's, hoping Pamela would show up. Jules waited until 11:00 p.m. and was about to give up. The bartender who'd served her and Pamela showed up from working the downstairs bar and immediately went over to Jules.

"Lemon Drop Martini?" he asked.

"Good memory. Last time I was here, you served Pamela and me in this very seat."

"I remember. I'm gonna miss her."

"Huh?" asked Jules.

"Oh, well, I assumed you knew. She stopped by today to say goodbye. Apparently, she got some sort of insurance claim, sold her house, and is moving away. She left me a five hundred-dollar tip and a French kiss. Good ol' Pamela."

"I didn't know her that well, actually. Did she say where she was moving to?"

"Naw, she just said some island where no one would ever bother her again. She said it was in the middle of nowhere and mostly private. I didn't pry any further."

Jules finished her drink, tipped the bartender, and left.

"Rick! She's gone. She got the insurance and split town. Johnie is screwed. We are never gonna be able to prove he didn't do it."

"Dammit! That throws a huge wrench into things," said Rick, slamming his hand against the steering wheel. He fired up the Ford and headed back to the condo, his frustration and disappointment showing on his face.

CHAPTER SEVENTEEN

Possum was up early making coffee when Carson knocked on the door. Rick had just awakened and Jules was moving slow, so she hopped into the shower to try and wake up. Carson handed Rick a flash drive.

"Rick, I've been trying to create a profile of the killer and can't wrap my brain around it yet. Kiefer Killian is a tall, large man. I can't see how either Pamela or Michelle could overtake him. If they drugged him first, then that's possible. I still haven't gotten the toxicology report for Kiefer because he was so badly burned. Once that comes in, I may change my profile. I have to ask you one question, then we can go over the flash drive. My profile is that a man killed Kiefer. Is there any way Johnie could've done this?"

Without a single millisecond of hesitation, Rick said, "Absolutely no way. He couldn't kill a fly. I've literally seen him catch a spider on the yacht and release it on the dock. Johnie is no killer."

"Okay, Rick. I had to ask. I'm gonna put my focus on the man who attacked Johnie. If we can place that tattoo, we'll have the killer. I'm certain of it. Now, let's go over the flash drive."

Rick popped the flash drive into his MacBook. A chart popped up on the screen.

"If you watch the video, you will see how I overlayed Google Earth over the chart and calibrated it with the GPS numbers we got off of Pamela's HumminbirdPC app. Based on the time frame she was there and the depth of water, I think she was there to get rid of something. Or maybe hide something. What could it be?"

"I've been thinking a lot about that. What would someone sink in the water that is valuable and something they might want to retrieve later? The jewels!" said Rick. "Pamela said Johnie stole the jewels from the safe, and they were in a watertight Apache case. Who keeps jewels in a waterproof case in a safe? There's no need. It's overkill, unless you plan on sinking them later for safekeeping. As soon as I finish this coffee, we are heading out to Hogtown Bayou. I'll keep Jules on the boat and show her how to use the fly rod for cover. It's a popular place to find redfish and specks. I'll use my small scuba rig and Pulse 8X metal detector and do a round square pattern in the area."

"That's a great plan, Rick. I contacted Lloyd's of London and they confirmed Pamela's insurance payment was indeed made. They do still have a million-dollar reward out for the jewels. If you can find them, this will go a long way toward proving Johnie was framed. He will at least be off the hook as the jewel thief. I had the knife and other forensic samples sent to Quantico for further analysis. No disrespect to Okaloosa's finest, but the forensic lab in Virginia is the best in the world."

Possum went to his room and brought out a large black duffel bag. Inside it was a mini pneumatic speargun and a dive knife.

"Just in case, Rick. A little protection never hurt. You want me to go with y'all?"

"No thanks, hombre. It's gonna be a beautiful day out there. We won't be there long, hopefully."

Jules made a thermos of coffee and packed her binoculars and a chart of the area that

Rick had given her. Rick used his app to have the boat launched before they arrived.

The water was still on Choctawhatchee Bay. Bait fish were breaking the surface and jacks chased them. Rick brought the boat up on plane and set the GPS for Hogtown Bayou. He used the exact coordinates that Carson had given him.

When they arrived, there were several boats in the area but none at the same coordinates. Rick pulled within thirty feet of the exact spot, set up Jules on the bow, and gave her a quick lesson on using the fly rod. She was a natural.

Rick looked around the area and when he saw no one paying attention, he lowered his scuba rig over the side of the boat. He moved to the stern and sat on the swim platform with his feet in the water and pushed *record* on his chest-mounted GoPro. He stayed there for a minute, making sure he was incognito, and slipped into the water. Within a few seconds, he had donned the rig and was below the surface. With his dive knife strapped to his right leg and the small speargun dangling under his left arm, he began to do a round square sweep of the area.

Jules was doing her best to look like she was trying to land a fish on the fly rod. She didn't even have a fly or hook on the end. Rick had placed a small BB weight on the line to make it easier to cast but not catch any fish.

A few minutes after Rick disappeared underwater, a small boat pulled up and dropped anchor near the spot where Rick was supposed to be. Jules went into the cuddy cabin and grabbed her binoculars. She zoomed in on the man. He was tying lures onto several rods.

Jules assumed he was there just to fish, so she returned to the bow. She made several more casts and kept scanning the area. The man closest to them continued to fish. Jules hung the BB weight on some seaweed and it ripped off. She reeled it in, climbed back into the cuddy, and tied another one on. She returned to the bow and cast a few more times. She glanced at the boat near her and there was no one aboard anymore.

She ran into the cuddy cabin and retrieved her binoculars. Hurrying back to the bow, she zoomed in on the boat. All three rods were on the boat, but the man was gone. Her heartbeat picked up as she scanned the water, looking for the man. There was no sign of him. She panicked. What was she supposed to do?

Rick swept the entire area, finding a few beer cans and old rusty lures. He continued his sweep and suddenly got a large hit. The needle pegged. Rick reached down under the silt and grabbed the object. It was a small bag of lead weights with a stainless line attached to it. He pulled on the line, and something large was stuck under the silt and weeds. He pulled as hard as he could and it came loose. Once the silt cleared, he pulled it toward him. It was an Apache waterproof case.

Bingo!

A sudden burning sensation and pain shot through his left side. Before he knew it, there was another. He spun around and saw a man with a long knife. He slashed it through the water toward Rick. Blood was pouring out of Rick's side, and the water was clouded up from the silt. Rick could see the man above him, kicking hard with the knife inches from his chest. Reaching down, Rick pulled up the speargun. In one motion, he jerked it forward and pulled the trigger.

The small spear blasted through the water, shattered the man's mask, and drove deep into his eye. His body stiffened and he rolled over, blood pouring out of his mask. Rick wrapped the line around his wrist and began to ascend. The lifeless man slowly drifted away. His buoyancy compensator was partially inflated. Rick kicked over to him and pushed the button on top of his Scuba 2 oral inflater, and the man shot to the surface.

Rick ascended slowly, trying to maintain his calmness through the pain and adrenaline. Once on the surface, he fully inflated his buoyancy compensator and blew his whistle as hard as he could. Blood gushed from his side.

"Jules, Jules! I need help!"

Jules had already begun to raise the anchor. She started the motor and moved the boat toward Rick. He guided her so he could grab hold of the swim platform. After killing the engine, she dropped the anchor again. She helped Rick get out of his scuba rig and got him on board. He collapsed on the swim platform, and she grabbed a towel and wrapped it around him.

"Put pressure on your side to try and stop the bleeding," she said in a rush.

Rick was getting lightheaded from all the blood loss.

"Jules, I need you to pull this line wrapped around my wrist, get it on board, and hide it in the cuddy cabin. There's a toolbox on the left side and a ratcheted cutting tool inside. It has blue handles. Cut the cable, dump it, and let the weight sink. Just get the box inside the cuddy. Hand me my phone. I need to call 911."

Jules handed Rick his phone and did as he told her. She wrapped the waterproof box in a towel, shoved it into the bottom of his dive bag, and put all his gear on top if it before stowing it in the forward compartment.

"Nine-one-one, what is your emergency?"

"This is Rick Waters. I am at the entrance to Hogtown Bayou and I have been stabbed twice. I have lost a lot of blood. Please send an ambulance and the coroner and deputies to Cessna Landing boat launch. We can motor to the dock. The man who attacked me is dead. I shot him with my spear gun after he stabbed me. I have everything on my GoPro. Please hurry— I'm very lightheaded."

"Hold the line, Mr. Waters."

A few seconds went by.

"Mr. Waters, are you sure the man is deceased?"

"He's dead as a door nail. He drifted away from me just a few feet from my boat. There's some current there, so I think he may have drifted deeper into Hogtown Bayou."

"Okay, help is on the way. Do you want me to remain on the line?"

"No, we'll make our way to the dock now."

"Help us! Can you help us?" screamed Jules.

The two men ran up to the dock to help Jules secure the boat. Their eyes grew wide when they saw all the blood on the deck of the boat and Rick hunched over holding the towel against his shoulder. By the time they had the boat secured, sirens were wailing nearby. Two EMTs ran onto the dock with a gurney. A sheriff's department cruiser showed up next, followed by two more and a fire truck.

"Can you speak?" asked one of the EMTs.

"Yeah, I've been stabbed twice in the side. One is deep, I think, and went through the side of my buoyancy compensator."

They placed Rick on the gurney and led him to the ambulance.

"Miss, we are taking him to Sacred Heart. Are you going to ride with us?"

"Yes, please."

"Jules, can you tell the deputy where we are going and point to where the body began to drift? I'm sure they can find him with a couple of divers. The deputy will have questions. Answer them as best you can and then have him give you a ride to the hospital. I'll be fine, I promise. Tell him he needs to talk to me. You didn't really see what happened underwater." "Okay, Rick. I'll be there ASAP."

Jules kissed his hand as they loaded him inside the ambulance. Her hands were shaking and her adrenaline was through the roof. The deputy waved her over and they walked toward the boat.

"I'm Deputy Pete Hansen. I understand you were on the boat. May I get your name?"

"I'm Juliana Castro. Yes, I was on the boat."

"What can you tell me about what happened?"

"I didn't see anything below the water's surface, but I was fly fishing while Rick went scuba diving. He's an avid diver and dives solo often. A man pulled up close to us and then when I wasn't paying attention, he slipped over the side of his boat with scuba gear on. He stabbed Rick twice, and Rick defended himself with his speargun. That's what he told me happened. You can talk to him in more detail at Sacred Heart."

"Do you know the man who stabbed your friend?"

"No, I've never seen him before."

"Where's the body?"

Jules pointed to the left of the area where the man's boat was anchored, just on the outside of Hogtown Bayou.

"Can you give me a ride to the hospital?" asked Jules.

"Sure, hop in my cruiser and we can head over there. I have the forensics team heading over and a couple of detectives will meet us there. I'll need to access the boat. Will that be okay?"

"You'll have to talk to Rick. It's his boat. I'm sure it's no problem. Can I grab my purse backpack and his dive gear off of the boat? It needs to be rinsed."

"As soon as forensics goes over it all, you can have it back. I promise."

"Can I at least grab my backpack? It was inside the cuddy cabin the entire time. Forensics won't need my purse. It never got anywhere near the water."

He thought for a second. "Are your ID and wallet inside?"

"Yes," replied Jules.

"Okay, go ahead. I'll need to look at them, though, before you can leave."

She stepped on board and the deputy held the boat steady. As soon as she got into the cuddy cabin, she grabbed Rick's dive bag and pulled out the waterproof box. She opened it and inside was a black plastic bag. She quickly shoved it into the bottom of her backpack and covered it with the leather flap that normally covered her computer. Then she put the rest of her personal belongings on top of that. She stuffed the plastic box back into Rick's dive bag.

Walking to the dock, she unzipped her backpack wide, showing it to the deputy. Her heart was pounding. He leaned over and pulled out her wallet and a couple things and put them back in. He unzipped the front pocket and pulled out the two breakfast bars she had stuffed in there, then quickly returned them and zipped it all up.

"Okay, let's go."

Jules followed the deputy to his cruiser, and he let her into the back seat. A crowd had gathered around the dock and several more deputies arrived. A coroner's van backed down toward the dock, and a dive team was gearing up to recover the attacker's body.

"Where is Rick Waters? Can I see him?" asked Jules when she reached the hospital lobby.

"Ma'am, he's in emergency surgery right now. Are you family?"

"I'm his fiancée! What do you mean surgery?"

She scrolled in her computer and confirmed that Jules's name was listed as the emergency contact.

"All I can tell you is that he suffered a splenic rupture and is in surgery now."

"What the hell is a splenic rupture?"

"Basically, when the knife drove deep into his side between two ribs, it nicked his spleen. Try and remain calm. He has the best doctor on the staff today. Please have a seat in the waiting room, and someone will be down soon with an update."

Minutes passed by that seemed like hours. Jules was a complete basket case. She texted Possum, and he, Gary, and Carson came flying into the hospital forty minutes later. Jules jumped up and ran to Possum, hugging him and crying.

"How is he, Jules?" asked Possum.

He held both her hands in his tightly. She could barely get the words out. She was crying and trying to speak.

"He's in surgery now. A man stabbed him in the back and it damaged his spleen."

"Who the fuck is this guy?" asked Possum.

"He's dead," said Jules. "Rick shot him with your spear-gun."

They all gathered around Jules, trying to comfort her.

"He'll be okay, Jules," said Gary. "He's Rick Waters. Just another day at the office."

That made her smile through her tears a little. A doctor came into the waiting room.

"Juliana Castro?"

"Hi, I'm here. How is he?"

"He sustained two knife wounds. One hit his scapula—I mean, his shoulder blade. I'll try and keep this in layman's terms. It gashed open a large cut on his back, causing a substantial loss of blood. The other wound went in between his shoulder blade and ribs and all the way through his spleen. He's very lucky. Another half of an inch and it could've been way worse. He's stable now and in the ICU. We are monitoring his vitals, and once he's out of the woods, we will move him to a private room. Luckily, his blood is type O and we had plenty here today. Juliana, I have your number and I will call you when you can come see him or if there are any other updates. I think he's gonna be fine. Shoving that towel into his shoulder may have saved his life. Did you do that?"

"Yes, he was bleeding badly all over the deck. It was all I could think to do."

"Well, it worked. Good job. He owes you one." The doctor patted her on the arm before walking away.

Jules wanted to stay, but Possum and Gary convinced her to go back to the condo and rest. They promised if anything changed, they'd haul ass back to the hospital.

"Gary, can you and Carson take Jules back to the condo?" said Possum. "I'm gonna go see Johnie and let him know what happened. It's hard to believe the entire crew of *Nine-Tenths* is in the same hospital at the same time!"

Gary and Carson led Jules to Possum's rented Navigator and headed toward the condo. Gary called ahead and set up some food to be delivered from Qué Pasa, his favorite Mexican restaurant. Once they were in the condo, Jules's hands were still shaking and she was full of anxiety. Gary offered her half of a Xanax, and she took it. It calmed her down quickly. She wasn't into drugs, but Gary reassured her it was safe.

"Johnie, how are you, bud?" asked Possum.

"I'm better. Way better. The swelling has gone down in my head and I'm just ready to get out of here and get back to the boat and work."

"Something has happened, and to say it's ironic is an understatement. Rick is in the ICU.

He's gonna recover, but the man who attacked him is dead. Rick was scuba diving over at Hogtown, trying to recover the jewels you were accused of stealing. It's a long story. Wow, so much has changed. I'll tell you everything."

Johnie pushed the button on his bed to raise it up and be able to look Possum in the eyes easier as he told the story.

"So, Carson figured out the exact GPS coordinates of where Pamela took her boat in the middle of the night. Rick and Jules went there this morning, and Rick was doing a sweep of the area when the man stabbed him in the back underwater. It only missed his heart by half of an inch! Jules never said anything about recovering the jewelry. I guess Rick didn't have a chance to find it. Anyway, to make a long story a little shorter, Rick shot the man through his eye with my little pneumatic speargun. He is probably at the morgue now. I'm sure we'll have his identity by this afternoon, if Carson hasn't gotten it already."

"Good fucking riddance!" exclaimed Johnie.

"No kidding, buddy. I'm gonna talk to your doctor and see if they have a time when you might be released. I'll be right back."

Possum found the head nurse on Johnie's floor and she paged the doctor. He came up to the nurses' station a few minutes later. He had an odd look in his eye, as if he were seeing a ghost.

"Didn't I just see you downstairs in regards to Rick Waters?" asked the doc.

"Yep, I'm also here to see Johnie McDonald."

"Wow, you guys really know how to make an appearance."

"No kidding. So, when do you think Johnie can return home, and is there any update on

Rick yet?"

The doctor pulled his file up on a computer.

"He's doing great. I think by tomorrow he can go home if he stays the same. The swelling has decreased to almost nothing and his vitals are perfect. As far as Rick goes, he's still stable with no changes at the moment."

"Thanks, Doc, we appreciate all you've done for us."

"Just doing my job, man," he said with a grin and walked off.

Possum relayed the good news to Johnie, said goodbye, and headed to the lobby to grab an Uber.

When Possum walked into the condo, Jules was on the couch watching the news, and Carson and Gary were at the kitchen table going over all the notes trying to figure out where this guy fit into the puzzle. Possum sat down at the table, and suddenly, Jules popped up and ran to the bedroom, then ran back out carrying a black plastic baggie.

"Now that you're all here—look what Rick found!"

She ripped open the baggie and dumped the contents in the center of the kitchen table. Jewelry tumbled out of the bag. Several huge diamond rings, a platinum brooch covered in rubies and emeralds, a woman's Jacob & Co. Caviar emerald watch, and a few miscellaneous loose stones. Possum's jaw dropped to the floor.

"Y'all found it. How the hell did you get it off of the boat with half of Okaloosa's finest on the scene without being caught?"

"I have my ways!" said Jules as she strutted back to the couch.

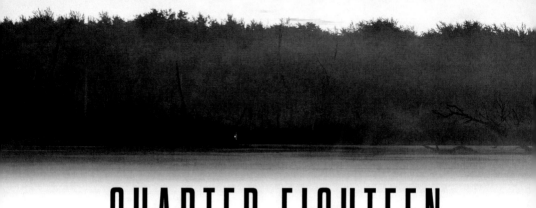

CHAPTER EIGHTEEN

Carson set his phone down on the desk and looked at the group.

"The police think the man who stabbed Rick was someone named Dale Clemens. He is assumed dead. They searched the area where Rick shot him with the speargun, but they believe the current dragged the body deep into the bay. He had rented scuba gear under an assumed name, but the photo on his passport matches Clemens. Does that name mean anything to any of you?"

"Dale Clemens?" repeated Gary, as Jules put a hand over her mouth. "Are you fucking kidding me? He's the guy who is suspected of sabotaging my plane and trying to kill us in Brazil. We took five big ones off of him, and he doesn't take that kinda shit lightly. How the hell did he get here? Isn't he wanted for money laundering and extorsion by the FBI?"

"That's exactly right, Gary. He had rented a room at the Emerald Grande. In his room, they found the fake passport under the name Greg Collier as well as a .40 caliber rifle. Ballistics on that gun matched the bullet that was lodged in

Nine-Tenths. His room was on the top floor of the Emerald Grande. They found a police monitor and listening devices in his room. We need to debug all the cars, the boat, and the condos. He has been tracking us for a while. It seems likely he's also responsible for attacking Johnie."

Carson's computer pinged with a new email. He turned the laptop so everyone could see it—it was from the lead investigator.

"Looks like these are some security photos of the guy. As you can see, there is a tattoo on his right bicep of a trident. Apparently, he was very fond of Maseratis and had several registered in his name in Foz do Iguaçu in Brazil. They are still searching for the body, but at this point, who knows if they'll ever recover it."

Jules shuddered, thinking of how close both Johnie and Rick had gotten to dying.

"How is he involved with Pamela?" asked Gary.

"I don't think he is. It's just an incredibly weird coincidence."

"You mean when he stabbed Rick, it wasn't to get the jewelry?" asked Possum.

"Maybe, or maybe not," said Carson. "It depends on what he overheard. He may have just been trying to settle a score with y'all, or maybe he heard us talking about the jewels and planned to kill two birds with one stone. We'll probably never know. We need to get that GoPro footage from Rick before anyone else does. Once he's moved to a private room, they should put his belongings in there. If Pamela lied about the jewelry and collected the insurance, as we know she did, then all we have to do is find her and return her to the authorities. Insurance fraud alone is a big deal. She'll do hard time for that. Plus, if we can prove she framed Johnie for that, they are gonna take a hard look at her for the murder of her husband as well. The problem is, we have to do this before Johnie goes to trial. At the moment, they have him dead to rights as the perp."

"Let's get this into motion then," said Possum.

Jules's phone rang. It was Sacred Heart. She looked down at the screen, afraid to answer. It rang a couple more times.

"Hello," she said apprehensively.

"Miss Castro? This is Dr. Cannon. I have someone who would like to speak to you."

"Jules, it's me, Rick."

"Oh Rick, I'm so glad to hear your voice. Are you okay, sweetheart?"

"I've seen better days, but I'm okay. They are taking me for another MRI shortly. I just wanted to hear your voice. I don't remember a lot of what happened once I got back to the boat. The doctor told me you saved my life. I don't know how to thank you, baby."

"You can thank me by getting all better and coming back home into my arms, that's how!"

"Was our trip to Hogtown a success? It's kind of all blurry now."

"Yes, Rick, we got the jewelry. It's on the kitchen table as we speak."

"That's so great, Jules. Please tell everyone hi for me, and I'll be home as soon as humanly possible."

"I will, sweetheart. Just take care of yourself, and I'll come visit as soon as you move into a private room. Can I speak to the doctor real fast?"

"Okay. I love you."

"I love you too, mi amor!" She waited for the doctor to come back on and then asked, "Doctor, when can I come visit Rick?"

"I'll give you a call back after we get the results from the MRI, but if I was to guess, maybe sometime tomorrow. I'll keep you posted. By the way, we are probably releasing Johnie today, so you might wanna arrange transportation for him."

"Okay, Doc, I'll let the guys know. Thank you again. You just made my day!"

"Goodbye, Miss Castro."

"Call me Jules. Goodbye, Doctor."

Jules slammed her phone down on the couch in joy and jumped up.

"Rick is doing great! The doctor said we might be able to visit tomorrow. He also said Johnie might be released today. Who wants to go get him? Should he stay here or on the boat?"

"I'll go get him in the Navigator. When will he be ready?" asked Possum.

"The doctor said he'd let me know."

"I'm sure he's anxious to get back on the boat," said Gary, "but we should put him up in the condo for a few days to keep an eye on him. I haven't started the demo of the unit next to mine. My mega bachelor pad can wait a few days." He chuckled.

"Okay, it's settled. I'll fetch Johnie, and maybe you can get his room ready in the condo next to yours?" asked Possum.

"Yep, I'm on it. I'll call the cleaning service and get fresh linens and stock a few things in the fridge for him. What kinda beer does he drink?" asked Gary.

"Free beer!" exclaimed Jules with a laugh.

"All right, I'll take care of him," said Gary.

"Can you run me down to the sheriff's office, Possum? I can rent a car, if need be," said Carson.

"This is ridiculous. What's your favorite color, Jules?" asked Gary.

"Blue."

"Do you like little SUVs?"

"Yep, like what?"

"Like RAV4s or Ford Escapes?"

"I like the Fords," said Jules. "Plus, Rick's a Ford guy. Why?"

"What color do you like, Carson?"

"Huh?"

"What is your favorite color?"

"I'd have to say green."

"Possum?"

"I'm pretty fond of gold, as in gold bullion! What are you getting at?"

"Anyone know Johnie's favorite color?"

"He loves black. All his clothes are black except for when he's out on the boat. Too hot. Every single baseball cap he owns is black."

"Okay, hang on."

Gary stepped out onto the balcony. He got on the phone with someone. After about fifteen minutes, he stepped back inside.

"Okay, in one hour we'll have five of the new Ford Badlands 4x4 Broncos delivered here from Gary Davis Ford. One Velocity Blue Metallic for you, Jules. An Eruption Green one for Carson. An Absolute Black for Johnie, and I got a Cyber Orange Pearl for myself. I had to go with an

Oxford White for yours, Possum. But we can repaint it gold later. Oh, crap, I forgot about Rick. What color does he like? Oh, wait…duh, red, of course. Hang on," said Gary.

He stepped back onto the balcony and returned after a couple of minutes. Everyone just looked at each other in amazement, thinking Gary had lost his mind.

"And a Race Red for the Rickster. Should I get one for Chief too?"

"Are you nuts? What are you doing?"

"I'm having fun. I figured we could all get Broncos and at some point, put Rick's business on the side in vinyl lettering. That's good advertising. We could even use them as loaners sometimes, or better yet, I'll start a small rental company that offers only Broncos with discounts on fishing trips. I was tired of bumming rides from Possum anyway."

"You do know I don't live here, right? Same goes for Carson," said Possum.

"Oh, I know. They need to stay in Destin. Unless you fall in love with yours, then you can just take it back to Houston and I'll replace it here. No biggie. You too, Carson. It's only a little fun money."

Carson let out a laugh and raised his eyebrows. "Fun money? The base price on the Badlands 4x4 model is $45,035.39, so if my calculations are correct, you just spent $270,212.34 before tax. That's before upgrades. You didn't upgrade, did you?"

"Oh yeah, I added the bigger wheels and tires and rooftop popup camping tents on each of them. It was a sweet deal. I told them to send them as is now, and we'd go in and do any other upgrades we want within a few days. I'll let y'all decide what you want." Gary had a devilish grin on his face as he popped open a cold beer.

Possum patted him on the shoulder. "You are one of a kind, Gary Haas!"

"That's what they tell me, haha!" He took a huge swig from his Destin East Pass Ale.

A little less than an hour passed, and a knock came at the door. Jules opened it, and a man walked in carrying a bunch of paperwork and sets of keys. She looked out of the window to see a car hauler unloading Broncos in the parking lot. Gary signed all the papers and passed out the keys to everyone. He tipped the guy five hundred for bringing the Broncos so fast.

"Who wants to go for a test drive?! I'll meet everyone at Dewey Destin's on Crab Island. Lunch is on me," said Gary as he jogged out of the door.

Jules threw on her sundress and shades, grabbed Chief and his travel cage, and hit the elevator, followed closely by Possum and Carson. They all went to their respective colored Broncos and fired them up. Each one had built-in GPS in the stereo. They each took separate routes to Dewey Destin's to check out their rides, and all arrived within a few minutes of each other. They turned a few heads as they parked next to each other by the water.

After lunch, Carson headed for the Okaloosa Sheriff's Department in Fort Walton, while Possum took off, bound for Sacred Heart. Jules had received a text during lunch that Johnie was being released soon.

She and Chief went for a ride down to Okaloosa Island. She took the top off of the Bronco and let the warm wind blow through her jet-black hair. Chief seemed to like the wind as well. She continued down to Mary Esther, and before she knew it, she was close to Navarre. She crossed the bridge and took the beach drive all the way to Pensacola and made the big circle back to Destin. It was a glorious day, but all she could think about was Rick. She was glad Chief was with her, at least, to keep her company. The poor little guy had no idea his dad was injured and in the hospital.

Possum got to the hospital to take Johnie home around 3:20 p.m. Rick was still in the ICU but doing better. The doctor said he would probably be moved to a private room the next day. The nurse wheeled out Johnie in a high-back wheelchair, and Possum pushed him the rest of the way out. It was hospital policy, apparently.

"Nice ride!" said Johnie.

"You should see yours."

"Huh?"

"Just wait, I'll show you."

Johnie shrugged off his comment, not knowing what the hell Possum was on about. He wanted to go to the boat, but Possum talked him into staying at least a few days in the condo next to Gary. He told him he could help with the investigation, as they were using Rick's kitchen table as the command center. That satisfied him.

As Possum pulled into the parking lot of The Palms condos, he parked right next to the black Bronco.

"Look, another one. That looks sharp in black," said Johnie.

Possum opened the glove box, pulled out the keys, and handed them to Johnie.

"What the fuck?"

"It's yours, dude. Gary bought one for each of us."

"But why?"

"You know Gary. Why does he do anything? That's just Gary."

Tears were welling up in Johnie's eyes. He didn't know what to say.

"Are you being serious right now?"

"Dead serious!"

Just as he said that, the bright orange Bronco skidded to a stop beside Johnie's door. Gary jumped out with a cold beer and more keys. He handed Johnie the condo keys and the beer and told him to head up whenever he wished. Johnie just sat there in amazement for a few minutes and couldn't move. He couldn't believe this. He finally opened his door and walked over to the black Bronco. Not only was it his favorite color, but he had been checking them out for a while and had been seriously thinking about financing one. But just like free beer, a free Bronco was better.

Johnie took the Bronco out for a spin, swung by the boat to get a few clothes and his overnight bag, and returned to the condo. He walked in and was greeted by a cleaning lady finishing up.

"Hola, Señor," she said.

"Hola. You speak English?"

"Sí, I mean, yes, I do. I almost done aquí."

"Take your time, darlin'. Man, they sure make pretty cleaning ladies here."

She blushed and continued to dust. Johnie opened the fridge and found it full of his favorite beers and some snacks.

Possum had left him some BBQ and the smoked fish dip he made from the blue marlin they had caught.

The cleaning lady was about to let herself out when Johnie asked, "What is your name?"

"Mi nombre es Mia."

"I'm Johnie. Nice to meet you. Will you be my regular cleaning lady?"

"Yes, Mr. Gary hired me. I can also make deliveries of food for you if you wish."

"I'm gonna be hungry later. How about you bring me two orders of Enchiladas Suprema from Qué Pasa around eight o'clock? One for me and one for you. I'll make margaritas."

"Mr. Johnie, I shouldn't. I'm working."

"Well, I don't see a ring on that finger and you will be off by then. Please just join me for dinner. I'm lonely."

"If you insist, Mr. Johnie."

"I do and just call me Johnie."

"Sí, Johnie. I will be back at eight o' clock."

She was blushing as she closed the door to Johnie's condo. She was stunningly beautiful. She looked more like a fashion model than a cleaning lady, and Johnie was smitten.

Carson returned from the sheriff's department and the morgue with some news to share with the team.

As the entire gang, Jules, Possum, Gary and Johnie listened intently, Carson began to speak.

"Clemens snuck into the country under a fake passport, as you know," he told them as they gathered at the kitchen table. "But what we didn't know is that he's been doing that for some time, conducting drug trades in Miami. The Feds were about to pounce on him when he disappeared.

Someone ratted him out for coming to the panhandle. They searched his room and found lots of evidence connecting him to the attacks on Johnie and Rick. There is nothing tying him to Pamela. We are fighting a war in two theaters, apparently. They did find the bike we saw on the surveillance footage. It was borrowed, aka stolen, from an employee at Moe's Original BBQ and left at the bike rack at Emerald Grande. His prints were all over it. They have the ballistics report back, and the bullet and shell casing are a match with the gun that was fired at Johnie.

"Unfortunately, the DA is not dropping charges against Johnie for the jewelry theft yet, although the FDLA has set up a special investigative unit to dig deeper into the Kiefer Killian murder. They still have this pinned on Johnie, but they are now looking into Pamela as a suspect. We are working against the clock here. Johnie could still go to trial for this, especially if they never find Pamela. The DA is young and aggressive and wants a win under his belt, and will be pushing the judge for an expedited trial."

"How do they know about the jewels?"

"I told them. As soon as I turn over the GoPro footage of Rick being stabbed, as well as the GPS trip showing Pamela's boat over the discovery site, I'm hoping the theft charges will be dropped. There is no chance we can keep those jewels and also get the reward, anyway. I'm sure Rick would want to turn them into the authorities. It's the right thing to do. Lloyd's of London will pay the one-million-dollar reward and then auction off the jewels at Christy's. They will recoup a lot of their money. An all-points bulletin for Pamela and Michelle was issued, also with Interpol. But if she fled to a country without extradition, there's no way to arrest her unless she comes back. I don't see that happening. It was her plan all along. If that's the case, Johnie is screwed."

Possum, Gary, and Jules all shared worried looks.

"What are we gonna do?" said Jules, biting her lip.

"I don't know," said Possum tightly. Hopefully once Rick recovered, he would think of some way to get Pamela to pay for what she'd done.

"For now, Possum, can you contact Lloyd's of London and get the process started?" said Carson. "I'll inventory the jewelry and put it in the safe."

"I'm on it."

Possum texted Johnie to see if he wanted to join them all next door for dinner.

I can't, amigo. I have a date.

Damn, that was fast.

Yeah, thank Gary for hooking me up. He knows how to pick a cleaning lady.

You dog!

Woof, woof.

Jules planned to make paella and headed over to the Tienda La Mexicana Y Taqueria, a small local Mexican restaurant and grocery on Airport Road, to get supplies. Possum got on the phone with Lloyd's of London and emailed some pictures of the jewelry they had recovered. They were extremely excited to hear of the find. They planned to send an agent from Atlanta over to identify the jewelry and cut the reward check in a couple of days.

Jules returned with all the supplies for paella. She had picked up several pounds of royal red shrimp and some scallops from Sexton's. She pulled out the plastic bag and showed it to Possum, who immediately began to clean them. Jules opened a bottle of wine and took the other half of the Xanax that Gary had given her. She texted the entire crew, letting them know dinner would be served at 7:30 p.m. and there would be appetizers before if anyone wanted them. She loved to cook but especially for Rick. She made sure to get some heavy-duty freezer containers, so Rick could try her paella once he was released from the hospital.

"Dinner, boys!" said Jules.

Gary, Carson, and Possum gathered around the table and tasted the coxinha appetizers she had made. They were tiny little chicken croquettes with a spicy Brazilian dipping sauce. Carson made a noise like his mouth was on fire.

"I'm not used to such spicy food," he said with a laugh. He washed it down with the homemade mojitos Jules made for everyone.

"Johnie doesn't know what he's missing," said Jules.

"He's in love," said Possum.

"What?"

"Yeah, he has the hots for the cleaning lady Gary hired. She's probably just getting there now for dinner."

"Good for him. He's a good guy who deserves to be happy," replied Jules.

"Yes, she's from Colombia like you, Jules," said Gary.

"Well, she's a winner then!" said Jules with a full mouth of coxinhas, laughing.

Her phone began to vibrate. She looked down and it was the hospital.

"Miss Castro, it's Dr. Cannon. I have an update on Mr. Waters."

"I'm gonna put you on speaker, Doc, okay? Everyone is here."

She put her iPhone on speaker and set it down beside the appetizers. They all leaned in to hear.

"Mr. Waters's vitals are all good. He's healing up nicely. We feel confident that we can move him to a private room in the morning. He should be here about four more days, then he can go home. It looks like there will be no permanent damage to his spleen. He's gonna be super sore for a few weeks, as the knife really did a number on his ribs. I expect a full recovery. Do you have any questions?"

"When can I see him?"

"I'd say ten in the morning is safe. We're gonna move him around eight after an X-ray. Unless I text or call you, that should be a good time."

"Thank you, thank you, thank you, Doc! You just made us all very happy. Do you like paella?"

"Paella? I love it, actually. Why?"

"I'll make you a plate and bring it to the hospital. It's the least I can do."

"Thank you, Miss Castro. That's very sweet of you. I will be on rounds tomorrow and that sounds delicious."

"Call me Jules, Doc. Call me Jules."

CHAPTER NINETEEN

Jules was up by six o'clock. Even though they'd stayed up late into the night celebrating Rick's recovery, she was wound up and excited to see him. She made coffee and surprised Possum for a change by beating him to it. Possum texted Gary and Johnie, and one by one they showed up at the condo, yawning but ready to work on Johnie's case.

"Jules, we all think you should go see Rick by yourself first and we'll all go later. We know how hard this has been on you."

"Thank you, Possum. I'm gonna sneak Chief in with Rick's backpack. I'll have both my injured boys in the same room."

"That's a good idea, Jules. Seeing you will totally lift Rick's spirits, but Chief will be the icing on the cake."

Jules was like a bull in a china closet. She paced around the condo and checked her watch every five minutes. It was only 8:15 a.m., and she had nearly worn a burn trail in the condo carpet. She decided to take the new Bronco out to the beach to kill some time.

She took the back beach road to Destin Commons to Scenic 98, past the Whale's Tail Beach Bar, and parked by the water. Chief stood up on her hand, and they took a stroll down the beach. The water was super clear that morning, with almost no waves. Chief did his best seagull impression, to the delight of a few passing tourists. By 9:30 a.m., Jules was chomping at the bit and jumped back in the Bronco bound for Sacred Heart. She arrived five minutes before ten and gave Chief a few grapes to keep him quiet inside the customized JanSport makeshift bird kennel, and soon stepped inside Sacred Heart Hospital.

"I'm here to see Rick Waters."

"Please sign in here."

After a few minutes, someone led her to Rick's room. He was asleep when she went inside. She pulled the door closed for privacy and tiptoed over to the bed. After unzipping the backpack, she softly placed Chief on Rick's chest. Chief stared straight into Rick's face from no more than two inches away. Rick slowly woke up, and when his eyes finally focused on Chief, a huge smile crept across his face.

"Chief, am I dreaming?"

Rick looked over and realized Jules was in the room.

"Hi, baby! I'm so happy to see you."

"Me too, Rick. How are you feeling?"

"Much better, since you are here. And you snuck Chief in too!"

"I knew you'd wanna see him."

Rick reached out with his left hand, and Jules grabbed ahold of it. With his right hand, he stroked the top of Chief's head. He just purred like a kitten, happy to be with Rick.

A few minutes later, the door opened. It was a nurse doing her rounds. Rick quickly tucked Chief under the covers. She moved closer to Rick and took his BP and oxygen level. She never noticed Chief squirming under the covers. Once she was gone, Jules got Rick up to date on what he had missed.

"Rick, the guy who stabbed you was Dale Clemens. The police are pretty certain he's the same person who attacked Johnie. Carson told us he had snuck into the country using a fake passport. They haven't found his body but he is assumed dead."

"He's dead all right. As soon as the spear went into his eye, his body stiffened and he started to float away lifeless," replied Rick. "How is Johnie doing? Does Carson think his case is looking any better now that we tracked down the jewels?"

"He's doing okay, but no, Carson doesn't think the jewels will be enough. Pamela is still out there somewhere, and she's the key to clearing his name. But don't worry about that for now, Rick. That can wait until you come home."

He opened his mouth to protest, but she placed her palm over his lips to stop him. "Hold out your hand and close your eyes," she told him.

He sighed but did as she said, no doubt thinking she was gonna put a Hershey's Kiss in his hand as she had done so many times before. But this time it was different. It was metallic.

"Okay, open your eyes."

"Keys? To what?"

"This!"

Jules showed Rick a photo of the new red Badlands 4x4 Bronco Gary had bought for him.

"What the hell? You bought this?"

"No, Gary did."

"I can't keep this. It's too much."

"Rick, he bought everybody one, even Carson. All different colors. Here's mine."

She showed Rick another photo.

"That crazy son of a bitch. He has more money than sense."

"He said he was tired of everyone bumming rides from each other with just your truck and Possum's rental. He wants to put *Nine-Tenths* and Rick Waters's Detective Agency on the doors in vinyl. I think he wants to live here now."

Rick's eyes glazed over a bit at the amazing generosity of his friend.

"He's an extraordinary gentleman. I'd love to have him as a neighbor. Maybe he'll even get his detective license. Can you imagine if we get a storefront down by the harbor?"

"That would amazing, Rick. You'll need a secretary, though."

"That's true. I wish you could stay, Jules. I know the dolphin research in Brazil is so important to you. I wouldn't even think of trying to coerce you into staying."

"Did I ever tell you what I did in college before I became a dealer?" asked Jules.

"No, let me guess, stripper?"

Jules playfully slapped Rick on his leg. "No! I'd never do that!"

"You have the body and face for it," replied Rick.

"The only person I'd ever strip for is you! No, seriously, I was a secretary in Barranquilla. We got some pretty rough customers there. I was really good at my job. So, if you ever need a secretary, I'm your girl."

"Are you saying what I think you're saying, Jules?"

"If you'll have me, Rick, I wanna stay."

Rick pulled her toward him and hugged her and Chief together. He had never felt happiness and contentment like this in his entire life. Tears were falling from both of their eyes.

"Yes, Jules, yes. I want you to stay. Now, we just need to find a storefront."

"I didn't wanna mention this, but I think Gary is already on the hunt. I told him I was gonna stay and help you on future cases, and I could see the squirrel running on a wheel in his head."

"You know, you're right. He's probably walking down HarborWalk as we speak looking for any vacancies. He's something else."

Jules spent the next thirty minutes loving on Rick. She must have kissed his hand a dozen times. Love was flowing from her and she was awash with joy.

As Rick stroked her hair, he asked, "Jules, didn't you say you saw a pamphlet of both the Maldives and Cape Verde?"

"Yes, that's right. Why?" She knew he was thinking about Johnie's case again, and how he could clear his name. He was always putting others before himself, even when lying in a hospital bed.

"Before I was stabbed, I was doing some research on both places and I had planned on letting the guys know. Anyway, what I figured out is because of the connection between both Pamela and Michelle and the Facebook group, Mephistopheles Cocoa, I have narrowed it down to the Maldives. Since the Maldives doesn't have extradition to the US, I think Pamela and Michelle took all the money from the insurance claim and the house sale and are living high on the hog on a beach somewhere. As soon as I'm healed, I think we need to take a trip. What do you say?"

"Let's do it!" replied Jules.

"We'll need Gary's help. Since he already hooked up with Pamela once, I'm sure I can talk him into doing it again. That satanism group they are both linked to has meetings, aka orgies on Cocoa Island in the Maldives. It's their headquarters and sacred temple. We just have to plant Gary there somehow. I'm sure we can come up with a reason to place him there. Then we've gotta get Pamela back to the States so she can confess. And we've gotta do it fast, before the trial. That's the only way we'll be able to clear Johnie of the murder charges for good."

Carson flew to Virginia to follow up on the forensics that he had forwarded from the Okaloosa County office. Possum, Johnie, and Gary were at the boat. Johnie had a charter leaving the next day, and he hadn't been on the boat since his attack. Possum helped him get it ready and get supplies for the charter scheduled for the next morning.

Meanwhile, Gary headed down to the HarborWalk, looking for any vacancies for Rick's new office. Once Jules had told him she was staying and planned to be Rick's secretary, he was full bore to make the brick-and-mortar idea reality. He was a tad hungry and spotted a woman in a cute, shiny Airstream selling grilled cheese. He remembered Jules going on and on about it, so he decided to try it.

"What a cool little restaurant you have here. I love the Airstream," said Gary.

"Yeah, the owner originally planned on renting a spot down by Emerald Grande, but they wanted fourteen thousand a month in rent for a small spot beside where they do the hatchet throwing," said the woman. "It's a third of the cost here. The owner already had this Airstream, so his startup costs weren't too bad. I've been here since day one. Oh, I'm Christina, by the way."

"Cool, Christina. I'm Gary Haas. Thanks for sharing that great story."

Gary ordered the Dude Melt—a sloppy joe/grilled cheese combo. It was messy but delicious. What was even better than the grilled cheese was the idea the Airstream put into Gary's head. Since Rick already had a badass '62 Ford F-100, if he would allow him to have it painted race red and then find a vintage-looking travel trailer, he could paint it to match and they'd have their storefront. He just needed to run it by Rick.

He found the rental office to inquire about a spot big enough to accommodate the truck and trailer. One of the t-shirt shops was closing up, and if Rick parked the truck sideways across the front of the travel trailer, it would fit. The rent was four thousand a month. He was as giddy as a schoolgirl. He gave the lady a deposit, hoping Rick would go for it, and thinking he probably would.

He jogged back to *Nine-Tenths* to run the idea by Possum and Johnie. They both loved it and were sure Rick would as well. Johnie gave Possum a lift in his new Bronco, and Gary said he'd meet them at the hospital. He just wanted to stop by the condo and grab something.

He ran into Jessica on his way back out.

"Hi, Gary, you gonna be able to come to the party?" she asked. "It's next Friday at your restaurant. Here's an invite. Please let your whole crew know they are invited."

"I'll let everyone know," he said. "So, are you really retiring?"

"Not exactly. I'm actually starting my own brokerage. I have worked for Keller Williams

Realty for longer than I care to admit. It's time for me to make my own mark."

"Good for you, Jessica. I know you're gonna kick some ass!"

She grinned. "Make sure y'all come to the party. It'll be a coming out of sorts for my new business as well as a celebration."

"We'll be there. You can count on it."

Gary arrived at the hospital just after Possum and Johnie, and they all went to Rick's room together. Jules smiled at them and stood up from Rick's bed.

"Rickster!" said Gary.

"Hey y'all, thanks for coming. It's good to see y'all's ugly mugs, haha. Gary, I have to ask you. Have you gone and lost your mind? I mean…buying what…six Broncos? What the hell, man?"

"I got the half-dozen discount," said Gary jokingly. "Listen, dude. I needed the tax write off, so don't think twice about it. There's something else I wanna run by you."

"Okay, shoot."

"We are all so happy that Jules is not going back to Brazil. She told me she wants to work with you. I'm sure as a secretary and also a secret agent, when you let her in on cases. The problem is, we need a better office than the back deck of your boat."

Rick opened his mouth to speak, but Gary held up a hand.

"Now, hear me out before you interrupt me. I've talked it over with the entire crew, and they are all in agreement that this is a good idea. But in the end, it's your call. It is your name on the business, after all. So, I did a little shopping, and I found a rental spot not far from *Nine-Tenths* by the boats and food vendors. My plan is to buy a thirty-foot vintage-looking travel trailer and paint it to match your '62 Ford. Park them both on the HarborWalk and make that the sales office for both Nine-Tenths Charters and your P.I. business. What do you think?" asked Gary.

"It's a great idea, but my Ford is patina-red and rusted."

"That's the other thing. You'll have to let me get it painted. Look, it's the last thing you have to do to make that truck a show truck. I'm sure you've thought about it before."

"I have. But I can't let you pay for all of that."

"How about fifty/fifty on the paint? I don't wanna be a full partner. How about ten percent of all charters sales and P.I. gigs? I wanna get my license too."

There was a long silence in the room; you could've heard a pin drop. Finally, Rick stuck his hand out.

"Let's do it, partner!"

Gary shook his hand, and they all hooted and hollered.

"What about you two?" asked Rick.

"Well, boss, I just wanna stay on as your first mate. The P.I. stuff I'll leave to y'all," said Johnie.

"Fair enough. And you, Possum?"

"I need to head back to Houston, amigo. I'm always a phone call or text away though. Plus, I ain't heading back until we clear Johnie of all charges," replied Possum.

"Okay, then it's settled. We'll all work Johnie's case and then we'll go full time with the new storefront. Hell, we should sell t-shirts and hats," exclaimed Rick.

"Damn right, we will," said Gary.

"Getting back to Johnie's case. I have a plan. I'm ninety-nine percent certain Pamela and Michelle have moved to the Maldives—Cocoa Island, to be exact. We need to get a confession from them and get them back on US soil. You think you can woo Pamela again, Gary?"

"Woo her? Are you kidding? She's like a rabbit. Keeping her from humping my leg will be a challenge." Gary chuckled.

"We need a cover story for you to be on the island. She will be incredibly suspicious if you just show up there," said Rick.

"No, she won't. I can guarantee it. Not only will she not be suspicious; she will freaking invite me. When I had my fling with her and Michelle, she gave me her WhatsApp number. I was so drunk I had forgotten about it, but I remembered later she said she was getting rid of her phone number and I'd need this to contact her in the future. Shit! I'll ping her right now. What time is it in the Maldives?" asked Gary.

Possum looked it up on Google on his phone. "It's twenty after midnight there. They are eleven hours ahead of us."

"Perfect. Knowing her, she's half in the bag now and partying as we speak."

"There's only one resort on the entire island," said Rick. "The other half is private. She most likely bought a yacht or a beach villa, and we all know she loves to drink, so she probably spends a lot of time over at the COMO Cocoa Island Resort. It's world class."

Two pings rang out from Gary's phone.

"She got back to me."

"Damn, that was fast."

"She said she's on vacation and wants me to spend her birthday with her. I asked her where. You'll never guess."

"COMO Cocoa Island Resort?" said Rick.

"Bingo!"

"When?"

"On the fifteenth. It's her birthday weekend. How soon can you travel, Rick? That's only four days away."

"I should be able to go by then. I might not be a hundred percent, but I'll be able to hold my own. Johnie, since you are out on bail, you can't leave the country anyway, so I'll need you to stay and keep the boat going. Plus, we can't take a chance of her seeing you. How about you, Possum?" asked Rick.

"I think I'll stay back and help Johnie on the boat. I'm kinda tired of traveling for a bit. I can be your point man here. You'll need one anyway."

"Great idea, Possum."

"Holy shit!" Gary slapped his forehead. "I just had an epiphany. Remember the night I hooked up with Pamela and Michelle? I went there with Jules, aka Valentina. Pamela is smitten with Jules. If I tell her I'm bringing Valentina and she's ready to play, it will be on like Donkey Kong!"

Rick frowned. "Jules doesn't swing that way."

"We all know that. It won't get that far. I have a plan. I'll tell her she needs to take it slow with Valentina, but she'll come around. Trust me, I know how to play this bitch."

"Jules, you ready to do your 007 act again?" asked Rick.

"I ain't kissing her!"

Rick held his side as he laughed. "Don't make me laugh. I don't wanna have to go back into surgery. All you have to do is make her think you're interested. That's it. We'll do the rest."

"Okay, then. But nothing more!" she replied emphatically.

"Rick, we'll let you rest," said Gary. "Oh, your realtor friend Jessica is having a big party on Saturday at Chief's Cockatoo Cafe. Will you be released by then?"

"I believe so. I'll make sure of it."

"All right. I take delivery of my new jet on the fourteenth. I ordered a Bombardier Global 7500. It has a range of, you guessed it, just over 7,500 nautical miles. I guess we can fly over the top and refuel in Dublin, drink a few Guinness, and have the plane serviced and thoroughly checked out. It's 3,600 nautical miles to Dublin and 5,500 to Gan International in the Maldives. I'd say that will be a great shakedown flight."

Rick raised his fist in the air.

"To the Maldives!"

CHAPTER TWENTY

Jules stood at the foot of Rick's bed two days later as the doctor went over his charts. He had been in the hospital for eight days total, counting the ICU. The doctor flipped through the papers one last time.

"Mr. Waters, you are free to go. You need to take it easy, though. I'm giving you a couple prescriptions for pain medication. Your rib muscles will take the longest to heal, and it may be awkward breathing at times, but everything else looks great. No scuba diving for a while. Haha."

"Thanks for taking such good care of Rick, Dr. Cannon. We are grateful," said Jules.

Rick shook the doctor's hand, and both he and Jules helped Rick to the wheelchair.

"You wanna push him out?" asked the doctor.

"Yeah, thanks, Doc."

Jules pushed Rick to the front entrance of the hospital, locked the chair, and ran over to get her Bronco. She pulled around the corner and stopped at the curb. It was a glorious day without a cloud in the sky. Jules had taken the top and doors off of the Bronco, and she looked stunning driving it, with her jet-black hair and bright yellow sundress. She helped Rick up to the passenger seat. He was moving quite well considering what had happened.

Once back at the condo, the crew greeted him with a round of applause. The only person missing was Carson, who was still in Virginia.

Possum opened a Divide & Conch'r beer for Rick and handed it to him. They all toasted. Possum took the lead.

"To Rick, our fearless leader. Stop getting stabbed all the time. Haha! Cheers!"

They clinked their beers together, and Rick tried to give Chief a taste. He just stuck his beak in the air defiantly.

"Rick, you made it back just in time. At 6:00 p.m., Jessica is having her party downstairs. Are you up to it?" asked Gary.

"Sure, man. I wouldn't miss it."

Rick lay down on the bed to rest a bit before the party, and Jules stayed with him, as Chief hopped up and down on the bed, running his beak along the duvet. They were one big, happy family.

Jules got up first to get ready for the party. With her help, Rick put on a Tommy Bahama shirt and some nice shorts, and they headed down around six-thirty with Chief in tow. The party was in full swing when they arrived. Possum, Gary, and Johnie sat at a large round table covered with appetizers and drinks. Gary pointed to the center of the room. There was a cool-looking bamboo tiki island with a swing in the center. A large sign on the bamboo read *Chief's Cabana*.

Rick walked over and placed Chief on the bamboo swing. People gathered around and took photos of him. He still had on his wing brace, but it would come off in a few more weeks. It was the same color as his feathers and didn't stand out too bad. Chief was a superstar up there on his perch.

Just as they sat down to enjoy some appetizers, Carson made an appearance.

"Hi, Rick. Congrats on your recovery. I'm glad you're doing well."

"Thanks, Carson. You didn't have to come all the way back here for the party."

"I know, I did and didn't, actually. I just left the DA's office. Come here, Johnie. You are gonna wanna hear this. They are dropping the charges against you for the jewelry theft. They have filed charges against Pamela for insurance fraud and giving false testimony to the police. There are now a lot of questions about the murder of her husband that don't make sense, and she is now a person of interest."

"Woohoo!" shouted Johnie.

"Don't get too excited yet. The DA still has murder as one of the charges against you, but at least they aren't totally focused on you, which will help your case. Also, this is an interesting twist. The forensics lab in Quantico confirmed DNA on the knife for you as well as the victim Kiefer but—and this is a big but—they also found DNA from a third yet undetermined person. It didn't match Pamela or Michelle. It's a mystery."

Rick frowned. "Wow, that is weird. Who could it be?"

"It's hard to say. It could be someone who cleans the house for Pamela, or hell, even someone who attended one of her parties who may have picked up the knife prior to the murder. They ran it through CODIS but got no hits."

"What's CODIS?" asked Johnie.

"It's the Combined DNA Index System. Basically, it's a database. Anyone ever convicted of a felony has their DNA there. Whoever is on the knife is not a felon," replied Carson.

"Well, I wanna drink up anyway. At least I'm not a jewel thief."

The party lasted long into the wee hours, and they all woke up the next day with hangovers. Even Chief. Jules found out he liked wine. A lot! It made sense, as his favorite treats were grapes.

They were all hungover but in full tilt to get to the Maldives as soon as possible, while Carson was trying to get an injunction against 23andme.com and Ancestry.com to get them to turn over DNA so they could try and find this mystery person who had touched or used the knife.

"It's here! She's here!" shouted Gary the morning of the fourteenth, waking up everyone but Possum, who was already up making coffee.

"Who's here?" asked Possum as he looked down at his watch.

"My jet landed last night at Destin Executive. I wanna go look at it and get her ready for the Maldives."

Jules and Rick stumbled into the kitchen.

"What's going on?!" asked Rick as he reached for the coffee.

"My jet's here. Wanna go see her?"

"Can I finish my coffee first?"

"Possum?"

"I'll hang back. I promised I'd help Johnie with some calibrations on the boat and then meet Carson at the forensics lab in Fort Walton."

The jet was spectacular. Comfortable seating for eight, and four of the chairs folded down to beds. It had a nice bar in the aft and two desks. They all returned and began to pack.

"Rick, I'm not so sure about my part in this with Pamela," said Jules, biting her lip as she folded her clothes. "Even the thought of pretending I'm interested in hooking up with her is just…making me nervous."

"I know, baby, and if you're not comfortable with it, we can come up with something else."

"I can tell you right now I will *not* sleep with that woman. I won't even kiss her."

"It won't come to that, Jules. You see this?" Gary spun his phone around and showed her a picture of a vial that read SP-117.

"What's SP-117?" she asked.

"It's commonly known as truth serum. My plan is to get her to admit she killed Kiefer by mixing some SP-117 in her drink. That will also make her drowsy. That along with some GHB, commonly called the date-rape drug, with leave her with no memory of the evening at all. If I can get her on a recording admitting to the murder, then all we have to do is get her to the States somehow. I haven't figured that part out yet. I'm working on it."

"I'm still not kissing her."

"Haha, I promise, Jules. No kissing. All you have to it look good and act interested. I'll do the rest. Are you down?"

She took a deep breath. "If it will help Johnie, then yes."

When they brought their suitcases out to the living room, Gary was waiting for them.

"So, the plan is the three of us will go," said Gary. "Jules, myself, and you, Rick. Also, I have a friend named Jamie who is a nurse practitioner, and a great friend of mine. We'll bring her along to make sure I don't overdose Pamela. She's hot, a freak, and into anything, so she'll fit right in with Pamela's group of degenerates."

"How soon are we leaving?" asked Jules.

"We need to leave this morning with a stopover in Dublin," said Rick.

"I know you met her once, Rick. Do you have a disguise you can wear?" asked Gary. "Yeah, I'll go with my banker outfit. Nice suit and full reddish beard. It's perfect."

They all boarded the plane and set off for Dublin. Rick had his banker outfit all ready to go. When they reached their destination a little over eight hours later, they checked into their two rooms at The Merrion Hotel, and planned to meet a half hour later at Napper Tandy's Pub for some Guinness and fish and chips. It was a great pub with lots of locals. They only had a couple, as they needed to keep their heads on straight for the rendezvous with Pamela at the COMO Cocoa. With the time change, it was already late at night.

They took the car back to the airport at 6:00 a.m. the next morning. The flight to Gan International took a little over twelve hours, and then they took the short hop over to Hulhulé, a small island with an airport roughly two kilometers from COMO Cocoa. From there they took a small speedboat transfer over to COMO Cocoa.

The resort was plush with small over-water tiki cottages, and a main resort area with a restaurant, bar, and infinity pool. Rick and Jules's cottage was next to Gary and Jamie's. They all settled into their rooms and decide to do the tourist thing. For Pamela's benefit, Gary walked with Jules, while Rick walked with Jamie, as if they were a couple. They had to play this right or she would get suspicious. Once at the pool, Rick ordered drinks for everyone, and they enjoyed the luxury of this five-star resort.

"Where could she be, Rick?" asked Jules.

"I don't know, but you see those guys over there arranging flowers and whatnot? I bet that's for Pamela's birthday party later tonight." "I bet you're right, Rick."

"I'm gonna message her on WhatsApp," said Gary.

> Hi Pamela, I'm here. I made it. I'm by the big pool and I have a surprise for you. A present, you could say.

> What is it? I can't wait. We are heading over from the yacht shortly.

> It's not a what, it's a who. I brought Valentina and she's ready to play. You want some?

> *Oh my God, yes! We'll be over shortly too. I also have a surprise.*

What?

> *Not a what, a who as well. You'll see.*

"Okay, Pamela and her gang are coming over from that yacht shortly," said Gary as he pointed to the big motor yacht anchored just outside of the resort. "She said she's bringing someone as a surprise."

Rick raised an eyebrow. "Who could she be bringing?"

"Probably another chick she wants me to party with. She's insatiable. She's very excited that you're here, Valentina," Gary told Jules.

"Whoopie," she said sarcastically.

About forty minutes later, Gary saw Pamela walking with Michelle hand in hand toward the pool. A man was following them. Gary jumped up and motioned for Jules to follow. He hugged Pamela and Michelle when they reached them. Rick and Jamie followed as well. "So great to see you, Pamela. You look stunning. So do you, Michelle."

Gary kissed them both, and Jules gave them hugs.

"I want you to meet my friends. Pamela, this is Steven and Jamie. They are good friends of mine from California. Steven is a producer out in LA, and Jamie is a realtor."

They all shook hands. Pamela couldn't take her eyes off of Jules in her bikini.

"Oh, I told you I had a surprise. We need to keep this on the down low, if you know what I mean. This is Kiefer, my soon to be ex-husband."

A silence fell over them, and Jules, Rick, Gary and Jamie all dropped their jaws in disbelief.

"Uh, I'm a little confused," said Gary.

Kiefer was a tall, thin man with a small amount of gray on his temples. He looked distinguished but carried himself like a frat boy, as if he were younger than he really was. He had a boyish charm about him. He stuck out his hand to shake. Gary shook what he thought was a dead man's hand.

"It's a long story, Gary. Are your friends privy to the incident in Destin?" said Kiefer.

"You mean the incident where you were stabbed to death?"

"Yeah, that one."

"Yeah, I told them Pamela was widowed. I guess she's not?"

"Like I said, it's a long story. Let's get some drinks and I'll clear it up for you."

They all settled around a table, and Pamela ordered several bottles of champagne.

When no one was looking, Rick turned on the field recorder he had in his backpack sitting beside the table.

"Where to begin? I'll keep this short. It doesn't really matter since there is no extradition to the US from here, but if we wanna party, you may as well know. A few months ago, I was looking at going bankrupt in my business because of some bad financial investments I had made."

"That's not all, Kiefer. Don't forget Biloxi," interrupted Pamela.

"Oh, yeah. I also had a wee bit of a gambling problem. I blame the coke mainly. I was on a heater at the Beau Rivage in Biloxi on the craps table. I was most of the way through an eight ball when I started drinking. That made me stupid. I took out several markers and before I knew it, I owed the house close to a million dollars. I was so drunk, high, and cocky, and I went to my room and partied until the sun came up. I ran out of coke and that's when the big guys knocked on my door. Let's just say they had crooked noses and they wanted their money. I told them I'd be down by noon to pay up. I always had in the past. This time I couldn't. I snuck out of the hotel and disappeared for a while. That's when Pamela came up with the idea of me getting murdered."

"So, you faked your death?" asked Gary.

"Long story short, yes. Plus, we framed some loser fisherman in Destin for the whole thing. It was Pamela's great idea to also frame him last minute for the jewelry heist, which gave us even more money to disappear with. It was beautiful."

"What about the dead guy they found that they think is you?"

"I'm not gonna get into all that. Let's just say a dead body is a dead body." Kiefer raised his glass and toasted. "To Pamela, happy birthday. The kinkiest little deviant I'll ever have for an ex-wife. Also the most clever." He grinned. "Gary, I know about you and Pamela and Michelle. Don't worry. I'm bisexual. I'm hoping we can take this party to a whole new level tonight. I know Pamela's beyond excited that Valentina wants to play."

Gary took a huge swig of champagne, trying to wrap his head around all of this and stay in character. Kiefer's sudden appearance changed everything. Not only was Johnie not guilty of murder, but Kiefer was alive and well. It hung him up. They still had to go through with the plan, but with Kiefer alive, they'd have to rethink it a bit.

They drank lots of bubbly and celebrated Pamela's birthday. Everyone was quite liquored up when Pamela announced they would have dessert on the yacht.

Jules was nervous. She looked over at Rick, and he gave he a strong look of encouragement. His courage made her feel a little better, although her heart was beating fast as they all took the beautiful teak and mahogany tender to the yacht. The hundred-and-fifty-foot yacht was decked out with every possible amenity. They all settled in the main salon of the boat and ate strawberries dipped in the chocolate fountain.

Pamela continued to make advances at Jules, and she played along as best she could.

"I want to get into something more comfortable first," she said.

"You all have to stay with us on the yacht overnight," Pamela told everyone. "I insist." She gave Rick and Jamie a room next to the master cabin, and then she invited Jules in to look at some of her lingerie. This was about to go down, and Jules wasn't ready. She didn't know what to do.

The crew had all gone below deck for the night. Michelle was making out with Pamela on the edge of the bed and kissing Gary at the same time. Jules was still in the dressing room and finally came out wearing a sexy black negligee. Pamela invited Rick and Jamie to join their threesome/foursome to turn it into a whatever-some.

They politely declined, but Jamie piped up, "Gary, how about I make everyone an after dinner aperitif like I made for you the last time you visited California?"

"That would be great, Jamie. Make us all one."

Jamie slipped into the galley. Jules knew she was spiking some of the drinks. Jamie reappeared carefully carrying the high-octane drinks in her left hand, and passed them all out. They all made a toast, and Rick and Jamie slipped away into their own room to wait. It wouldn't take long.

Kiefer and Michelle passed out first, and Pamela began to slur her words and call for Jules. She hid the pen video recorder in her negligee top and stepped inside, to get Pamela on the record.

"Jules, come kiss me. I always wanted to kiss you."

"I will, Pamela, but first please tell me, why did you fake Kiefer's death?"

The truth serum was working and working well.

"Kiefer already told you. We had to disappear. It's as simple as that."

"Where did you find a dead body to frame the fisherman?"

"I'm so bad. You're gonna be mad at me." Pamela covered her mouth like a child.

"Just tell me. I won't be mad, then we can be together," said Jules, taking her hand to encourage her.

Pamela bit her lip. "Okay, since you promised you won't be mad. I was trying to find a dead body from the college in Tallahassee, but I got tired of waiting because the guy

I paid to get me one wasn't coming through. He was a pre-med student there. He was getting cold feet. He said he was gonna turn me in for trying to steal a dead body. I got scared. So, I told him I'd give him a blow job if he'd try again. He met me at my house and I took him into Kiefer's study. I went down on him and had him lie on the couch. When he was really getting into it, I reached behind the couch, pulled out the big knife I had hidden there, and stabbed him repeatedly! He died with his cock in my mouth. The whole thing made me incredibly horny."

Jules just listened in disbelief.

"So, why did you frame the fisherman?"

"That was actually by happenstance. The original plan was to just burn a body in Kiefer's car to make it look like he was the one murdered. I was so horny; I went to happy hour at Harry T's and that's when I ran into Johnie. He was okay looking and I really needed to get laid. We went back to my place and he was so drunk he could barely walk, and that's when the idea hit me. I sent him into the safe to get my sex toys that I keep in a black box. We had sex and he passed out. I killed two birds with one stone. It was the perfect setup. I couldn't have planned it any better. That loser will get convicted and sentenced to life for a murder he never committed. Come here, Jules. I want you."

Jules moved slowly toward Pamela, who sat on the edge of the bed. As Pamela reached out to put her arms around her, Jules pulled out the syringe that was tucked in the garter behind her left thigh and drove it into Pamela's shoulder. She looked back with wide eyes, confused, then fell over, completely out cold.

"Rick, come quick! I got her to confess on video," yelled Jules.

Rick ran in and saw Pamela, Kiefer, and Michelle passed out.

"Gary, what's your plan?!"

"I think it's time these three get repatriated!"

CHAPTER TWENTY-ONE

The car alarm and horn were going off at a deafening volume. The smell of the exhaust lightly came into the windows of the van. Kiefer looked out of the van's front windshield, unclear where he was or what time it was. The last thing he could remember was sitting around the pool in the Maldives, bragging to Gary and his friends about how he'd made himself disappear and start a new life on the islands. He heard a noise from behind him and saw Pamela and Michelle beginning to wake up under a blanket they were lying under.

"Please turn off your car alarm and engine," said the deputy to Kiefer.

Kiefer looked at him as if he were seeing a ghost.

"I'm sorry, what?" said Kiefer.

"Please turn off your vehicle's alarm and engine. I'm not gonna ask again," replied the deputy.

"Where am I? How did I get here?" asked Kiefer as he turned off the van.

The alarm stopped as well.

"Have you been drinking, sir? I need you to step out of the van."

The deputy shined his light into the back of the van. Bodies were moving under a blanket. He immediately grabbed his weapon and pointed it at Kiefer.

"Step out of the van now! Who's in the back of the van?"

"Uh, that's my wife and her girlfriend. I'm confused. What's going on?"

The deputy called for backup. He'd had enough of Kiefer not following his orders, and opened the van door and ripped Kiefer out in one motion.

"Spread your feet and place your hands on the van."

When Kiefer spun around and did as the officer told him, on his back was a clear plastic baggie with the words written in large black permanent marker: *I'm Kiefer Killian, I faked my own death. Watch flash drive.* A small flash drive and two passports sat at the bottom of the bag. The deputy removed the baggie that was pinned to the back of Kiefer's shirt and handed it to the deputy next to him.

"What's your name?"

"I want a lawyer."

"You got it, buddy," replied the deputy as he slammed Kiefer hard against the van and handcuffed him.

Two other deputies had removed Pamela and Michelle, who also had similar plastic baggies attached to their backs. They hauled all three of them into the station for questioning, which wasn't far, as the van was parked sideways right outside of the sheriff's department. They were all brought into separate rooms to be questioned. Kiefer waited for a lawyer, as did Pamela, but Michelle, not knowing any better, started to answer questions from one of the investigators.

"Why did your friend park the white van in front of the sheriff's department with the alarm going off?"

"I don't remember. I don't remember anything. Where am I?"

"You are in the Okaloosa County Sheriff's Department."

"Florida?"

"Last time I checked, yes. Fort Walton, to be exact. What kind of bender have y'all been on?"

They continued to interrogate her, but the evidence in the plastic baggies really told the story. All the baggies included flash drives of the video of Pamela's confession, the audio tape Rick had recorded of Kiefer bragging at the pool, and both the real and fake passports for each of them.

Rick's phone rang.

"Hello?"

"Hey, Rick, it's Carson. I just spoke with the DA and all murder charges have been dropped for Johnie. Apparently, Pamela, Michelle, and the undead Kiefer Killian all turned themselves into the sheriff's department. It's gonna be all over the local news, and teams from Fox and CNN are rumored to be coming in today. This is a huge story. I'm on Okaloosa Island heading to Destin. How about I come over and we can all discuss the case at your condo? Can you get Johnie over? He's gonna be ecstatic. Don't tell him anything, just get him over there." "They are all here right now. Come on over."

"You got it."

About twenty minutes later, Carson arrived.

"I want everyone to turn off their cell phones and place them on the center of the table. It's for your own protection."

They all did as he said. He pulled out a C9 bug detector and scanned the entire condo. It was clean.

"Okay, here's what I have on the record. Pamela is formally being charged with murder and insurance fraud. Kiefer is being charged with insurance fraud and pseudocide, aka faking his own death. Pseudocide is technically not a crime, but there will be more charges soon regarding hindering a police investigation as well as conspiracy to commit murder. Michelle has agreed to testify against them for a plea deal. She is currently being held for conspiracy to commit murder and the other charges as well."

"But Kiefer's not dead. How is it murder?"

"Okay, off the record now. I know that you know that body was not Kiefer's, and I know they didn't get to Florida on their own. The body was exhumed and matched by DNA with a premed student from Tallahassee. But you already knew that, right? I wanna hear the entire story. Look, I'm retired FBI and those sons of bitches are getting what they deserve. I just gotta know how you did it. It doesn't leave this room."

Rick began to tell the story. The only thing that would have made it better was if they were sitting around a campfire.

Halfway through, Johnie grinned and said, "What about my charges?"

"I'll get to that, once Rick finishes. I promise," said Carson.

Rick continued, "After the birthday party on the island for Pamela, we all took their beautiful mahogany tender over to his mega yacht. The only thing on their minds was an orgy. We used Jules as bait because Pamela was so obsessed with her. Once we all got to the bedroom, Gary had his nurse friend make some special after-dinner shots. Two were laced with propofol and GHB. And one with SP-117 and GHB. That's the one we gave to Pamela."

"Truth serum and the date rape drug?"

"Yep, the perfect cocktail mixed by a nurse practitioner. As soon as that began to work on Pamela, she started singing like a canary. She admitted the entire thing on a hidden camera Jules was wearing."

"I know most of this. What I wanna know is how the hell did you talk them into returning to the US and turning themselves in?" asked Carson.

"Are you sure we are off the record?"

"One hundred percent!"

"Once the three of them were comfortably numb, we carefully and quietly carried them to the tender. The boat ride to Hulhulé only took forty minutes. Once we got there, we loaded them on the plane and Jamie, the nurse practitioner, kept them asleep with an IV drip of saline and propofol. You know, the drug that killed Michael Jackson. When dosed properly, you can sleep for days. Once we arrived in Destin, I sort of borrowed a white cargo van and drove them to the sheriff's department, placed Kiefer in the driver's seat, while wearing a facemask of course, and rode another borrowed bicycle back to my Ford, which I'd parked not too far from the station behind a closed business. The rest is, how you say? History."

Carson just shook his head and smiled. "That's freaking genius. Do you know how many laws you broke bringing them back?"

"A couple?"

"Uh yeah, and some biggies too, like kidnapping and taking someone against their will across state and federal lines. Don't worry, your secret is safe with me. I will say, placing the empty Jägermeister bottles in the van was a slick move too. The deputies thought they were hammered and just couldn't remember how they got there. Jäger has the nickname 'mind eraser.'"

"Am I free?" yelped Johnie from the edge of his seat.

"Free as a bird, my man. I spoke with the DA and you will most likely get a formal apology from the sheriff's department and the DA's office. It's up to you if you wanna pursue civil action against them. You have a rock-solid unlawful arrest case plus a libel suit," replied Carson.

"I'll think about it. I mostly just want it behind me now. The few days I spent in the Crestview Hilton, better known as Okaloosa Corrections, made me realize how precious freedom is and what it's like to be behind bars for something I didn't do. That's pretty scary. There were a few guys in with me who were innocent as well. If I do sue them, I'd like to use the money to start an innocence project. I saw that on TV once."

"That's an admirable plan, Johnie," said Carson.

"Now what?" interjected Rick.

"Well, that's it. It will most likely go to trial, but with that recorded confession and all the other evidence, Michelle's testimony against them, they will do hard time. You can go back to running your charter boat...unless..."

"Unless what?" asked Rick.

"When I was done at the DA's office, I stopped by to meet with the lead investigator over at Okaloosa Sheriff's Department. While I was waiting, I scrolled through some files sitting on his desk. The top one is right up your alley, Rick. An up-and-coming blues guitarist from Mobile named Kyle Rife is missing near the crossroads in Mississippi. His car was found on the side of the road and there were satanic symbols found nearby. The police think it was a kidnapping, but there hasn't been a ransom called in yet. His father is the owner of one of the biggest casinos in Biloxi. He is offering a million-dollar reward to anyone who can help solve his murder. You interested?"

"Hell yeah." Rick grinned. "Jules, you ever been to the Mississippi Delta?"

The End

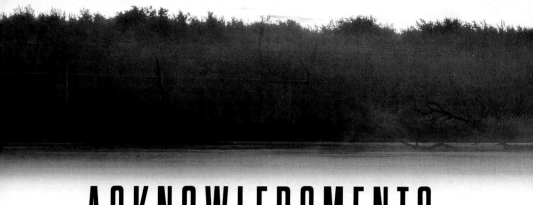

ACKNOWLEDGMENTS

I'd like to thank my friends, fans and readers. I am blessed to have so much positive support.

I'd like to thank my mentor Wayne Stinnett, who never fails to answer a question or give me advice.

I'd like to thank fellow writer Bob Adamov, for all his insight and cool marketing ideas.

Thanks to my amazing narrator and fellow writer, Nick Sullivan, who always does the most amazing job narrating and bringing my characters to life, but also is always there for a quick answer to a question or to shoot me some advice.

I'd like to thank my formatter Colleen Sheehan, the best in the business.

Thanks to my editor Stephanie Slagle, who helped me steer the story in the right direction and speaks very good Southernize.

I'd like to thank Rebecca Juliano for all the photography advice.

Thanks to Gretchen Douglas, my proofreader, for finding things everyone else missed.

I'd like to thank my graphics artist Les, who does a great job and is also quick with revisions.

I'd like to thank my good friend Vebjørn Bråthen, who's always there when I need to vent, or drink a beer with over Zoom.

Special thanks to all my beta readers. Y'all all do a great job! Bavette and Dennis Battern, Mike Keevil, Ron Dalton, Carroll Scadden Shroyer, Chuck Springs, Yvonne Edwards and Terry Gillard.

ABOUT THE AUTHOR

Eric Chance Stone was born and raised on the gulf coast of Southeast Texas. An avid surfer, sailor, scuba diver, fisherman and treasure hunter, Eric met many bigger than life characters on his adventures across the globe. Wanting to travel after college, he got a job with Northwest Airlines and moved to Florida. Shortly thereafter transferred to Hawaii, then Nashville. After years of being a staff songwriter in Nashville, he released his first album, Songs For Sail in 1999, a tropically inspired collection of songs. He continued to write songs and tour and eventually landed a gig with Sail America and Show Management to perform at all international boat shows where his list of characters continued to grow.

He moved to the Virgin Islands in 2007 and became the official entertainer for Pusser's Marina Cay in the BVI. After several years in the Caribbean, his fate for telling stories was sealed.

Upon release of his 15th CD, All The Rest, he was inspired to become a novelist after a chance meeting with Wayne Stinnett. Wayne along with Cap Daniels, Chip Bell and a few others, became his mentors and they are all good friends now. Eric currently resides in Destin, Florida. Inspired by the likes of Clive Cussler's Dirk Pitt, Wayne Stinnett's Jesse McDermitt, Cap Daniels Chase Fulton, Chip Bell's Jake Sullivan and many more, Eric's tales are sprinkled with Voodoo, Hoodoo and kinds of weird stuff. From the bayous of Texas to the Voodoo dens of Haiti, his twist of reality will take you for a ride. His main character Rick Waters is a down to earth good ol' boy, adventurist turned private eye, who uses his treasure hunting skills and street smarts to solve mysteries.

FOLLOW ERIC CHANCE STONE

WEBSITE:

ERICCHANCESTONE.COM

FACEBOOK:

FACEBOOK.COM/RICKWATERSSERIES